ORCHARD OF

THE FOX

Kassandra Keator

Cover design by: Sophie Morse

Printed in the United States of America

Third Edition

ISBN: 979-8-218-51767-0

https://linktr.ee/kkeator_books

CONTENTS

PART III: FINIS VITAE SED NON AMORIS

Absorbism

Noun

A rarely documented condition in which an individual experiences animalistic changes in bodily form due to intense bouts of emotion—both from themselves and others. The culprit is always the strongest emotion that had surrounded the individual at birth. Both factors differ from case to case, but the animal forms are always warm-blooded.

The more the individual encounters their afflicted emotion, the more their human form deteriorates. Those with this condition do not usually live in human bodies past the age of 35.

Further research is yet to be done to come to a solid conclusion regarding the cause of this disease. Currently, scientists have found it to be linked to a genetic abnormality of the amygdala that is extremely heritable.

<u>Chapter 1</u>

The sun's hands stretched across the sky as it greeted the early birds and tapped the sleepyheads awake. Its influence waned as autumn set in, animals and trees alike showing off their skeletons. Soon they would be as bare as the humans they shared their home with.

Chestnut eyes awoke, light revealing red hair and freckles as it flooded the girl's dry room. It splashed color onto the walls and flowed across the rickety wood floor. Finally, it submerged the room's owner. She sat up, heavy eyelids blinking. It'd been a long week. She didn't want to get up. Still, she forced herself to her feet. The floor creaked under her weight, still unfamiliar with its new resident.

Her room was the only bedroom on the second level of this house, it sat next to a bathroom. The room was rather plain, a few boxes still waiting to be unpacked. The walls were white with pale wood adorning the floor. Her twin-sized bed lay beneath an arched ceiling, obviously old and covered in even older sheets. It was accompanied by a nightstand and lamp. Across the room was a vanity and double-door closet. To the left of the bed were two windows with a dresser wedged in the space between them.

As the girl crossed her room, the floor continued to groan in protest. She ignored it and sat at her vanity for a moment. Faded scraps of stickers spelled "Adelie" on the mirror, letters worn down by the sands of childhood. The face staring back at her had matured greatly in the last few years. She was almost eighteen now.

Her face no longer looked round and friendly, but rather sharp and thin. It matched the rest of her fragile frame. Red side bangs rested across her forehead, the tips of them blending in with the rest of her long, straight, thin hair. She used to have much shorter, much thicker hair as a child. It looked like not even her hair could cope with everything that had happened over the past few years. She briefly brushed it before heading downstairs.

The wooden stairs descended to the first floor and stood flush to a wall on its left side. She ignored the old family portraits that decorated that wall. They seemed to stare at her as she went down. The door to the backyard stood in front of her. It was about an acre in size and lacked a fence. A few trees stood at the end of it, giving their home some privacy from a house that was another acre away, a little way past the line of brush. Adelie had already spent some time out there under those trees last night, anything to get away from her mother for a while. The moon was much more welcomed company.

She turned to face the kitchen and living room, where more boxes were strewn about. These areas were small, but then again, the house was pretty small, too. Couches, a TV, and a small fireplace made up the living room. The door to her mother's room stood just beyond it. As for the kitchen, it was just about as average as a kitchen could be, really. Nothing special there. The scent of coffee greeted her before her mother's voice did.

"Good morning."

It was a stiff hello.

Adelie nodded as she walked past her, tension as thick as the butter sitting on the kitchen counter. Her mother's eyes dipped down to the mug in her hands. The reflection wore a shameful scowl like her daughter's.

After a quick and quiet breakfast of scrambled eggs, Adelie returned to her room to get dressed. She pulled on jeans, an old t-shirt, and a forest green flannel. Her trusty pocketknife found itself in her pocket. Once she pulled on her favorite boots, she practically flew down the stairs to head out of the house. Passing her mom again, she gave her a tap on the shoulder and uttered her first words of the day.

"I'm taking the bus to school."

"Okay, have a good day," she replied as she watched her daughter leave.

It came upon deaf ears as the door squeezed her words between the locks.

Once outside, Adelie closed her eyes and took a deep breath of cool, crisp air. It was tangy with the scent of earth and evergreens. It made her smile. Opening her eyes once again, she made her way to the bus stop and waited. The much fouler scent of exhaust would carry her to school soon.

❖

It's always weird to be suddenly dropped into a new place. First the house, now the high school. Standing with her backpack hanging from one shoulder, Adelie observed her surroundings for a moment before walking to her first class. She saw two front buildings, one for classes and one for lunchtime. Beyond them stood a library and flowery garden. Sidewalks connected each place and were surrounded by trees and bushes. It wasn't bad, but she was still glad to be in her senior year.

School dragged on as slowly as the hands of a watched clock. Though Adelie loved to learn, she hated being confined to a desk. She hated the icebreakers, the busy work, the meaningless group activities. Each class change felt like torture as she maneuvered her way through the hundred or so students. At least this was a small town, meaning the student population wasn't *too* overwhelming. By the time her last class rolled around, she had begun to regain hope in the fact that the school day was almost over. She wanted to explore her new town and the neighboring forest instead of being trapped in a tiny classroom.

The bell rang and Adelie's name had already been included in the roll call when three students strolled in. The first had light olive skin, dark hair, and blue eyes, seemingly the leader of the pack of pupils at his heels. The nonchalant style of his step caught her attention right away. It said, *"I really don't care that I'm late."* He wore jeans, a red hoodie, and black converse.

The second was a few inches taller and paler skinned than the first. He had green eyes and his brown hair that was styled up into a quiff. He also wore jeans but had a football jersey on instead of a hoodie. Ordinary sneakers covered his feet. He looked friendly enough, a casual smile on his face, but something about his eyes spoke *"mischievous."* It looked as if he was just going along with what the group was doing, no arrogance to be found.

The last boy was shorter and darker skinned than the other two. He had a buzz cut and brown eyes that appeared almost playful. His entire outfit looked expensive, from his long-sleeved button-up, to his slacks, and finally his bright, white sneakers. He stuffed his hands in his packets and walked with a relaxed gait.

The group sat down at their desks after a brief scolding from their teacher. In the middle of all the movement, the first boy glanced her way, seemingly caught off guard by a new face. She returned his gaze with a glare just as the teacher spoke up to resume roll call.

"Owen Smit!"

The raven-haired boy smirked as his arm jutted up. He had a slight snaggletooth.

"Present!"

His voice oozed haughtiness. Adelie rolled her eyes. A few names were called between his and his brown-haired friend's name.

"Jace Tendale!"

The boy raised his hand without a word. He was shortly followed by the third late student.

"Damien Vark!"

"Here, Miss," he answered, his voice sounding a bit tired.

After that, the class carried on as expected, mindless small talk and syllabi crumpling under uncaring fingers. The final bell's ring came from an angel's harp as it hit Adelie's ears. She ghosted out of the classroom, seemingly unseen by her classmates, and headed to the bus loop.

Settling into a greasy blue seat, she felt her eyes grow heavy. The backpack in her lap felt even heavier. As more students filled the bus, the whirlwind of voices added to her drowsiness. She didn't want to deal with it. As the bus started up, the vibrations soon lulled her to sleep.

Addie.

A bump in the road.

Look at me.

The crunch of metal.

It'll be okay.

Adelie jolted awake to find herself on the floor. She was the last student on the bus. A steady hiss flowed in through the broken dashboard. There was steam rising like morning mist. The front door had popped open. She went through it.

The bus driver was outside, angrily grumbling into his phone. They were on one of the side streets leading to her house. Adelie could see the skid marks on the road, the collision between vehicle and tree. It took a minute before the driver noticed the student observing the scene. He apologized and made sure she was okay before returning to his phone call. Help would be there soon. Still, Adelie felt much less annoyed than she should've been. She was finally in the forest.

Trees surrounded them, leaves softly fluttering around their feet. Everything was red and gold. Still, a different shade of red caught her eye—a flash of fur in the foliage. The reason for the crash? Glancing back at the bus driver, she decided to let her curiosity get the best of her. She walked off the road and into the woods.

After a few moments of walking, she came upon a fallen tree. The upturned roots had created a mound, which then became a den. She could see a mother red fox with three kits.

A baby was crying. The moon illuminated the new face. A clock struck nine.

The baby girl had bright red hair and freckles. Her crying soon dissipated when she noticed her parents watching her. They wore smiles and soft eyes. Soon the baby wore a coat of fur and a bushy tail. She was now a fox kit. The parents expected this. Still, they were surprised at the form she took and the emotion she'd absorbed. Love would be an incredibly tricky one to live with.

Years later, when the baby had grown into a child, her parents explained to her what her condition was. The three of them were hunched together on the carpet of her childhood room.

"You have absorbism. It means that when you were born, we loved you so much that you soaked in our emotions like a sponge," her mother squeezed a stuffed toy for emphasis.

"Then, whenever your body comes into contact with this emotion now, you turn into a fox. Everyone who has absorbism turns into a different animal depending on their personality. Everyone also has a different emotion that affects them. The emotion is the one that surrounds them the most at birth."

The girl stared, eyes wide. Her father nodded before speaking up.

"I have absorbism, just like you! In fact, you probably got it from me. That happens sometimes. For me, I tend to turn into a big ol' grizzly bear when I get mad," he reached forward and tickled his daughter, who giggled in response.

"So try to stay outta trouble!"

The mother, though smiling, spoke again.

"Yes, and don't tell anyone or reveal yourself. It's dangerous."

A small box appeared in the father's hands. He opened it, revealing a pocketknife.

"I always had this to keep me safe from those who might harm me. When you get a little older, it'll keep you safe too."

As the fox turned to leave the den again, her eyes met Adelie's. They locked onto each other. The vixen was hostile, and rightfully so. This was her territory. They were her children. However, after a minute, the fox let her guard down and stared at the girl with newfound curiosity. She sniffed the air, whiskers twitching. This human smelled different. She *was* different.

The vixen stepped closer, close enough to touch. Adelie longed to stroke her hands through her beautiful fur. Still, she stopped herself from doing so. It was wrong. The fox seemed to know her inner turmoil too and quickly stepped away. She began to trot off in the opposite direction. Adelie followed.

On the cusp of the girl's adolescence, the household's air became thin. The parents were struggling financially. Her mother was quiet while her father was loud. Sharp teeth and claws threatened to break through his human skin. Something was going wrong with work. There was a lawsuit. He would have to defend his company.

The girl didn't know what these words meant, but she knew that she heard growls outside her door at night.

The girl and the fox ran side by side, a few feet of dirt and stones separating them. Their eyes never left each other. Despite the chill in the air, Adelie felt warm.

The freckled girl sat in the messy playroom; a few other children scattered around her. She was a bit too old to get along with them. Her father and mother were currently in a nearby courtroom. One stood tall while the other tried to hide away.

The case appeared to be going well. Her father was confident and smart. The opposing party seemed to be running out of options. Still, they found a loophole. A crack to squeeze through. A bullet to dodge.

The father became angry.

A wiry arm reached up from the ground. It grabbed the fox's paw. The animal's body slammed into the earth.

Adelie realized it was a snare. The air went cold again.

A roar.

Splintering of wood.

Screams of human terror.

Her father was no longer a father, but a bear. It stood on all fours, a destroyed desk beneath its claws. Its eyes found the judge, who then became the judged. A flurry of fury enveloped its mind while a flurry of panic fought to escape the room.

His wife was the only silent entity. She crumpled into her chair.

Teeth bared, the bear let out another deafening roar. It was followed by an equally deafening cacophony of screams and scraping feet.

The animal began to move. It bounded down the path between the seats. People quickly shied away. Fangs nipped at the stragglers. Doors flew open upon its weight.

It was out.

The fox cried and struggled against the pull of manmade fingers. Adelie froze, pupils blown wide in fear.

More screaming souls greeted the rampaging beast. Its only goal was to destroy. To hurt. Anger continued to surge through it, erasing any human memories. Glazed and dark, feral eyes rolled around in a wild skull.

Still in her chair, the woman sobbed and hugged herself. It took her a moment to remember her third family member. Even then, she was hesitant to leave the safety of the now empty courtroom. Eventually, she did.

The sound of screams and footsteps jolted the young girl out of her boredom. She snapped up and looked out the narrow window in the playroom door. People frantically ran past her room, paying no regard to the children in danger. That was when she heard a familiar growl. The other children cowered behind her. Terror gripped her heart.

Another door greeted the bear. This door had a window. It peered inside, eyes still glazed over. Its brain screamed for it to break in and destroy what was inside. A young face stared back. Amber eyes met black ones.

Time stretched in that moment; a string pulled tight enough to snap.

Adelie rushed over to the distressed animal, pocketknife in hand. The fox coiled and screamed at her. It did not trust her any longer. She must've done this. Adelie noticed this distrust and glanced at her knife. Manmade. Slowly, she slid it back in her pocket. She stretched an open palm toward the vixen.

Teeth nipped at her fingertips. She pushed the pain back. She let it come closer at its own pace. After a few moments of sniffing and staring, the fox looked her in the eyes once more. Their connection was back. Adelie reached back into her pocket and pulled out the knife once again. Swiftly, she cut the vixen free.

Her eyes were flames, melting away the rage that had waxed itself into the father's brain. He was still there. He could be human. He could care. He'd done it all before. He had a daughter. She was right in front of him.

With a blink, his mind was back, but his body was not. The fury was threatening to consume him again. The disease was too strong. Shaking his head, he turned away from the girl's face. He was ashamed.

As if on cue, his wife came upon the scene and gasped. She thought he was going to kill their daughter. Screaming, she urged him to stop. To leave. To go away.

Fear and rage fought within him. The animal wanted to kill her. The human wanted to run away. He'd let everyone down and exposed himself. His own family now hated him.

Without a second thought, he turned tail and ran. Ran until he found an exit. Ran until his lungs screamed along with his brain. Ran until he couldn't hear anything any longer.

Paws met asphalt. Cars screeched and surged around him. He could see trees in the distance. He fixed his eyes on them and did not stop until he was a part of them—until human feet could not follow.

Police swarmed the streets in search of the rogue animal. News agencies flocked around the court building, a few strays sneaking in. This was the first time in quite a while that absorbism had become relevant in society. They weren't going to miss this chance to profit off misery. Audiences would be disgusted yet intrigued. They wouldn't dare change the channel.

The freed fox bolted away to safety.

Back in the playroom, the other children escaped in search of their own parents. They became mixed into the sea of reporters that cascaded through the hall, washing up any information they could get. That's when they spotted

A voice rang out, snapping Adelie back to reality. The bus driver stepped into view.

"Hey! The bus is all fixed up. I can getcha home now."

She could see the yellow bus clearly now. There was no steam, but there were two new men on the scene. They held guns and wore camouflage. Adelie heard a rustle behind her. She turned to look. The mother fox had returned for her kits.

Time stood still again.

didn't know how to cope. However, both were happy to have found a safe place. School went well for the daughter. She stayed out of the house as much as she could.

That's when the fighting started. Her mother wanted her at home. After all, misery loves company. Despite not having much of a hand in her rearing, the mother took it upon herself to keep her daughter on a leash. It didn't work for long, the teenager escaping her grasp when she could. Of course, around that time, her mother claimed to have seen reporters lurking in the neighborhood. She began the moving process again.

The daughter resembled her father in that time, angry teeth threatening to bite. She even began to go through his old things. That's when she found the pocketknife that was rightfully hers. It found its way onto her person at all times.

Verbal and physical fights continued to ensue. She didn't want to leave this place just because they each had different ways of dealing with their life. At 16, all she could do was kick and scream.

The mother won. They moved to Orchard Hill by the time the daughter was nearly 18.

Before Adelie could even take a breath, the vixen had shot off in another direction. The hunters stared after her, their eyes twitching. One of them cursed quietly.

Adelie could see the want in their eyes.

She felt anger rise in her, not only at them, but at her mother. They'd just moved into this town— a town her mother had picked herself. She'd chosen a hunting town just to deter Adelie from being out and about.

"Leave her alone."

The men gave her a confused look before laughing. This only made Adelie more irritated. The bus driver leaned in close.

"They hunt. It's what they do," he stood up straight again and faced the two.

"Sorry fellas, she's new around here. First time on my bus today."

The hunters gave Adelie a look-over before speaking up again.

"Better get her home before dark, then."

With that, the bus driver led the new girl down to the bus. The vehicle was still in rough shape but fixed up enough to make it back to town. The rage began to water down into helplessness. She was alone in this fight. Looking over her shoulder, she could see the men walk deeper into the woods.

Boarding the bus felt like a mistake. The closing of the plastic doors sounded like the rattling of a cage. She looked out the window with hot tears pricking at the sides of her eyes.

Later on, miles away, the same hunters were stomping out the life of that fox. Ribs snapped under forceful boots, stabbing vital organs. Her mouth hung open. Blood spilled from her tongue and nose, staining the dusty ground. The life in her eyes vanished along with the evening sun. Once the deed was done, the men slung her over their shoulder. They carried her out like a prize.

A while after Man had gone, the kits huddled together in the dark. They surrounded the soiled dirt, unsure of what to do. They were alone now. They had no chance.

Adelie felt the same way.

<u>Chapter 2</u>

Adelie's gut told her that the vixen couldn't have stood a chance.

When she got home, her mother went on and on about how she should've called her. That she was worried sick. That she should know better. That she loved her. That she'd be in real trouble next time. As Adelie climbed the stairs, she uttered a short response.

"I know why you made us come here."

She slammed and locked her bedroom door without waiting for her mother to reply. Her backpack hit the floor just as her body hit the bed. Dying threads of light wove its way through her room, walls white as bone. She felt as pale and vulnerable as the thin outline of the moon outside. It hung alongside teardrop stars.

Adelie hid under the sheets to escape the howl of the wind outside. It was like the mother fox was crying for help. Fear and guilt reached through the walls. They gripped her until she fell asleep in their grasp.

Soon, her mind was filled with colorful visions. Wisps of orange and red. Bright yellow eyes. Cream teeth and tails. They danced and called to her. She curled around them, bodies flush and safe. The sun nestled them in warmth.

Adelie slowly blinked her eyes open. The sun drenched her in light, making her eyes bleary. She swore she could still see the ghosts of her dreams circling the room. With a burst of determination, she swung her feet over the side of the bed. Standing tall, her mind played one thought on repeat.

No death today.

Glancing at the clock, she noticed it was about an hour before she needed to leave for school. She looked down at herself, immediately noticing that she was still in her flannel and jeans. Quickly, she hopped in the shower and rinsed off yesterday's grime.

The house was quiet as she exited her room, backpack in hand. Again, the scent of coffee wafted through the house without its creator. Her mother must've been up. Still, she was nowhere in sight. Grabbing a to-go cup, she quickly filled it with coffee to avoid a possible confrontation with said mother. She stepped out the front door before taking a sip. The air was crisp and cool. At that moment, she thanked herself for having coffee. She also thanked herself for throwing her wet hair into a ponytail. After a few minutes, the clanking of metal signaled the vehicle's arrival.

A small part of her grew anxious that the bus would have the same driver from the day before. That he would encourage her to keep quiet. To blend in. A sigh of relief puffed from her lips when the bus doors opened to reveal a stranger. She climbed the steps with confidence before finding a seat. It wasn't long until she was back at school.

The first few classes of the day went by quietly. As usual, she kept to herself and did her work as assigned. By the time lunch rolled around, she wasn't hungry. Her last meal was over a day ago, but her stomach had no quarrel with it. Her brain couldn't fight it either.

The cafeteria was swarming with students—bees in their own little clumps of hives. The building was tall with bright white lights casting down upon the equally white tile, one or two of them flickering from time to time. Food was handed out from the left side of the hall while everyone sat themselves at the sporadically placed tables along the right side.

Adelie wandered around for several minutes trying to find somewhere she could be alone. Yesterday's search had been just as difficult. She was met with judgmental stares and snorts. She gave up about halfway into the lunch period and planned to scout out the bathrooms next. She stayed there yesterday and would do it again as a last resort.

"Hey! You can sit here if you'd like!"

A squeaky voice managed to climb its way above the noise. The girl turned around, very much caught off guard. The voice's owner was a younger boy with glasses and curly dirty blond hair. He sat at a small table, seemingly alone. Adelie was in shock. She looked at him and pointed at herself questioningly. He immediately perked up.

"Yeah! Here," he kicked a chair out in her direction.

Adelie stumbled over the chair, a bit startled. Still, she didn't want to be rude, so she sat down.

"Uh, thanks," she avoided eye contact.

The boy beamed.

"You're welcome! I noticed you were having trouble finding a spot. People usually avoid me, so you'll always have a seat here if you need it!"

Adelie felt a pang of both sorrow and gratitude for the mystery boy. She smiled weakly at him and nodded.

"Oh, forgive me! I'm Jeremy," his hand sprung out for a shake.

Adelie blinked a moment before getting the message.

"Adelie," she hesitantly shook his hand. He returned it with enthusiasm.

"Adelie! Cool name. Are you from around here?"

She shook her head. He spoke up again.

"Me neither. I've seen that people here don't respond well to new kids."

Staring ahead, she could see the boys from yesterday sitting at a large table together, the "leader" of them placed in the middle. It looked like a pack of wolves digging into their kill, laughing and yapping as they ate. What was his name? Otis? She couldn't remember. Not important.

Shit. Otis looked back. He was frowning.

"Yeah, I can tell," she muttered in return.

Adelie thrummed her nails against the plastic table as Jeremy filled the silence between them. He had a lot of spirit for an ostracized freshman, she'd give him that much. Though a bit high energy, he was very kind and patient. She humored him by playing along with his ramblings and nodding when necessary.

Soon enough, the bell rang. On the other hand, all too soon, the girl noticed the other boy making his way to her and Jeremy's table. His lackeys trailed behind him. Taking a deep breath, she quickly thanked her new friend as she attempted to escape from the crowded lunchroom. The attempt was futile as she was swept directly into the group of boys instead.

"Hey, redhead," he folded his arms.

"That's not my name."

Adelie meshed into the crowd again. She gained some ground before she heard the loud thumping of running sneakers. Leaving his pack behind, he managed to jump in front of her, thwarting her second attempt to escape.

"HEY, whatever your name is, we gotta talk."

The boy was only a few inches taller than Adelie, his frame rather scrawny. Dark hair formed a mop on his head. A few longer strands hung near his eyes and past the base of his neck. His bright blue eyes caught her attention before his words did. They were icy, almost lonely.

"I don't 'gotta' do anything, Otis."

"Otis" let out an offended gasp. His friends chuckled from a few yards away.

"First of all, it's Owen. Second, I'm the son of one of the top hunter in this town. He said you were messing with one of our traps."

Adelie raised an eyebrow, slightly amused at what seemed to be his masculinity on the line. If she didn't know better, she'd think he was trying too hard.

"Okay?"

Owen frowned.

"I wouldn't do that again if I were you. Could get you in big trouble. Everyone knows everyone around here," he puffed out his chest.

"What's your name, anyway?"

"Amelia," she fought to keep a straight face.

"Amelia. Amelia. Well, Amelia, I hope you took my words to heart today. Would hate to see you get hurt," he slowly backed away and into his friend group again.

"Will do, Otis," she headed to her next class without another word.

The boy practically grew red with embarrassment.

❖

The rest of the day went particularly well for Adelie. The lunchroom ordeal had put her in a good mood. She still felt confident as she entered her last class, where Owen would surely be. After sitting down, it was only a few minutes before the group of boys paraded in. The leader seemed to have recovered from the earlier trauma. His eyes simply skimmed past Adelie, no notice given. The teacher commenced roll call as soon as the classroom door clicked shut. The girl's name was eventually called out.

"Adelie Henderson!"

Like yesterday, she raised her hand quietly. After lowering it, she shot a glance Owen's way. At first, he frowned deeply, no doubt in realization of the fake name from earlier. After a moment, though, his face softened, exposing some sort of inner epiphany. He appeared to be so lost in thought that it took him a second to realize his name had been called.

"Present," his mouth was a straight line, the word barely making it out.

It was a much different reaction compared to the arrogant one from yesterday. His buddies shook his shoulders and whispered to him quietly, trying to bring him out of his mini episode. Owen nodded and quickly got out his materials for class.

Though she also thought he was acting strange, she shrugged it off and enjoyed the much quieter atmosphere of the class. Before long, school was up for the day. Adelie felt his eyes on her as she hustled out the door. Not only did she have the kits to find, but she also did not feel like dealing with whatever sudden realization the boy had come to.

❖

Adelie let out a sigh of relief when she finally got onto her bus. Her current plan was to get out at whatever stop brought up any trace of the kits. Instead of settling into her seat, she sat upright, eyes and ears open. She hoped her animalistic senses would help her.

The first twenty minutes of the trip brought nothing but anxiety for Adelie. The bus was about half empty now. She figured she only had another twenty minutes or so to pick up on where they were. Her nails dug into the cracked cushion beneath her. All the trees outside were a blur as they sped on. The sound of laughter and radio static blocked up her ears. All she smelled was the musk of teenagers. Another ten minutes and two stops passed with nothing. It wasn't until they got to the stop before hers that she heard something. Not a fox, but a dog.

There was a brown dog tied up in someone's yard. The house sat at the edge of the woods— the edge of the stretch it took to get to Adelie's house. The animal was on its hindlegs, trying to break the rope. It was barking and lunging at seemingly nothing. Adelie caught a whiff of something familiar. Her mind might've been playing tricks, but it was the only thing she had to go off. Shooting out of her seat, she made it behind the other students exiting the bus. As her foot touched the ground, the doors closed, and the vehicle made its way to its next destination. It would get there without its passenger.

The dog was still barking. Before she had time to think, her body was running. It ran past the canine, swerving between the trees and bushes with ease. Her backpack hit the ground. The familiar smell came to her again. Adelie stopped. The scent danced about the forest. She swore she could see its shadowy form. It was like her dream. It was like this morning. It had to be the kits. When she looked down, there were splotches of crimson that had mingled with the fine earth. It smelled of fox and death. Their mother really was dead. Swallowing thickly, she carried on a little farther.

That's when she saw the fallen tree. Her lips pulled into a soft smile and her heart immediately swelled. They had to be close. She longed to see them, to hold them close and keep them safe. Adelie could feel the tell-tale sign of pre-transformation—her hair thickened and stood on end. She let it happen without a fight.

The whites of her eyes turned black, and her mouth chattered as her teeth sharpened into a canine set. Thick, red fur sprouted along her body, covering her skin and growing over her clothes without damaging them. Rounded ears became pricked black ones that moved to the top of her head, the hair there now meshing with her neck. Adelie dropped down on all fours, hands and feet turning to paws that itched at the ground as her body shrank, a bushy tail forming soon after. Another few moments and she shook off, her human form gone.

She now stood as a red fox, a welcome guest among the falling leaves.

The kits crawled up from their burrow below the tree as soon as Adelie was on all four paws. Still, they looked confused and hesitant. They were thin, shaking, and covered in dirt. Adelie sniffed about the burrow. It was finely covered in their scent, but there was another smell still lingering. It was their mother's. The kits nosed at the dirt and whined too. This was all they'd known. Now it was empty.

She looked at the three of them again, eyes burning with both sadness and determination. In one motion, she circled around them all and rubbed them with motherly comfort. She nuzzled into them, wanting to earn their trust. They shriveled in fear and confusion; why did she smell both human and animal? After a few minutes, though, they began to loosen up with the realization that she would not hurt them. They could sense that she already loved them. She reminded them of mother.

Soon enough, one of the kits began to bark and nip, wanting to play. Bursting with adoration, Adelie humored them and played along. The four foxes frolicked through the golden forest as their red coats blended in with the foliage. Birds chirped as they flew south. Leaves crunched deliciously beneath them. Beams of sunlight filtered in through the withering canopy above them.

Joyous as it all was, Adelie knew what she had to do. She slowed down to a trot before stopping altogether. The kits tilted their heads. Motioning for them to follow, she began to sniff about the forest floor. She needed to show them what Man's tricks were. They sniffed with her, though unaware of what needed to be found. A few hundred feet later, she found it-- a fox snare.

She stood between the kits and the snare to signify a no-touching rule. This wasn't something safe. It was something to fear. One of them leaned forward and touched their nose to the steel. Adelie immediately growled and pushed them away, hackles raised.

Bad. These are bad. These will hurt. All three of them backed away, tails between their legs.

Something shifted nearby. There was a new scent. She sniffed the air, confused by what came. It was someone else's fear. It was familiar, albeit a bit different from when she had encountered it before.

Owen Smit.

Well, in theory, it wasn't very surprising that he was out here. He did say his father was one of the leaders of this hunting town. Still, it piqued her curiosity. What was this cocky kid afraid of?

Sensing that their new mother was on high alert, the kits huddled close and used her fur as a shield. Adelie's nose and ears twitched as she tried to gather more information.

He walked rather slowly, the earth hardly trembling under his feet. His sweat caught on the breeze, and so did the scent of a gun and trap. She put the pieces together in her head.

This boy was afraid—petrified—of hunting and killing.

Though she suspected that the four of them would be safe, she kept her guard up anyway. This kid was turning out to be a very mixed bag. Perhaps it would be best to take the kits away and create a new den for them. Adelie urged the kits to move quickly but quietly.

As they walked, his fear-scent became more and more apparent. He must've been following them. Curious, she looked over her shoulder. A few black hairs and a puff of breath poked out from behind a nearby tree. He was setting up a trap and seemed nervous. In a way, so was Adelie. She would do anything to protect the kits but was a little apprehensive about exposing herself as an Absorber. If he made a move, she would most certainly turn back from fear and anger.

It seemed that the universe heard her thoughts and decided to make them true. The slight clank of metal echoed in her ears. She immediately turned around, the three others behind her. Owen's scent only strengthened. Adelie could see his face. He stood up after finishing up with the trap. His hand was on his gun, though it shook. Still, it was enough to send a jolt of terror through her.

No death today.

"Stop!"

She surged forward, jumping into the air and morphing back into her original form. The vixen disappeared in a blast of fur and Adelie now stood on two legs, her human face staring right back into Owen's. The remnants of her pelt fell in clumps onto the forest floor. A yelp came from behind the bush, the boy falling and scuttling back into a tree. He hit his head and immediately cradled it with his hand. The kits scattered and hid in various locations around them. Adelie stood her ground, expecting the worst. The other human spoke up.

"I-I knew it! You're an Absorber! You're—"

"Yeah, yeah, a freak and—"

"You're the girl from the news a few years back!"

Owen pointed an accusatory finger.

Well, that wasn't what Adelie expected. She blinked, taken aback. The air around her felt tight. Her skin felt a size too small. She feigned innocence.

"What?"

This made the boy frown. Collecting himself, he got to his feet once more and took a step toward her.

"Your dad. He's an Absorber too. He fucked up really bad."

Adelie's mouth felt dry. She looked away to keep him from seeing her vulnerability.

"In all honesty, I felt bad for him."

She looked up again, surprised to see Owen's face soften.

"I felt bad for you, too."

Adelie closed her eyes and replied.

"I don't know what you're talking about."

The boy sighed.

"C'mon, I know it was you, *Adelie*. I remember the name now. It's close to my mom's name, Adalia," he quickly trailed off the subject and shook his head.

The silence gave Adelie time to grasp the situation at hand. This was all so confusing. He knew who she was, *what* she was, but wasn't pulling out a torch and pitchfork.

"Alright, fine, you're right," Adelie finally replied.

This brought a smug smile to Owen's lips. Still, this was her chance to ask him some questions. She was the one to point now, his smile dropping.

"I've got questions for you, now. What is your deal? You strut around like a show-pig, yet you crawl through here sweating bullets. I could smell your fear a mile away."

The boy gulped.

"Plus, why are you okay with the fact that I'm an Absorber? Why aren't you freaking out? It's a scary thing, right? People hate it! You know something I don't?"

Adelie could practically see the marbles rolling around in the other's head. He was being attacked, possibly nothing he'd experienced before. She wondered if she'd put a scratch on his ego. Dazed as he was, he took a breath and answered her.

"Fine, alright, now you're the one that's right," the gun that hung around his neck fell to the ground with a loud thud.

"I don't like it, okay? I wasn't even going to use this gun. Just don't say anything at school."

The girl's eyebrows furrowed together.

"What do you mean?"

Owen stuffed his hands in his pockets, visibly flustered now.

"I can't tell you. I *can* tell you, though, that I used to have a friend that was an Absorber. He died when I was younger."

"I'm guessing you know how to keep a secret, then," Adelie inquired.

The boy took a moment to respond as he pondered.

"*Maybe* if you stopped coming out here and left things alone—"

He didn't have time to finish as Adelie took hold of his ear and yanked down, hard. Owen squealed in pain.

"You really gonna try to act tough now? You tell no one. Got it?"

He nodded relentlessly as he strangled out a *yes*. Only then did Adelie let go.

The other inhaled deeply as he stood up straight, hand now cradling his ear instead of his head. The girl wasn't done. She stepped up close to him again.

"And you tell no one about these kits. If one of them dies, it's on you."

"Trust me, I think I'd rather kill myself than have you hunt me down."

The comment made her let out a small laugh. Owen laughed a little too, though still a bit shaken.

Shadows began to fall in place, the sun slowly burning out. It was time for them to go home. Owen gathered the fallen gun.

"Well, uh, I'll see you around," Owen swiveled and began to make his way back up the hill to the road. She could vaguely see the shape of a bike sitting at the top.

Looking around, Adelie saw the faces of the kits slowly come into view again. She motioned for them to go back to their old burrow for now. To be careful and quiet. They did as she said. Now she needed to call her mom for a ride. She didn't want to, but she had no choice.

Adelie tapped her pockets, only to find them empty. Right. She'd dropped her bag by the bus stop. It held her phone. It was possibly a mile or so away now. Sighing, she started walking in the direction she came from. Owen, now settling onto his bike seat, took notice.

"H-Hey, where ya goin'? There's not much down that way," he called out to her.

She froze. Oh, no. She did *not* want help from him.

"I left my bag somewhere. It's no big deal!"

"I can give ya a ride! You can stand on the back!"

"Uh, I'm good!"

Owen frowned and rode his bike up the road at her pace.

"C'mon, I'm trying to make peace here!"

She ignored him and continued to walk.

"I'll tell my friends to be nice to you!"

"I don't give a shit what you guys think!"

The boy cussed to himself in frustration. After a moment, a better idea came to mind.

"I'll tell the hunters to lay off of you!"

The girl stopped. That was an appealing deal. It would give her more time to investigate.

"Fine," she trudged her way up to the road, only to be met with a cheesy smile.

"This doesn't mean we're friends. Just take me home."

Owen gave her a salute and a "yes ma'am." She rolled her eyes as she stood upon the bike pillars. His shoulders served as her handlebars. With that, they rode off toward the bus stop. Her backpack was still sitting where it'd been dropped. In fact, the previously barking dog was now curled up asleep on it. Thankfully, she pulled it out without disturbing it. Owen gave it a pat.

As they left and headed toward her house, Adelie checked her phone.

4:32 PM

Mom: ADELIE??? WHERE ARE YOU???

4:50 PM

Mom: I DON'T KNOW WHAT YOU THINK YOU'RE DOING BUT IT'S CHILDISH

5:11 PM

Mom: I love you just please get home safe. I'm worried about you.

Adelie sighed and shoved the phone back in the bag. She wished she had somewhere else to go home to. Unfortunately, they got to her house sooner than she thought they would.

"We're here. That one's mine."

Owen skidded to a stop, nearly throwing the girl over the front. She frowned and smacked his shoulder. He flinched and apologized.

Adelie stepped down from the bike and dusted herself off.

"Thanks. See you at school," she quickly turned and walked up to her front door.

A dark figure watched from the window, no doubt her mother.

The boy looked like he might've said bye too if it weren't for the tense atmosphere. He decided leaving would be for his own good, too. It'd been a weird night.

Chapter 3

As predicted, Adelie's mother chewed her out as soon as she stepped in the door.

"Well, here in walks misses 'I'm too good to send my mom a text when she's worried sick about me.'"

Adelie was tired. *So* tired but knew if she didn't say something then this would be an ordeal for the entire night.

"It wasn't on purpose."

Her mother's face twisted angrily.

"Like hell it wasn't! You get a kick out of giving me heart attacks. You always have. You want to put me through that same pain your father did *again*?"

Ah, there it was. The "Dad" card. Adelie faced her, some energy renewed through the irritation rising in her gut. Her words flew out in a flurry of sarcasm.

"*Yes*, Mom, I *planned* to accidentally lose my phone for a minute. In fact, I was running away but changed my mind. Would that make you feel better?"

The mom sucked in an astonished breath.

"After what we've gone through, I find it unbelievable that you would joke about that. It's been hard enough without your outlandish behavior. Go to your room. I don't want to see you the rest of the night."

So much for wanting to make sure she was okay.

"You're not the only one having a hard time, y'know," Adelie ascended the stairs to her room.

Sleep got away from her for the second night in a row. Perhaps this night was even more difficult than the previous. Now, several unanswered questions cycled around in her brain. Not only did she wonder about how and why the hunters were really killing things, but she also pondered on how to get Owen to spill such information. He'd said 'I don't like it either.' He was unhappy and putting up appearances. She would have to get closer to him to find out more, as unpleasant as it sounded.

The sun eventually rose again as Adelie went through her morning routine. When she was done, she descended the stairs as usual. Unusually, though, her mother sat on the couch in the living room. They made eye contact, a tense silence following. Her mother cleared her throat.

"I got a job in town. Won't be around much."

Adelie wanted to say that it wouldn't make a difference anyway. She held her tongue.

"Okay. I probably won't either," the girl replied.

The mother's eyebrows raised.

"Oh?"

"After school stuff. Projects and all that"

Adelie was born to lie.

The woman took a sip from her coffee.

"You need to tell me what's really going on."

Adelie tightened the hold on her backpack.

"You wouldn't approve of it anyway."

"I'll find my own way, then," it was said as a threat.

"I have to go. I'll be late for school."

She went outside to wait for the bus. The mother continued to sip at her coffee.

❖

Adelie didn't expect to see Owen so soon after getting off the bus. Yet, there he was with his pals just yards away from the bus loop. Before she could even attempt to be friendly, the group of them had spotted her. They soon walked alongside her as she made her way to her first class.

"Hey new g—"

Owen jabbed the other boy in the ribs.

"I mean, uh, Adelie! Sorry! Hi! I'm Damien!"

She glanced at him before replying quietly.

"Hi, Damien."

Owen moved between them to be next to Adelie.

"I know you said that you don't care what they think, but I told my friends that you're cool, anyway."

The other boys smiled and nodded. Thankfully for her, the school bell rang out, signifying that classes were starting in a few minutes.

"We'll have to do introductions later. See ya!"

Owen waved to Adelie as he and his pack separated from her. He looked sad. This wasn't good. She just wanted information. Sure, she'd said that she needed to get closer to him, but it would all be superficial. This was very foreign and risky territory for her.

Lunch came around again, and so did Jeremy's familiar face. Adelie smiled softly as she sat beside him. Her friend? Was he a friend? Returned it with an overblown grin as he nudged something across the table.

"I noticed you didn't eat a lot yesterday. Here, have half of my sandwich!"

Adelie looked down at the offering. In all honesty, it made her stomach turn. She hadn't been very keen on food lately. Still, she didn't want to upset the only friend she was alright with having.

"Oh, thank you."

She plastered a wide smile to her face as she picked up the sandwich. Jeremy seemed to be very pleased. If he had a tail, it'd be wagging. As she went to take a bite, she made eye contact with Owen from across the cafeteria. He noticed and told his friends to wave. This resulted in four pairs of hands signaling to her, one she didn't recognize. He was taller than the others, all blond hair and muscle. She quickly took a bite and looked back at Jeremy. The boy seemed to notice, though, and glanced over his shoulder to see who or what she was looking at. He turned back, face a bit somber.

"Hey, uh, I noticed that one guy that came up to you yesterday. Are you friends with him?"

The piece of sandwich caught in her throat as she attempted to swallow it.

"No."

Jeremy's frown deepened. He leaned forward.

"Is he bullying you too?"

Adelie immediately felt the hurt behind his words. It hurt her too.

"Uh, no. Is he bullying *you*?"

Jeremy looked away. He seemed almost ashamed for even bringing it up.

"I'm new, but I've been here since summer. There's this ice cream place in town that I found and really love. He likes to go there too, I guess, with one of his friends. It was their hangout. Last time I went, he," he paused, eyes getting a little glossy.

He took off his glasses to wipe at them.

"You don't have to say if you don't want to. I get it," Adelie reassured him.

"No, no, it's okay."

He took a deep breath.

"He slammed my head into the sink and pushed me to the ground. Almost broke my glasses, even."

Adelie winced.

"I've never been so scared," he wiped at his eyes again and put his glasses back on.

"I don't want him to hurt you, too."

Adelie felt sorrow and anger all at once. She wanted to hug Jeremy while she punched Owen in the face. Instead, she reached forward and put her hand on his shoulder.

"I'm sorry. Don't worry, I'll hurt *him* before he ever lays hands on *me*. I won't let him hurt you, either."

He perked up at that.

"Thanks."

She nodded before looking across the lunchroom again. A glare was sent the other boy's way. He felt like a stranger all over again. She would set him straight.

Adelie settled back into her seat to eat the rest of the sandwich. She really felt like she owed him now. He munched down on his half, too. The rest of lunch was spent in pleasant silence before the bell began to ring. As Jeremy got up from his seat, he spoke up again.

"I know it really hasn't been long, but I think we could be good friends. Us outcasts gotta stick together," the smile reached his eyes.

"I think so too," Adelie smiled back.

❖

Luckily for Adelie, her final class offered her a chance to talk to Owen again: a group project where each group had to research and discuss the importance of different kinds of biomes. They were given temperate forests. Her teacher assigned her to a three-person group that included her, Owen, and Jace. Damien was placed in a different group. Owen, of course, seemed to be ecstatic.

When school was out, the three of them walked together and discussed plans about arrangements for the project. Soon enough, though, the conversation turned to boyish banter and teasing. A swift look from Adelie discouraged them from trying any of it on her. She took the sudden silence as her opportunity to bring up Jeremy.

"You guys know Jeremy, a freshman?"

The two of them blinked dumbfoundedly at the question. Jace answered first.

"Uh, I've seen him around, but I don't really *know* him. Why?"

Adelie crossed her arms.

"Funny. I think your friend here knows him pretty well. Well enough to think it's fine to assault him for no reason."

Owen looked horrified. Jace turned to him in confusion.

"What is she talking about?"

Adelie barked out a laugh. This was too good.

"Oh my god. He didn't even *tell you?*"

Owen didn't speak, his eyes the size of moons, showing all the words unspoken-- fear, shame, shock. Adelie's blazed with the passion of a new-born sun.

"You must be stupid if you thought it was fine to do what you did, that you'd get away with it. I see you two have a lot to talk about."

She left them wide-eyed and speechless as she made her way to the bus loop. When she looked over her shoulder, she noticed Owen speeding away from his friend in a state of complete disarray. His hood was up, shielding his face. She hoped this was a sign of a second epiphany for him. Nevertheless, Adelie boarded her bus and got comfortable in her seat as the vehicle carried her to her precious kits.

When she got to the stop that was just before her own home, she hopped out onto the sidewalk with the other students. Though the same dog was barking, it was not at another animal, but rather the coughing of the bus. Adelie sighed in relief. Making sure she kept her backpack on this time, she ventured into the woods.

Leaves spiraled to the forest floor as she enjoyed her walk. She let herself breathe another sigh of relief at all the warm-colored foliage. The fact that it was Fall meant that the kits would have no problem hiding when needed. They surely blended in, at least for now. Adelie's red hair also matched her surroundings. It was like an extension of her being.

A cool breeze blew in from the East, scattering the leaves and bringing the kits' scent to her. Slumping off her backpack, she smiled and allowed her body to change form. Now on four paws, she continued her walk by trotting with the wind bristling her fur.

After a few moments, she came upon the den, the three kits poking their heads out hesitantly. Adelie looked around, ears pricked. She made sure the coast seemed clear before signaling for them to wander out from their home. Instead of wandering, though, they all sprang out at once and knocked their surrogate mother over. The four of them rolled around in the soil and squealed with delight. A few yips and chewed ears later, they all gathered themselves up and shook off the dirt.

Once they were eye to eye, Adelie was able to get a better look at them. She didn't have enough time before to identify their age or sexes. Now, two males and one female stood before her.

The first male, who she decided to name Birch, was a bit taller than the others. His coat was browner in color, and he had a small tear in his ear already—no doubt from some rough play.

As for the second male, she named him Aspen. He was smaller and leaner in stature than Birch. Not only this, but he had a bit more of a playful spark to his eyes. He always looked like he was smiling.

Lastly, Adelie named the female Maple. Though much smaller than the males, she was feisty and never let them overtake her during play. Her coat was a very bright red, perfect for her to blaze through the forest. In all honesty, Adelie already felt a bit more of an attachment to the little female. Still, all of them were precious to her.

For starters, all of them were at least weaned off milk, and looked relatively healthy, though a bit hungry. She would need to teach them how to hunt and find food. It would be hard to follow in their true mother's footsteps, but she would make it work. She had to.

As another breeze surged through the forest, it seemed to bring her a bit of luck. Grasshoppers began to hop up from their hiding places, jumping all around the kits. They already looked intrigued, heads bouncing along with the movement of the insects. Though the human side of her didn't want to do this, she turned her head and snapped one out of the air. The three others watched, ears pointed in interest as it crunched under Adelie's teeth. They seemed to get the message, though, because they were soon jumping around and chasing after the little critters. These grasshoppers were small fry, for sure, but at least it was a start.

While they ran around, Adelie noticed some berry bushes nearby. With autumn already settling into the land, they probably wouldn't be around much longer, but they would give her more time to fully show them all how to hunt. She wouldn't have to worry about them starving in between sessions. Grabbing their attention, she directed them to the bush and took a bite of a couple of them. Almost immediately, the kits began chomping down on the berries, making satisfied little growls all the while. The sight made Adelie happy. It was nice to see them with so much energy, especially with how the past few days had been for them. Now their faces were covered in juice and grasshopper wings.

Adelie decided to use all their newfound energy to her advantage. They needed to find a new den to call home. This uprooted tree not only had painful memories, but it had been noticed by the hunters that terrible night. She called the kits and had them follow her once again.

Though there were many good places for them to call home, many of them seemed to already be occupied—by foxes or otherwise. Along the way, she caught the scent of a badger, and decided it was best to move on to a different area. The kits wouldn't stand a chance against a badger, and she didn't want to accidentally settle them into the other animal's home. Still, the three of them began to whine from having to walk so much. Adelie needed to find something as soon as she could.

The ground began to move up on a steady incline. That's when she noticed the large amounts of boulders and hardened soil that started to make walls around them. She walked up to one of the piles and looked between the lowest rock and the ground. Inside, the rocks were not stacked as low as the outside one. There was enough space for the three of them, and even her, to be in there. Plus, there was also an opening on the other side to serve as an exit.

Excitedly, she began to dig under that low rock to broaden the entrance. The kits assisted her, and they were done in no time. All four of them ducked into the new space. Though there was always the danger of a rock falling, Adelie was willing to take that chance to avoid another human discovering them. The latter seemed far more likely.

Just as the kits cozied up inside their new burrow, a screech bore its way in from the outside world. All three of the babies froze in fear, fur fluffed up and bodies clinging to each other. Adelie tensed up too, the sound sparking a burst of adrenaline through her. It sounded like another fox.

Once she made sure that the kits were accounted for, she scooted her thin body from under the rocks and stood on alert. Another scream pierced the air. It was definitely a fox. Not only that, but a fox in extreme distress. Adelie's heart pounded in her chest and urged her to go to the sound. She started to run, body changing back to normal along the way. The animal's screeches continued to echo all around her. They got louder and louder.

Coming upon her backpack, she quickly scooped it up and grabbed her phone from the outside pocket. She then discovered the source of the sound—a few yards away, there was a fox in a snare. It was a familiar scene. This time, though, there were two men stomping down on it with their boots. The scene made her want to leap out and scream their heads off, but she knew better. She needed evidence.

Holding up the flip-phone, she quickly snapped a few pictures of the violence. As she took the last photo, she could hear the fox's breaths becoming ragged and sparse. Adelie was about to get up to stop the hunters when another noise caught everyone off guard.

A dog was growling.

Looking to her right, Adelie could see it standing atop a nearby hill. This was not the same dog that inhabited the house at the bus stop. Rather, it was a husky, adorning a black and white coat and pale blue eyes. It barked with intent, those same icy eyes staring daggers into the two men. This distracted them, giving the fox a moment to catch its breath. Adelie also took this chance to creep closer to the frightened animal, pocketknife in hand.

The dog began to move closer, its lips curled back into a snarl. A bit intimidated, the men backed away while saying "easy boy." It continued to pad towards them, its stare unwavering. With their backs turned, Adelie quickly sprang into action and began to saw away at the wire around the fox's paw. Though the animal was afraid, it did not have the energy to fight her. Maybe it knew she had good intentions. Maybe it was just continuing to catch its breath.

Unfortunately, the husky's intimidation did not last for long. One of the men began to get irritated.

"This is bullshit!"

Adelie continued to cut. Almost there.

The dog snarled. The angered man raised up his gun.

Snap.

The fox bolted, the dog barked, and the startled man shot off a bullet into the sky.

Now it was Adelie's turn to flee. Shoving her phone in her pocket, she got away just as the men spotted her. The mystery dog sprinted in the opposite direction. The two hunters looked both ways and could not choose who to go after. They decided to give up and argue with each other instead.

Once Adelie reached the road, she picked up her phone again to call her mom. No answer. Right, she had a job now. She wouldn't be around. There was no choice but to walk the three miles to her house.

The walk was long and cold, hardly any cars passing her by. About halfway through it, the sun began to set. The sky burst into flames for a few minutes before the moon's waters extinguished it. Adelie was only about a mile away now, but she was shivering. Her left arm wrapped around her torso while her right arm held out her phone, the screen's glow serving as a flashlight.

After what felt like an eternity, she finally began to see houses. One had something familiar on its lawn—Owen's bike. It was strewn across the grass like an unwanted hand-me-down. Adelie continued to walk until she stumbled upon her own home. No car. She checked the time on her phone. Damn these shorter days. It was only 6 P.M, yet it felt like midnight. The walk felt a lot longer than an hour, too.

Unlocking the door, Adelie let herself in and grabbed an apple from the fridge. Her mom wasn't home. She then wandered up to her bedroom and dumped her backpack out onto her bed. Grabbing her binder, she took out her notes for the group project. She also took out a scrap piece of paper. She doodled the black and white dog on and off through the evening. Just as headlights turned into the driveway, she fell asleep. Her untouched apple sat on the bedside table.

<u>Chapter 4</u>

The next day at school, Adelie walked around the crowds of students with her book flipped open to her sketches of the husky. Though she desperately wanted to hear a "yes," everyone said "no" regarding missing a dog. No one seemed to even recognize the canine. As she got ready to put the sketchbook away, she noticed Owen and Jace near the bus loop. She rushed over, the boys giving her a surprised look.

"Hey. Know anyone missing a dog? Saw one like this last night," she thrust the pictures closer to their faces.

The two of them squinted and took a closer look. After a few seconds, Jace spoke up.

"Oh, that's just Ace."

"Ace?"

"Yeah, a stray that hangs out around here sometimes. He likes to mess with the hunters, so they call him 'Ace' as a joke. They hate his guts!"

"Hm," she turned the book around to look at the sketches again.

"I guess I could've guessed that."

Owen spoke up, suddenly curious.

"How come?"

Adelie stuffed the drawings into her backpack.

"The hunters I saw last night nearly shit themselves when they saw him."

Owen let out a little laugh at that.

"Must be a pretty scary dog then," he assumed.

"Not necessarily. Maybe just a smart one," she guessed.

❖

A few hours later, it was lunch time again. Adelie entered the cafeteria only to see Owen standing at *her* usual table, Jeremy sitting at one of the chairs. The two of them were in deep conversation. Though Jeremy seemed a bit tense, it was Owen who looked the most anxious. With one hand behind his neck and the other in his pocket, the boy appeared to be in the middle of an apology.

Adelie made sure to hang back until she saw Owen slink away to the other side of the lunchroom. As she made her way over, Jeremy grinned and waved her down. She smiled back and sat down beside him.

"Hey. That kid giving you more trouble?"

She motioned to the dark-haired boy reuniting with his pack. Jeremy looked a bit startled.

"Oh, uh, *no*, actually."

Adelie raised her eyebrows.

"He said that he was sorry. Sorry for what he did," he fiddled with the zipper on his lunch bag before continuing.

"Did you talk to him?"

Adelie sighed and took out her lunch—a granola bar.

"Honestly, yeah, I did. I'm sorry."

"No, no, it's okay. I just—"

"I know. An apology should've come without anyone holding his hand," she sighed and took a bite of her food between her words.

"But, really, he never would've realized. That idiot has walls up so high that he can't see those who live below it."

Jeremy stared at her, intrigued.

"He won't be a threat to you anymore. Don't even worry about him," she reassured.

The boy smiled wide, his eyes bright.

"Thank you, Miss Adelie."

The redhead nearly spit out her snack.

"'Miss'?"

"Sorry! Got ahead of myself! I am just very happy to have you as a friend."

Adelie tapped her chest to get the cough to go away. Jeremy kept talking.

"Well, it's not *totally* uncalled for. You *are* older than me."

"Hey," she pointed her granola bar at him.

"Don't push your luck, or *I'm* gonna be the one beating you up."

The two of them laughed and joked around until they had to go back to class.

❖

Hours later, Adelie met up with Owen and Jace at the library to work on their project. They climbed up the spiraling staircase to the second floor. Walking alongside the lesser-known friend gave Adelie a clearer view of his appearance. Jace was at least a head taller than Owen. A few freckles trailed down his cheeks and arms. His green eyes brightened with mischief as he elbowed Owen in the ribs playfully. Owen winced and rubbed at his side.

While the first floor was filled with mostly shelves full of novels and comics, the second floor carried many rows of textbooks and tables for students to use. The trio picked one out and sat down and unloaded their backpacks.

The three of them dove into the schoolwork in front of them, pausing now and then to get foolishly off-track. Those instances were mostly Jace and Owen being as loud as possible to get the librarian pissed off. It worked, and both the lady at the desk and the girl in their group gave them nasty looks. An hour and a half of temperate forest research passed before Jace's phone started vibrating. He flipped it open and answered the call before swiftly shutting it again.

"Guess who's off the hook," he smirked.

Owen immediately frowned.

"Aw, no, c'mon man! We're not done yet!"

Jace shrugged and threw a devilish grin their way before rushing off to the main doors. Owen cursed under his breath and let his face fall nose-first into the book on the table. Adelie simply glanced at him and cleared her throat, hand still writing down notes. He adjusted himself slightly, eyes now visible over the pages.

"Why is it that every time I end up alone with you it looks like you wanna rip my throat out?"

Adelie set down her notebook and raised an eyebrow.

"You're not entirely wrong, but you're safe today. I saw you talking to Jeremy. "

Owen perked up and returned to a normal sitting position.

"O-Oh yeah, I, uh," he stammered, as if deciding on putting up a façade or not.

Adelie's unrelenting stare broke down his wall.

"I felt bad. What you said made sense. I'm sorry," he finally uttered.

The statement made her sink into her chair with a smug grin.

"Never thought I'd hear you admit that you were wrong, or better yet, *sorry* about something."

Owen returned her smirk with one of his own.

"I'm full of surprises," he shrugged.

His words sparked a sudden realization in her. Something she needed to do.

"Speaking of surprises," Adelie reached for her phone.

Flipping it open, she quickly found the pictures from the day before.

"You said something about 'not liking it either' the last time we talked. Did you mean this shit?"

Owen blinked as a bright screen was shoved in his face. He was met with incriminating photos of the hunters attempting to suffocate the fox. The men's faces and intentions were clearly visible.

Blue eyes grew wide with fear as he quickly smacked the phone down on the table. Owen gritted his teeth against the unavoidable clang. The noise caught the attention of other students, who momentarily glanced their way before returning to their work. When he looked back at Adelie, he could see her eyes turning as red as her hair. She took in a deep breath but was cut off.

"Shh! Shh! Just, c'mon," Owen scooped his stuff up and beckoned for Adelie to follow.

Now she was fuming. Not only did this boy smack her, but he shushed her too. However, she wanted to know what was going on, so she followed his lead. The two of them found themselves in a more secluded corner of the library. Owen plopped down on the floor between two bookcases, one at his back and one at his feet. Adelie sat next to him.

"I know you wanna kill me for that, but it was for good reason," he whispered.

She stared at him and waited for him to explain himself.

Owen sighed and slicked some hair back from his face. It was as if he had just pushed something to the back of his mind, too.

"I really, *really* can't tell you much— but, yes, that's what I was talking about."

Gears began to turn behind Adelie's eyes. They urged him to spill more information.

"There's a lot of hunters in this town. They all want money, so they bend the rules to get more of it," he stared at the dirty carpet below them.

"What do you mean?"

Owen jumped at the question, a tight wire of tension wrapping around his body.

"L-Look I can't keep talking about this."

Adelie looked around.

"There's no one here. You're fine."

"You don't understand," he kept staring at the floor.

"I don't understand because you won't tell me."

The silence that followed was interrupted by Adelie's phone vibrating. She flipped it open to read the text message. Cursing, she slammed it closed. Owen glanced her way.

"My mom can't pick me up until later," now she was the one staring at the floor.

Owen took advantage of the change of subject.

"I could probably get my dad to carpool you home," he began to lighten up a bit.

Adelie did the opposite.

"Oh, no, I'll just wait here. It's fine."

Owen was about to speak again when Adelie cut him off.

"I'm getting a sense of déjà vu. How come you're scared of me, but the next minute, you want to do everything in your power to be nice to me?"

"I'm full of surprises, remember?"

Adelie rolled her eyes.

"You're full of somethin' but I wouldn't call it surprises."

Owen chose to ignore the comment as he dialed his father's number. He walked away from Adelie as he conversed with him. After a few moments, he came back over and gave her a thumbs up. She begrudgingly offered a small smile back. The two of them wandered back up to the main entrance to wait. They sat on a nearby bench, backpacks in their laps and lips sealed.

Adelie tucked a strand of hair behind her ear.

"Didn't you say that your dad is a hunter, too?"

The boy stiffened and stared at the ground again. He took a while to answer.

"Yes."

"Hm," she sighed and leaned into her backpack.

"No idea how you convinced him to let me ride with you guys."

Owen blinked before sitting up straight, chest puffed out.

"I have a way with words."

For maybe the hundredth time that afternoon, Adelie rolled her eyes. She texted her mother that she was getting a ride home from school.

A car honked outside. The two of them jumped.

"Ah, that's him. Let's go," Owen hurriedly got up from his seat.

Adelie quietly followed behind him. She was met with a tall truck complete with an equally tall driver. He had dark hair and blue eyes—where Owen must've gotten it from—and a fair amount of facial hair, including a thick mustache. His skin was tanned and showed signs of wear and tear. The man stared at them sternly, his face hardly moving when he talked.

"Get in," he ordered.

The two teens obliged. Owen went to grab for the backseat handle before flinching away and climbing into the front seat instead. Adelie took this as her cue to sit in the back by herself. She squeezed into the narrow space, garbage and bottles lining the dusty floor. As soon as all doors were shut, they were off. The truck grumbled and coughed. It covered up the awkward silence. They made one pit stop at the front of the school to pick up Owen's bike and toss it in the tailgate before continuing.

Owen's father stared straight ahead, seemingly fixated on something other than the road. His son fussed with the straps of his backpack and did the same. Adelie's nose scrunched up at the smell of gasoline. Still, she felt the need to say something.

"Thank you," she cleared her throat.

The man simply grunted. The drive fell silent again, save for the growling of the vehicle. It felt like hours had passed by the time they arrived at Adelie's house. After she hopped out, she looked into the front window and nodded at them both. The man still stared ahead. The boy stared at her instead.

As Owen's father put the car back in drive, Adelie noticed a desperate sadness in the boy's eyes. They were blue in every sense of the word. She could tell that he wanted to leave the vehicle, too. However, he soon looked away and tightened his grip on his backpack. The truck made a swift U-turn and Owen disappeared altogether. About a block away, it turned into its destination—the melancholy bike's home.

Once again, Adelie was greeted with her own empty house. She was almost glad when her stomach growled and gave the quiet something to chew on. She needed something to chew on, too. Looking through the cupboards, she was met with more emptiness. Same with the fridge.

She groaned in frustration as she trudged up the stairs to her bedroom. When she set her backpack down, she noticed the apple sitting on her bedside table. The poor, beautiful thing had been abandoned the night before. Adelie quickly picked it up and took it down to the kitchen. She rinsed it off with care before taking a big bite out of it. It was perhaps the best thing she'd ever eaten, at least in that moment.

Hours later, the moon had risen by the time Adelie spotted her mother's car outside. The lights burned her tired eyes. She didn't want to go down to see her, but her stomach was already begging for food again. The sound of the front door opening only intensified the conflicting feelings. Stomach winning against brain, she headed down the steps to the first floor.

The woman who faced Adelie was disheveled, hair full of frizz and purse spilling across the hardwood floor. She hardly looked like her mother, yet here she was.

"Sorry I couldn't pick you up. Boss wouldn't let me leave work."

Adelie raised an eyebrow.

"Boss?"

Her mother took down her ponytail and sighed in annoyance.

"Yeah, something 'Smit.' Nice guy. He had to pick up his son from school."

All the blood in Adelie's body grew cold. She wasn't sure about everything that was going on in this town yet, but she had a bad feeling about that man. He was a hunter, which normally wouldn't bother her, but in this town, it did. Owen flinched at his father's every movement, every word. He seemed to completely change whenever his dad was brought up in conversation. This had to mean that either he was abusive or that he was the very reason for the fox killings—or both.

Shaking off the tornado of thought, Adelie made sure to reply innocently.

"He's actually the one that got me home. His son's name is Owen. He's a... classmate of mine."

"Oh, good, good."

Her mother turned away to gather her things off the floor. The daughter still couldn't help throwing some spice into the sugarcoated exchange.

"There's nothing to eat here."

Her mother cursed and dropped the wallet she had just picked up.

"Shit. I've been eating out. I didn't get groceries. I'll get you something in the morning."

Adelie's empty stomach overpowered her mother's empty words.

"I'm hungry now, though. I've *been* hungry."

That got her mother's attention. She snapped her head around, eyes sharp as bear claws.

"Well, I've *been* working. We can't all get what we want when we want it."

Warmth returned to Adelie's blood. In fact, it boiled.

"Dad always had food on the table. He always made sure we were fed."

Her mother quickly stood up now, eyes threatening to tear into her own flesh and blood.

"Why are you making me the bad guy? He's the one who left. I'm the one who has stayed, or have you forgotten?"

Adelie swore she might get slapped, but her words stung just as much. Scowling, she charged back up the stairs and gave her last words for the night.

"It's getting harder to remember!"

Thankfully the mother was too tired to go up to her door and demand it to be opened. Instead, she simply yelled from where she stood.

"Well, you better think real hard! You wouldn't even be here without me!"

Adelie slid to the floor just behind her door. Her fingers found their way to her scalp and began to tug. She clawed at herself until a few strands fell to the floor. It was the only way to get all the anger out. The only way to punish, not only herself, but the whole universe, too.

She was about to move on to her skin when she heard a loud bang from outside. Then she heard yelling. Her feet carried her to her window. Just down the street, she could see the silhouettes of two people. She then spotted the shape of a bike.

The people were outside Owen's house. It quickly became apparent that it was Owen and his father. The boy had been shoved and was currently picking himself back up. Though his body cowered, his voice spat across the quiet air. His father's voice roared in return. Before long, Owen hopped onto that same, sad bike and rode off into the dark.

Sleep didn't come easily that night.

<u>Chapter 5</u>

It was no surprise for Adelie to find her morning void of a proper breakfast. What did surprise her, though, was her willingness to eat from the school cafeteria. The combination of no sleep and no food had her in a vice grip. She joined the dozens of other teens hobbling up to the glass-shielded counter. Sadly, most of the food options made her sick just from looking at them. Moving along the line, she settled for some fruit and a few pieces of French toast before facing the register.

When the cashier asked for money, Adelie reached for her pocket only to feel her knife. No money. She swore she had brought a few dollars just for this purpose. Cursing quietly, she apologized and was about to tell them to throw out the food when someone spoke up.

"Hey, wait, I can get it!"

A curly, dirty-blond head bounded over to the checkout. His glasses slid down his nose. It was Jeremy in all his glory, and he was here to save the day.

"Jeremy? No, you don't have to—"

"Here you go ma'am! This should cover it," he handed over three dollars and some change.

Adelie smiled a little sheepishly and picked her tray back up. The two of them walked toward an empty table and sat across from each other. Adelie reached for her fork.

"You didn't need to do that. I can pay you back."

Jeremy sipped at an orange juice cartoon until it was empty. He must've eaten already.

"Don't even worry about it. I can tell that you haven't been eating much. Plus, I didn't expect to actually see you in line for school food."

Adelie let out a little laugh. She ate a few strawberries before replying.

"Thank you."

The boy smiled and took his Gameboy out to play some games before classes started. The girl munched away, finally glad to have some nourishment in her system.

❖

Today was the day that Adelie and her group would have to present their project to the class. Since she had done most of the writing work, the others agreed to do all of the actual talking. As the room filled up with her classmates, she noticed that Damien had arrived before Jace and Owen. He looked worried. So was Adelie. She'd noticed Owen's absence at their table during lunchtime and wondered just how bad the previous night had been for him. This kid was weird, but she would never wish for him to deal with even worse crap than Adelie did from her own mother.

A few minutes later, said boys wandered in. The bell rang the second they stepped through the door. Adelie wasn't surprised to see a cut on Owen's lip, a bruise on his cheek. She wasn't even surprised to see him plop down in his seat without a word whilst wearing the same clothes as yesterday. What caught her attention was his ability to smile at her despite her being the most likely reason he even wore such a beaten face. Guessing from what she had seen through her window, his father must've gotten angry at Adelie's inclusion in the ride home last night.

Questions nagged at her. Why was he here now, but not at lunch? Why was he with Jace but not Damien? These thoughts were cut short when her group was called to the front of the classroom. She got her USB ready and set up their PowerPoint. The boys took it from there.

When Owen's role came around, his voice was tired. His frame curled into itself, eyelids threatening to do the same. In a bold move, Adelie stepped forward and finished the rest of the presentation for him. She hated every second of it, but it was worth it to see Owen perk up a little. Even Jace looked a little happier. At least the topic was an easy one. Adelie could talk about the importance of forests all day. When they returned to their seats, Owen muttered a quick thank you and offered a second smile.

Eventually, both the class and the presentations came to an end. Owen waved goodbye to Jace, Adelie, and Damien before shuffling into the hallway. Jace hurriedly followed, perhaps against Owen's wishes. It was weird to see Owen be the hasty one. Now she knew what she must look like daily. As she gathered up her things, Damien approached her. His dark eyes were pools of concern.

"Hey, uh, Adelie?"

Adelie zipped up her backpack and slung it over her shoulder.

"That's me. What's up?"

"I think you were the last one to see Owen yesterday, right? Did something happen?"

Adelie didn't know how much she should reveal in terms of Owen's father's behavior. She really didn't know the entire situation, either. To avoid any misgivings, she offered a little fib.

"I was the last one, but I'm not sure what's wrong, either."

Damien sighed.

"I know his dad is a dick, but he never really says much else. I saw how his face looked and was just worried, sorry," Damien's eyebrows knitted together.

Adelie almost wanted to say something. Not yet.

"Don't be sorry. *I'm* sorry I can't help. I can try to talk to him, though."

The boy's face lifted a little. He spoke up again.

"That would be great. Please let me know what he says."

"Will do," Adelie nodded.

With that, the two of them went their separate ways.

❖

The sky was peppered with gray clouds when Adelie found her way to the kits. She was on all four paws, bushy tail and all. She ducked into the den to find something extraordinary— the kits were all eating off a crow! In fact, it took them a second to notice that their mother had returned to them. They soon flooded her with nuzzles and licks. She couldn't have been prouder of them. It was nice to see them doing well, especially at something she hadn't extensively taught yet.

From how puffed out Maple's chest was, Adelie guessed that she'd been the one to make the kill. The little vixen was quickly becoming the leader of the group despite her size. Birch, the biggest of the three, quickly pinned her down to play before she could get too cocky. The two of them tussled for a moment before Aspen joined in too. She gave them a few minutes of playtime before breaking them up.

All four foxes crawled out of the den and into the cool air. Adelie surveyed the surroundings, judging their safety. The youngsters cautiously sniffed at the wind. Sensing nothing, she had them follow here through the woods. A few raindrops fell as the sky darkened. The smell of wet earth was refreshing as it washed over their senses. It began to come down stronger, little pools appearing on the ground. The kits lapped out of them, happy to have fresh water. Adelie was about to cut their hike short when something made Maple freeze and crouch down. The others stopped as well, ears perked.

There was a rabbit. It was taking shelter under a couple logs. Adelie guessed the three of them were still hungry if they were about to try for another kill. Maple took a few small steps before shooting off toward her prey. Mud flung into the air and coated her fur. The rabbit shook and took off running, too. Birch and Aspen rounded the scene to try to cut it off. It slipped past them. Now it was coming right for Adelie. It jumped in a last-ditch effort to get away but was immediately caught by Adelie's jaws.

Though she had caught it, she didn't have the nerve to kill it. It was squirming and screaming. As the others rushed over, Adelie let go of it. Both the rabbit and the kits started running again. This would be good practice for them.

After a few rounds of catch and release, Aspen was the one to finally grab it by the throat. It wasn't long until the poor creature was dead. This was how nature was. Adelie licked his head as a congrats. All of them headed deeper into the forest, Aspen proudly carrying his prize. The rain let up for the moment. That was when Adelie caught another scent.

Owen was here again. She wasn't sure where yet, but close. He didn't seem to be a very big danger, but she remained hostile. As they neared a large clearing, she spotted him.

The boy was sitting at the edge of a pond with his hood up. A couple ducks splashed around with glee. He was looking at his reflection when he turned toward them. His eyes grew a little, seemingly surprised at them being there. The kits took notice and tensed up beside their mother. Owen pulled his hood closer to hide his beaten face.

"I don't mean any trouble. I'll leave if you want me to."

Defeat leaked from his words. Adelie pitied him. That pity made her want to talk to him. She had promised his friend she would, after all. She spun around and guided the kits back to their den. She made sure they were safe, warm, and feeding on their second meal before she bid them adieu.

Adelie walked back to Owen on two legs and her backpack over her shoulder. When she returned, he was lying on his back. Cold rocks supported him as equally cold rain hit his face. He quickly sat up when he saw her make a second appearance. A small smile tugged at his lips.

"I thought you got pissed and left."

Adelie scoffed and sat next to him. She pulled out a small umbrella from her backpack and popped it open. It shielded them from the downpour and cold wind.

"For once, no."

The two sat silently for a minute before Adelie spoke again.

"I saw you last night, your dad kicking you out. I can't help but feel like it was my fault."

"You saw?"

"I don't live very far from you guys. I heard yelling and looked out my window."

Owen pushed some stray hairs from his eyes.

"I won't lie, then. Yes. He was mad that I was with you."

A part of Adelie, perhaps an old part, would've given anything to make sure Owen was as far from her as possible. However, the motherly part of her felt deep sorrow for him. Yes, he was pathetic, obnoxious, naive—but that didn't seem to be his fault anymore. Parents either make or break their children.

"I guess I'm not surprised. I'm sorry," Adelie sighed.

"Don't be. It was my decision to get him to pick us up."

Silence took over again.

"Listen," Owen whispered, the rain nearly washing away his words.

Adelie was all ears.

"I want to tell you things. I think we're safe out here. The hunters don't like to come out in weather like this."

Well, this kid really was full of surprises.

"Okay," Adelie approved.

Owen fidgeted, hands and feet trying to find something to do while his lips moved.

"There's a lot going on. I haven't really talked about it with anyone before. Jace knows but it's only because his dad is in cahoots with mine."

"Why are you telling me, then?"

He turned and looked her in the eyes before answering.

"You're the only one in a long time who's been able to look right through me."

At that moment, it felt like the opposite. Owen continued.

"Damien and Colby would probably blab or not take it seriously. But you--- you've been through shit. You know how much the world can suck."

A different name. Colby. Probably the other friend Adelie hadn't recognized at lunch. Though she was extremely put aback, she had to give credit where credit was due.

"That's not true. Just after class today, Damien talked to me. He's worried about you. I'm sure your other friend is, too. They want to know what's going on."

Owen anxiously turned his attention to the soaking ground.

"I know. I know they want to know. It's just so hard."

"They're your friends. Friends are supposed to hear you and support you. I've never really had friends, but that's what I always thought it was all about," she urged.

"You're right," he sucked in a deep breath.

"I'd like to tell you first, though."

Adelie obliged by nodding.

Owen's fingers fiddled with the fabric of his jeans.

"I'll just come out and say this. My mom died when she had me. It was twelve years after my big brother. It wasn't expected. Andres, my brother, said that my dad was never the same after that. Always drinking and yelling," his fingers balled up into fists at his sides.

"I'm sorry."

"It's fine. After my brother moved out a few years ago, things got worse. Money was getting low. My dad was desperate to get it any way he could. He'd always had a hunting hobby, but he teamed up with his own friends to turn it into a business. Normally this wouldn't be that bad, but some of his friends had connections in the DNR. They all worked together to slip through the cracks when it came to regulations and reports. Basically, they've been killing all they want without penalty. These woods used to have a lot more animals— lots of bears, bobcats, even wolves sometimes. They're gone."

Adelie listened with bated breath. Words spilled from his mouth like the water that spilled onto the earth around them. A floodgate had opened.

"What's worse is why everything is gone, only foxes really remaining. Their goal is to make certain species disappear from this area by obtaining their coats. With a plan like this, it means that the coats became ten times more valuable since they are harder to obtain. They raise the prices even more by making sure that the furs aren't damaged in any way. They do this by, by—"

"Suffocating them instead of shooting them," she finished his sentence.

Owen nodded, looking a little queasy.

"Exactly. The guns are all just for show."

Adelie's hand shook with rage, the umbrella nearly falling over.

"I hate it. I hate all of it. He forced me into it, and I've been playing along just to get by. I've never killed a single animal. I don't want to be a part of it," Owen gritted his teeth.

Adelie pushed her own anger to the side to console Owen.

"Now I see why you act like that. Still, you really should talk to your friends. They deserve to know."

Owen put his face in his hands and nodded.

"I know. Thank you for listening. Maybe you could help me figure things out?"

Adelie playfully punched him in the shoulder.

"We know each other's deepest, darkest secrets now. I'm not goin' anywhere."

The boy's eyes lit up with newfound hope. Still, he smirked.

"See, I told you, I'm—"

"Full of surprises. Yes, yes, I know. Shut up."

The atmosphere turned tense for a moment before the two of them cracked up in quiet laughter. Adelie scooped her phone from out of her backpack. She flipped it open to check the time just as a big gust of wind whipped through the forest. The two of them shivered.

"It's fucking cold. We should head home," Owen stood up.

Adelie quickly realized that her previous plan to walk home had backfired. She felt stuck. Before she could say anything else, Owen spoke again.

"Lemme guess, you were gonna walk?"

"Yep."

"Well, you should know by now that I mostly get around by bike."

Adelie stood up and put on her backpack again.

"Is that an invitation?"

Owen spread out his arm, motioning for her to walk ahead of him.

"Ladies first."

❖

Adelie was drenched to the bone by the time she reached her front door. After finding her keys, she left her backpack and boots on the porch to let them dry. Her mother wasn't home yet. As soon as she got up to her room, she hopped in the shower. The hot water felt like honey. It soaked her body and mind in warmth. It helped her take in everything she had learned today.

When she finished up, she heard the front door open. Like an alarm, it made her stomach growl. Adelie decided to lay in bed and relax for a minute. Though hungry, she really wasn't sure if her mother had bothered to get food. Her eyes closed.

Adelie didn't even realize she'd fallen asleep until she heard her name being called. She was immediately flooded with the smell of spices. Replacing her robe with pajamas, she raced to the head of the stairs. Could it be?

The dining room table was set, dishes of food and all. Her mother had made spaghetti with tomato sauce filled with garlic, basil, and parsley. A small tray of garlic bread sat between the two piles of pasta. It looked and smelled amazing. Granted, it was a cheap meal, but it was a welcome sight, nonetheless. Her mother stood at the bottom of the stairs. Her hair was in a messy bun and her eyes were tired.

"I know it's not much, but I was able to do some shopping."

Adelie couldn't help but smile a little as she descended the stairs. Her gait was a bit slow as she observed the scene. She glanced at the clock. Not only had her mother gotten out of work early, but she'd finally gotten food. She even made a hot meal for the two of them. Wasting no time, Adelie quickly pulled up her seat and began to dig in. After a few bites, she paused.

"Thank you."

Now her mother was the one in shock. Her fork twirled up some spaghetti as she replied.

"You're welcome."

They ate their food in pleasant silence. The mother began washing dishes as soon as they were both done.

"That boss of mine, Richard, or Mr. Smit, rather—he seems like a real gentleman. He let me clock out a little early today to make sure I got you some grub."

All the food in Adelie's stomach wanted to purge up her throat.

"How did he know?"

"I had mentioned it while working. I guess he remembered it," her mother smiled to herself.

"What is your job, exactly?"

Her mother wiped off her hands.

"He runs a fur and taxidermy shop in town. I run the register. Why?"

"Nothing. I just didn't know."

"Well, it's nothing to get fussy about. Hardly anyone even goes in there."

Adelie thought a moment before replying.

"Kinda weird he hired you, then."

Now the mother was mad, a hand smacking down upon the granite kitchen top.

"You'd better be *happy* he hired me. We need it. He's a fine and generous man."

❖

A father and child were planting a garden. The little girl struggled to use the watering can, the object's weight nearly knocking her over. The father smiled and helped her hold it. Water flowed onto the fresh soil. The girl smiled, freckles sprouting on her sun-kissed skin. As they began to dig at a new spot, something appeared in the ground. She grabbed at it, unsure of what to expect. It was thin and coiled. Man-made. It didn't belong in a garden. A growl sounded from next to her.

A bear sat where her father used to be. It snatched the object away. The girl covered her eyes in fear.

Now she was in a courtroom full of tall men in suits. Her father was there too. He was smiling again.

Adelie woke up with a start. Sweat traced her body. She felt hot and cold at the same time. Her mind rifled through the dream, trying to make sense of what it meant.

She had an idea.

<u>Chapter 6</u>

Adelie caught sight of Owen when traveling between classes. He was standing outside the bathrooms, no doubt waiting for one of his buddies to finish his business. His eyes were glued to something in his hand. She fought through the traffic to get to him, tapping on his shoulder when she reached him. He jumped a little.

"Ah! H-Hey!"

She glanced down to see a Tamagotchi in his palm. He quickly shoved it in his pocket, cheeks a bit red. She raised an eyebrow.

"Don't judge me. It gives me purpose."

This boy really *was* something else.

"Whatever you say. Hey, I've got an idea about what we talked about yesterday."

A boy emerged from the bathroom and struck Owen in the side. He was tall with blond hair and blue eyes. He also had a little more muscle on his frame. What was his name again?

"Adelie, Colby. Colby, Adelie," Owen introduced the two, excusing his momentary embarrassment.

Adelie offered a small wave. Colby high-fived it. His hand was damp from washing his hands.

"You're the new girl from the other day, right?"

She wiped her hand on her jeans.

"Sure."

"I told you her name was Adelie," Owen corrected with an exasperated sigh.

Colby snapped his fingers and nudged Owen. It seemed his friends really loved abusing their leader.

"I knew it. See ya 'round!"

He grabbed Owen by the arm and began to tug him down the hallway. Owen was able to wiggle his way out of the other's grasp after a few feeble attempts.

"Just get to class without me! I'll be there!"

He ran back over to Adelie.

"Don't take it personally. He's an idiot but he means well."

Adelie snorted at that. It was weird to hear him say that.

"Anyway, you've got a phone, right? We could text!"

Adelie blinked. Sure, her mom had texted her before, but she rarely used the feature herself. Pressing buttons several times to get one letter never appealed to her much. Thinking back, she'd maybe only sent a handful of texts back to her mom before.

"I'm not really into that sort of thing."

Owen's heart might as well have stood still.

"WHAT? It's the way of the future! It's great! Here, gimme your phone."

Adelie frowned and took out her phone but didn't let him take it.

"Just tell me what to do."

"Fine. See that button? Push it and then hit to make a new contact."

Her fingers lingered over the numbers. She slowly pressed the right keys but ended up on a different page. It was taking her to the internet.

"NO, no, don't go there. Ugh, just give it a minute to stop."

The bell rang.

Owen cursed as the two waited for the program to shut down. After a few more seconds, it finally did. Adelie sighed and handed him her phone.

"Just do it for me, then."

His eyes were stars. Quickly, he punched his number into her phone. She then told him her number to put in his. The bell began to die down.

"See ya!"

He sped down the hallway the same way that Colby had gone. Adelie jogged the other way and headed up the stairs to the second floor. Just as she entered the classroom, her phone vibrated in her pocket. She sat down before sneaking a look at the screen.

10:16 AM

Owen: Hi :-D

❖

By the end of the day, Adelie had not only Owen's number, but Jeremy's, Jace's, Colby's, and Damien's, too. Jeremy had happily entered his number into her phone during lunch, eyes gleaming with excitement to have someone to text. On the other hand, Damien, Owen, and Jace basically played hot potato with the device during the class they all had together, even giving her Colby's number without his presence.

Owen was about to leave with them to the bus loop when Adelie cleared her throat. He told the others to go on without him. Adelie could still see the worry in Damien's eyes as she and Owen made their way to the library. She hadn't gotten to talk to him yet.

Luckily, they were able to find an empty, secluded spot. It was very near where they had attempted to talk before. Adelie hoped that they wouldn't be noticed. She wished they had somewhere better to talk, but the forest wasn't safe right now. The rain had gone, and the ground had dried up. Hunters would surely be out and about. She became lost in her own thoughts, only awakening when Owen poked her shoulder.

"Psst. You said you had an idea," he whispered.

She blinked a few times and allowed her vision to come back to her.

"I had a dream. I feel like it was trying to tell me something."

Owen glanced around. Coast clear. He waved for her to continue.

"I think we need to find my dad. He could help us fight this. We don't know anything about law or rules, but he does. I bet he could make a case against them if we got more info."

Owen furrowed his brow.

"What? Isn't your dad practically just a bear now? Sorry, that was bad of me to say. What I mean is, you haven't even seen him since that big incident, right?"

"No. I haven't seen him. No one has."

"How would we find him, then?"

Adelie held her backpack closer to her chest and sighed.

"I don't know, but he's gotta be out there. If he's a bear, maybe we could track him," she offered.

He thrummed his fingers along his chin as he pondered.

"Hmm, I could ask some of the hunters if they've heard any news of bear sightings nearby. They even have some friends out of state that are basically doing the same thing as them when it comes to hunting. If he's a person, though, what should we do?"

"His absorbism was bad. Really bad. If he's alive, he's probably shifting form constantly. It could go either way at any given time."

Adelie looked around to make sure no one was watching or listening. Talking about her father put her on edge. It didn't help that she was also afraid of the two of them being caught talking to each other.

"That makes sense. I'll see if I can find anything out," Owen replied softly.

The offer was extremely gracious. It was clear that his father did not like Adelie or Owen mingling with her. This could mean more danger for him, more hurt that she had only seen an ounce of.

"Be careful. I'm gonna feel like shit if your dad turns rogue on you again."

"He usually does, anyway. I'll be fine."

"Only if you're sure. This... isn't just about me, now."

A wide grin lit his face.

"Wait... are you *actually* starting to like me? Kinda sounds like you care," he teased, but a spark of excitement was still palpable.

Adelie sighed a *pfft* and snuck a smirk back at him. Unfortunately for her, she *did* care.

"Don't get used to it."

They stood up and dusted themselves of the information they'd just disclosed. She texted her mother to see if she would take her home, knowing that she had today off from work. The two teens were walking to the front when she replied back.

3:56 PM

Mom: Yes, but don't make a habit of missing the bus. This is my day to relax.

Regardless of the backhanded comment, Adelie was glad to not have to ask Owen for help home again, especially after what he had already agreed to do for her.

Owen spotted her texting.

"Do... you need help getting back?"

"Nah, my mom's gonna pick me up in a bit. I've had just about enough help outta you for now," she kidded.

Owen laughed and waved, walking towards the front door.

"Alright, well, I'm gonna go then. I'll talk to you later."

Adelie waved back and sat down at a bench outside after Owen left. She texted Damien. He deserved a follow up, but she made sure not to spill too much information.

Adelie: Hey. Owen's dad hit him but he's OK. I think he needs time to talk about things.

Twenty minutes later, her phone vibrated as she stepped into her mom's vehicle.

Damien: tht makes sense. thx adelie

A few weeks went by. The chill in the air turned into frost on the ground. The trees continued to show their rainbow of colors, some slowly turning brown. The kits grew at an extraordinary pace, their bodies and smarts improving every day. School continued to be school.

Owen and Adelie rarely met up due to fear of exposure. They mostly communicated by text, which they would both delete directly after. Owen was not having luck finding anything out about her father so far. None of the hunters said much, and when they did, they did not know of any bear sightings. Sadly, word got around to Owen's dad about the boy's inquiries. He constantly interrogated his son about his weird questions. Owen lied with a silver-tipped tongue.

It was a Saturday evening when Adelie received a text from Jeremy.

5:46 PM

Jeremy: Hey! Wanna get ice cream? <=D

She took a moment to reply, a bit of surprise in her eyes. Smirking, she quickly punched out her text. These weeks of texting had really improved her speed.

5:47 PM

Adelie: OK, but I don't have a ride. :P

5:48 PM

Jeremy: My mom can drop us! Address? <B)

❖

Adelie and Jeremy entered a little ice cream shop, no doubt the place that Jeremy had spoken of in the past. A small bell tinkled from above and the floor was colored in white and blue tiles. Pastel pink tables were accompanied by pale yellow chairs against the walls of the small space. Though modest, the place had a large counter with dozens of flavors to choose from. A smiley, round-faced gentleman stood behind the register. It was hard to imagine anything bad ever happening here.

"I hadn't been here since what happened, but now I have a friend to come here with," Jeremy grinned.

Adelie smiled right back at him.

"I'm glad."

They looked through the glass excitedly to survey the flavors available. There were the classics such as vanilla, chocolate, and strawberry, of course, but many were new to Adelie. One was called "Pot-Hole," which consisted of chocolate ice cream, chocolate sprinkles, Oreo, and ribbons of white fudge. Another unique one was called "Ms. Bits" which was made of vanilla ice cream with pieces of every chocolate bar they had available. Since Jeremy was familiar with the place, he quickly pointed out the treat of his choice.

"I'll take a double-scoop cone of the 'Mr. Hero,' please!"

Adelie looked at the ingredient list curiously. Blueberry, strawberry, and mango ice creams all mixed into a colorful concoction. Looked pretty good. Soon enough, though, the cheery employee was awaiting her choice. Unsure of what to choose, she picked plain strawberry in a cup without a second thought. She chose to adorn it in rainbow sprinkles. Once they made it to the register, she slammed down her wallet and eyed Jeremy.

"My turn, alright?"

He blinked, a bit stunned. It soon turned to amusement.

"I guess you knew that I planned to pay again, huh?"

Adelie simply raised an eyebrow as she happily handed over her cash to the cashier. Once done, Jeremy joined her in sitting at a table. They enjoyed their dessert in blissful silence for a few moments. Old school pop played softly from the speaker in the ceiling.

"Thanks for inviting me," Adelie smiled.

Jeremy was caught by surprise, a little bit of "Mr. Hero" making its way onto his glasses. He took them off and wiped them on his shirt, grey eyes squinting.

"Oh, of course! Friends don't always have to just hang at school, y'know. I also, uh, felt better about coming here ever since Owen apologized."

Adelie nodded in reply and continued to dig in. Jeremy piped up again.

"I've seen you around with him sometimes. Keepin' him under control, are we?"

Now Adelie was the one to look surprised, both at his words of choice and the fact that their time together had become obvious. Jeremy stifled a laugh.

"Of course. He's annoying, though, and always finds his way back to pester me," she covered up her tracks.

The bell rang again as more customers entered the shop. Adelie and Jeremy turned to look.

"Speak of the fuckin' Devil," Adelie huffed under her breath.

It was Owen and Jace. All four teens made eye contact. Jeremy stiffened.

"Welcome, welcome! Choose any flavor you'd like," the employee sang.

The third-party interruption was enough to disrupt the tension in the air. Owen smiled, Jace poked Owen on the shoulder, Jeremy relaxed, and Adelie continued to eat her ice cream. She could tell how eager Owen was to speak to her, but they both knew they still needed to lie low. They couldn't risk the other boys getting caught in the mix, either. Jace disrupted the silence this time.

"Table for four?"

Jace pulled up a chair without an answer to his question and sat in it backwards. His chest was against the backboard, legs popped out from both sides. Owen grabbed a chair and sat down normally while flicking the other in the ear. It seemed they were always messing with each other.

Though Jeremy had previously relaxed, he tensed up again when the two other boys cozied up next to them. He became too nervous to eat. Ice cream began to drip down his fingers. Jace, who was the closest, took notice. He angled his chair toward him.

"I never got to apologize for the shit that happened that day. I'm so sorry, man. I didn't even know it happened. This idiot never told me," he glanced at a now extremely embarrassed Owen.

Jeremy blinked behind his thick frames as his hand got messier and messier. Jace now turned to Adelie.

"Also, thanks for calling him out on his bullshit."

"Anytime," she replied.

Owen avoided eye contact with the other until he noticed a giant glob of ice cream fall onto the table from Jeremy's double-scoop. He pulled out a few napkins from a nearby dispenser.

"Here, uh, you've got a little," he tilted his head toward the puddle.

Jeremy jumped in both surprise and embarrassment.

"Oh, god, thank you," he grabbed the napkins and quickly wiped up his hands and the table.

For once, Owen helped clean up a mess instead of starting one. Adelie was glad to have witnessed it.

Owen and Jace got their own cones a few minutes later. Though Jeremy and Adelie soon finished up their own treats, they stuck around to hang out for a while. Jeremy, though shy, began to open up and engage in conversation. His fear was slowly dissipating and being replaced by his normal, bubbly self. He would periodically glance at Adelie and send her a smile, cheeks a bit pink.

It was a rather odd feeling for Adelie to be sitting amongst, well, friends. She was almost completely silent during the last half hour the four of them shared a table. Friends talk, laugh, eat ice cream. They look to you to see your reactions to their jokes, their stories. It was all new to her. She soaked it in, much like the Absorber she was.

A car honked outside. All of them jumped a little and then turned to the windows to investigate. Peering closer, Jeremy realized that it was his mom.

"Oh, uh, my mom's here. Adelie?"

Adelie, filled with the newfound excitement of growing friendships, could only think of one answer.

"Your mom got room for two more?"

Jeremy's mouth hung open before flipping up into a smile once more.

"I think so!"

Owen and Jace sighed in relief. Jace exclaimed as he got down on one knee in front of the frazzled freshman.

"Thank God, we got dropped off at the library to do schoolwork, but we got bored and left. Please take us home!"

"O-Of course! Let's go!"

Jeremy's mom giggled in delight as everyone piled into her SUV. Her son sat in the front while Adelie became sandwiched between Jace and Owen in the back seat. She suddenly regretted this idea.

"I never thought I'd have a full car with this one," Jeremy's mom joked while tussling with her son's hair.

He quickly swatted her hand away, a bead of sweat on his brow.

"Mom, stop! Just be cool," he reached for the volume knob and turned it way up.

Complicated by Avril Lavigne proceeded to play at full blast.

<u>Chapter 7</u>

The next time that Adelie hung out with the group of boys again, it was nearly Halloween and the air was getting colder. She had been invited to come to Damien's place along with Owen, Jace, Colby, and Jeremy to carve pumpkins. It was no doubt Owen's suggestion to tag her and Jeremy along. Her mother was excited to see Adelie interacting with others her age. Adelie, however, felt apprehensive. Getting ice cream with them wasn't a big deal, but going to someone's house felt a little scary— especially someone she barely knew. She'd never really done that before. A first for everything, right? Maybe she would get closer to everyone. Plus, when was the last time she had gotten to carve a pumpkin for Halloween?

Her mother dropped her off on the way to her work shift. The drive through the subdivision was impressive. Row upon row of impressively large houses covered the neighborhood, a far cry from the smaller rustic house she lived in. They were out near a more populated town, yet not too far to justify Damien being placed at a different school. A middle point. Adelie was the last to arrive and was relieved about it. Less awkward one-on-one conversations.

The house was surprisingly huge and fancy looking. It wasn't surprising that it was Damien's, but rather that Adelie had never laid eyes upon a home like this before. It was almost like a mini mansion, the outside rising high with pale pillars and a perfect lawn. Statues lined the front entrance and the shrubs surrounding the front of the house were perfectly cut. As she was wondering what the inside would look like, she had barely knocked when the door was swung open. It was Damien, cheery and bright, his brown eyes glowing.

"Adelie, hey, welcome, welcome!"

Adelie forced a small smile on her face to not look too rude.

"Come on in," he insisted as he moved aside.

Stepping in, she was immediately blown away by how tall the ceilings were, complete with a few shining chandeliers. The floors looked like marble and everything, from the furniture to the electronics, looked pristine. Damien's parents walked up and looked just as elegant as the household itself. Both were dressed in formal clothing and smelled like fresh flowers. Damien looked a lot like his father, the man having a buzz-cut and similar skin tone. His mother's skin was maybe a shade lighter, curly hair delicately sitting on her shoulders. Hazel eyes looked to Adelie with interest.

"Welcome to our home. You must be new?"

"Oh,uh, yeah. I moved here about two months ago," Adelie answered.

Damien's dad popped into the conversation and leaned in closer to Adelie.

"How are you liking it? Settling in okay? Any trouble?"

Trouble is an understatement.

The questions seemed innocent rather than interrogatory. His dad's peppy attitude was surprising from his previously composed, statuesque appearance. Damien waved a hand at him, stepping between him and Adelie.

"*Dad,* leave her alone! She's just here to have fun, not talk about personal stuff."

Said dad tapped at his own lips, eyebrows shooting up.

"Oh, of course, sorry! Everyone's out in the backyard with everything. Go ahead," he stepped to the side to reveal a pathway to a sliding glass door in the distance.

Looking through it she could see the other boys setting up a table and chairs, pumpkins sitting at their feet waiting to be carved.

"Thank you," Adelie nodded and headed their way, Damien just behind her.

A gust of crisp autumn air caressed her face once again when she opened the door. The porch she stepped onto was perfectly clean and the tile shone in the late-afternoon sun. A far too exquisite-looking table and chairs covered a good portion of it. The backyard was huge with an equally huge white privacy fence. The grass was somehow still extremely green, its blades with no hint of wear and tear. One lonely tree clung to the ground of the back left corner. It looked like they kept up on their raking, too— or maybe a leaf blower? Who knows, but the only leaves in sight were the ones still attached to branches.

She didn't get too much time to admire the property, the boys jumping to her in an instant.

"Hey! You actually came," Owen exclaimed with surprise in his voice.

Jeremy shuffled over too, pumpkin carving kits in hand.

"Adelie, hi! We were just setting up to start carving," he explained with a grin on his face.

It was weird how Jeremy was terrified of Owen just a few weeks ago. It already felt like a distant memory. Almost. Adelie still held resentment at the back of her mind for what he did, but what was most important was making up for a bad deed. Most everyone was deserving of a second chance. Owen had learned that kind of behavior from his father, no doubt about it. She was glad to see Jeremy look so happy and comfortable with everyone.

Colby and Jace waved to Adelie as they placed pumpkins on the table. Still a little unsure of how to interact with so many people, she waved back to them and turned to Owen and Jeremy.

"Yep, I'm here," she replied simply.

Colby called everyone over once everything was set. Jeremy distributed the kits to each person and planted himself in a seat next to Adelie. Owen and Jace sat at the side directly facing them and Jeremy while Damien and Colby sat at the opposing ends. Books filled with image ideas lay strewn across the table.

Colby piped up as he began sifting through pages from one of the image books.

"So, what are we all carving?"

Damien flicked Colby's shoulder. Was that their main form of communication? She'd seen Jace and Owen do it before. Jeremy looked happy to answer Colby, an index finger raising high, when Damien did instead.

"Dude, we can't tell each other that. It's gotta be a secret until the very end!"

Jeremy slowly lowered his hand and looked around bashfully.

"Oh, I have no idea what I'm gonna carve. I was hoping someone would give me an idea," Colby blinked and rubbed at the back of his neck.

"Well, I would've helped you with an idea, but *someone* said that it was inappropriate," Owen joined in, shooting a faux annoyed glance toward Jace.

Everyone stared at the two boys and waited for an explanation. Jace sighed, resting one of his elbows on the table with a hand supporting his head.

"Normally I wouldn't have cared but there's kids, man. Trick-or-treating is still a thing," he vaguely answered.

The other teens leaned their heads closer, hovering over the table with anticipation. Damien questioned them first.

"Spit it out! What was it?"

Owen's mouth curled into a devious grin.

"Something that begins with a 'P' and ends with an 'S.' Get my drift?"

It took only a few seconds for everyone to put the pieces together. A heavy rush of exasperated sighs and small laughs followed. Owen shrugged, seemingly proud of his previous idea. Adelie face-palmed and slowly dragged her fingers down her face. Why was she friends with him again?

Adelie pinched the bridge of her nose and looked Jace's way.

"Thank God you stopped him," she retorted.

"*Anyway,* let's get goin'. My parents are gonna have you guys leave by the time the sun sets," Damien butted in.

That slight threat pushed everyone into action. Hands got to pulling guts and seeds out of the gourds. Jeremy didn't like the texture, so Adelie did it for him. The other boys didn't seem to mind. In fact, they made a small game of splattering some of the stringy bits on each other's faces— except Damien, who reminded them not to waste time.

The sun dipped lower, but the pumpkins shone bright by the time everyone was done, candles nestled delicately inside of their carved cages. Adelie made a fox with a witch's hat on, the brim of it covering its ears. It came out quite nice, especially with her not having done something like this since she was a child. Jeremy made a simple jack-o-lantern face with pointed teeth and triangle eyes. Colby somehow carved a twisted-end candy with football strips down the middle of it. Everyone had to admit it was clever. Damien made a "pi" sign, that nerd. Jace carved a "cool S," which Adelie had never heard of, but apparently people drew it all the time these days.

Owen blew everyone away with his handy work when he revealed his design to be an extremely intricate wolf. It stared straight ahead with intent, the fur created with swirls of both kept and unkempt pieces of the pumpkin. The circle of a full moon glowed behind it, popping out the lines of the wolf's face. Everyone's jaws dropped to the ground. Damien shouted exasperatedly.

"You telling me you could make something like *this* when you considered making something so stupid before!?!"

Owen appeared proud but embarrassed at the same time.

"Well, yeah, I like to… whittle in my spare time. I don't usually show stuff like this, though, 'cuz I thought I would look lame. Like, what cool guys whittle?"

Colby lightly punched Owen in the shoulder with a huge grin on his face.

"What are you talking about? That's *awesome*! If you've got talent, you shouldn't hide it," Colby encouraged.

Jeremy agreed and gave Owen a thumbs up.

"Yeah, it looks amazing. Good job," Jace looked between the pumpkin and Owen's face with a warm smile.

The crafter blushed profusely at the compliments. Adelie tapped him on the shoulder.

"You should make me something sometime-- a gift for all the trouble I have to put up with around you," she teased.

Jeremy and the others laughed at the suggestion. Everyone but Owen collected their pumpkins to bring to the front of the house to take home. Adelie was joining them when she noticed Owen not participating, simply staring at his creation. She stopped, set her pumpkin down, and walked over to her friend.

He looked... *sad*, all the pride drained from his features. When he noticed her next to him, he quickly pushed hair back from his eyes and attempted a smile. She didn't buy it.

"Are you okay? Second-guessing your design? You shouldn't," she tried to reassure him.

Owen stuffed his hands in his hoodie pockets and let his fake smile drop into a frown.

"No, that's not it. Uh... I... can't bring this home. My dad would just destroy it or throw it away," he admitted, words strained.

Honestly, damn that man. Adelie pondered over what she could do for him for a few moments. Something to make him happy again, give a way out. There was no way she was going to let anything bad happen to the one thing Owen had shown confidence in.

"Oh, well... I could take it to my place, if you want? It'd be safe there. Even my mom wouldn't stomp on a pumpkin."

Her offer was laced with both care and humor. It cracked a smile on Owen's face.

"Yeah, that would be good. Thanks," the simple reply of gratitude held a heavier meaning than any word could say.

The two of them walked together out of the house, a silent bond of friendship growing with each step. The others wondered why they had taken so long to join them. Adelie glanced at Owen before smirking.

"Oh, his pumpkin was too heavy for him. I had to help him pick it up," she lied with ease.

The friends took it as truth, continuing to kid around with each other until Damien's parents took a snapshot of them, a group of smiling faces and decked out pumpkins. They would later make copies for everyone to keep.

Later that night, a fox and a wolf sat together and brought light to the darkness.

<u>Chapter 8</u>

A few weeks later, winter finally found its grip on the town. Every tree stood naked, save for the small patches of snow on their branches. The lucky evergreens stood tall, plump, and green against the white scenery. Squirrels scattered to and fro in last ditch efforts to find food. Straggler flocks of birds began their belated journey south. Deer huddled together for warmth and safety. Foxes, however, stayed out of sight as much as they could. Sadly, unlike in Autumn, their bright coats shone like blood against bone. Adelie's kits remained cozy in their den with a small pile of prey piled up beside them. They rarely left their home at this time, their mother sometimes bringing them store-bought meat and fruit to keep them healthy.

Thanksgiving was almost here, but Adelie rarely felt anything for it anymore. Her mother was always either too busy or too tired to create a feast for them. Sometimes they both decided to call it off since it would only be the two of them. However, this year, she was in for a surprise when she received a card in the mail. It was from Jeremy.

Dear Ms. Adelie and Ms. Henderson,

I decided to write to you guys the old-fashioned way! My family and I would like to invite you to our Thanksgiving dinner. We would really enjoy your company. Hope to see you guys!

Sincerely, Jeremy Rider

Truth be told, Adelie hadn't received a card from someone since she was a little girl. Her eyes sparked with interest as she read the words. She wanted to go.

❖

Adelie and her mother stood at the Riders' doorstep. The redhead wore a thick, black coat with a deep blue sweater lying underneath it. A cream-colored scarf hung from her neck and was accompanied by a simple gold necklace. She had straightened her hair and given her eyes a touch of mascara. This was a special occasion, so she wanted to look and feel special. Her mother was dolled up, too. In fact, she had helped Adelie piece her outfit together. Adelie guessed that it was something to be thankful for.

After a tentative knock, Jeremy's parents answered the door. His mother was a curvy woman with equally curly dirty-blond hair. Though Adelie had met her before, she looked so different as she stood in a red dress. Her big smile was the same as always, though, and her husband placed his hand around her waist as they welcomed them into their home. He was a tall, lanky man with brown hair and glasses. Though quieter than his wife, he was just as wholesome. It was easy to see where Jeremy had gotten his disposition from.

As they stepped in, a wall of pleasant heat soaked their cold bodies. Adelie and her mother took off their coats and boots before walking any further. The living room laid before them, pristine couches and fireplace begging to be praised. A pair of stairs suggested that the rooms of the house were on the second floor, but beyond that wall was where the dining room was. The four of them journeyed toward the dining room but came upon the kitchen first.

Adelie couldn't believe her eyes as she ran directly into Jace and Owen. The two boys were pigging out on hors d'oeuvres when they stopped mid-chew.

"Ad-feffliee?"

Owen sounded like an idiot with his mouth full. Adelie cleared her throat. He got the message and swallowed down his food. Jace cracked up and jeered at him. Jeremy was nearby, a piece of bread in his hand. He looked as if he might drop it from the mere sight of his friend showing up for dinner. Stepping forward, he leaned in and gave her a hug.

"You came!"

Adelie turned a little stiff. They'd never hugged before. Hell, she hadn't even hugged anyone in recent history. Still, though, she gently placed her hands on his back and reciprocated. She threw a smirk at the other teens.

"I did. You invited these losers, too?"

"Us losers gotta stick together," Jeremy played along.

"For your information, he asked us *first*, and in person!"

Owen defended his and Jace's dignity, though Jace didn't seem to care as he stuffed some rolled-up ham down his throat.

"Like that's so hard? I got a nice card. He *paid* to invite me," Adelie remarked, a certain slickness dripping from her rebuttal.

Owen couldn't compete with that. Jeremy turned a little red as the two sets of parents giggled at the faux drama occurring in front of them. Adelie couldn't help but feel like something was missing.

"Are Damien and Colby coming too?"

"I invited them but they're spending time with their own families," Jeremy answered.

Everyone soon ventured into the dining room, though Jeremy hung back and beckoned for Adelie to join him. She obliged, curious as to what he wanted.

"You, um, look really nice. I'm glad you could come!"

His voice shook a little and his face looked flush. Maybe he was just nervous about having so many people over? Whatever the case, she was flattered at his compliment.

"Oh, of course, and... thank you. My mom helped me," she laughed a little and pushed some hair from her eyes.

It seemed like he was going to say something else but was cut off by his father announcing that the turkey would be done soon.

"We should probably find our spots at the table. All the sides are ready so when they cut the turkey, we can dig in."

"Sounds good."

The two of them made their way to the table, which was covered in half a dozen different sides: green beans, mashed potatoes, home-made macaroni and cheese, stuffing, a basket of biscuits, and a giant gravy boat. Owen and Jace openly drooled like starving strays. To be fair, it did look a lot like *The Last Supper*.

The two mothers conversed while Jeremy's father handled the turkey in the other room. The two women really hit it off as they talked about their children. Too bad Adelie knew just how fake her mom could act when with company. It almost made her too disgusted to eat. Almost. As if on cue, her mother turned toward the teens.

"Now, what were your names again? Jake and--?"

"Jace, and I'm Owen," the raven-haired boy corrected.

"Owen? As in Owen Smit?"

Suddenly all eyes were on him.

"Yes? Why?"

"I work with your dad! He mentions you all the time."

Owen froze up.

"He does?"

"Yep! Your brother too. Andres, was it?"

Owen nodded while taking a long swig of water. The condensation on the glass mirrored the sweat forming on his skin.

"I heard that he was in college, sounds like a smart kid. You're very lucky to have such a cool big brother."

"Thanks," Owen's lips barely moved.

"Do you plan on going too?"

"*Mom*, leave him alone. You're so nosey," Adelie intervened.

"What? I'm just asking harmless questions!"

Just when the redhead was about to counter the statement, Jeremy's father burst into the dining room with two huge trays of turkey meat—one white and one dark. He set it down with care, his eyes showcasing the pride he had in his cooking. Jeremy sat down beside Adelie.

"Everyone dig in! No need for prayers. I can tell these kids are ravenous," he laughed as he spotted Jace already reaching out to grab a turkey leg.

No one fought him on that as they all began the ritual of filling their plates to the brim. Things became a little hectic when the gravy boat didn't travel fast enough, but everyone recovered and soon became enraptured in the meal before them. Adelie, after grabbing her own pieces of turkey, hid a few extra pieces in her pocket to give to the kits later. A few minutes of happy chewing passed before Jeremy's mother spoke.

"Now, I know we said no prayers, but we have one condition—we all have to say what we're most thankful for on this wonderful Thanksgiving!"

Adelie's mother agreed, of course. Jace, Owen, and Adelie groaned. On the other hand, a light bulb seemed to appear over Jeremy's head. Jeremy's mother motioned for Adelie's mother to go first.

"Well, I'm very thankful for the hospitality of the people of this town! We've only been here a few months, but it already feels like home."

Adelie could just gag. Jace was next.

"I'm thankful for this food. It's really, *really* good."

Owen's turn.

"Yeah, me too. The food, I mean."

The adults laughed but quieted down when Jeremy stood up from his seat.

"I'm thankful for so many things! At first, I was very unhappy here. I felt out of place. I was bullied—" Owen looked away in shame.

"--But now that bully is my friend, and I don't think he's gonna bully anyone ever again, right?"

Owen nodded rigorously.

"Still, there's one person that I am the most thankful for. She's sitting next to me just like when we're at school," his eyes now focused on Adelie.

"Ms. Adelie showed me kindness when no one else would. She still does! She's amazing, and I'm so very glad to have her in my life."

Those gray eyes locked onto Adelie like bolts of electricity. They pulsed through her. Wait, no, that was her own pulse. Her heart beat in her ears as her skin warmed. She felt the hairs on her neck stand straight up. Her red locks thickened.

No. God, no. Not now. Not him. No.

Was he falling in love with her? With their age gap and everything? It felt like more than just a friend's appreciation. She was about to change form in the middle of a Thanksgiving dinner party.

Her body flew up from her seat as if by its own control. Everyone stared at her, particularly Jeremy who was waiting for a response to his very subtle confession. Her mother eyed her curiously. Owen, Jace, and the other parents stared in confusion.

"I-I'm so glad I met you too! I, uh, don't feel so good, though. Excuse me."

With that, she rushed past everyone and into the nearest bathroom.

Everyone looked a little dumbfounded. Jeremy's father appeared to be worried about not cooking the turkey thoroughly enough. Adelie's mom, though, caught on quickly. She got up from her seat.

"I'm gonna go check on her. Everyone, please, don't worry! She's probably just flustered from everyone's kindness!"

Jeremy smiled a little and sat back down. He mumbled to himself, most likely trying to talk himself into thinking things were fine. That he didn't mess up.

Adelie's mom knocked on the bathroom door. Inside, Adelie fought to contain her absorbism. Her teeth had sharpened. Her red hair puffed out in all directions. She pushed the palm of her hand against her forehead like her dad used to do when she was little. He said it helped to push the animal back. Though it probably didn't work, it comforted her.

"Adelie, it's me. You alright?"

"W-We need to leave," her voice and body quivered.

"Are you—"

"Yes."

Her mother proceeded to apologize to the others on her behalf. Though Adelie expected her to make a huge deal out of it, she was relieved to hear her speak to them with true concern in her voice. Jeremy's eyebrows furrowed together in worry.

"Is she okay?"

Another wave of absorbism cascaded over Adelie.

"Yes, don't worry. She just needs to get home."

❖

10:34 PM

Owen: U ok? <:-(

Adelie glanced at her phone when the screen lit up beneath her sheets. Mascara ran down her face from the tears that she'd cried. She had ruined everything. Jeremy was the sweetest, most kind friend that she'd ever had and now she didn't know what to do. Part of her felt flattered. Part of her hated herself. Most of her knew that she couldn't continue to be near him anymore. She had to protect him from the truth, even if it meant destroying their friendship. If she distanced herself, he could move on from his crush and Adelie would be safe from exposure.

10:37 PM

Adelie: No

Flipping her phone off, she placed it on her bedside table and turned off her lamp.

<h1 align="center"><u>Chapter 9</u></h1>

Adelie made the mistake of turning on her phone while on her morning ride to school. She'd had it turned off the whole holiday weekend, spending most of her time tending to the kits—who really enjoyed all that leftover turkey. Sadly, the cellphone instantly blew up with messages, most of them from Jeremy. The wound was still fresh. Tears pricked at her eyes as she dared to read them. They were all from Thursday night.

She quickly shoved her phone back in her pocket to avoid crying again. Before she had got on the bus, her mother had checked to see if she was doing okay. Just being asked about her well-being almost broke her down. Her mother offered to let her stay home from school. It was strange for her to even care. It was even stranger to have to be in this situation. Either way, Adelie decided to push through her emotions and show up to school.

During her class before lunch, Adelie locked herself up in a bathroom stall, phone in hand.

She guessed that was his stupid way of saying "yes."

❖

It was time to go to lunch. Adelie tied her hair back in a low ponytail and pulled up her hood. This way her bright hair wouldn't give her away and her face would be as hidden as possible. If she needed to, she would resort to sitting in the bathroom, but she was hungry and didn't feel like eating on a toilet. Not only that, but she wanted to talk to Owen about what had transpired. As she entered the cafeteria, she noticed that Jeremy was already at their usual table. He held his face in his hands, elbows supporting them. His finger scooted his glasses up his nose as he glanced around the crowds. The string around Adelie's heart tugged in two directions— to Jeremy and to Owen.

He's helpless. He's looking for me. He doesn't deserve this. He has no other friends.

I can't. He can't know. No one else can know. I can't start over again.

In the end, she ducked her head down and swiftly moved to Owen's table. She strategically placed her back to where Jeremy was and Colby was surprised at her sudden appearance.

"Hey. You feelin' better?"

Jace inquired, his green eyes wide. Adelie gave him a curt nod. Damien and Colby remained confused, but not confused enough to stop eating. The redhead flashed her amber eyes toward Owen. He returned it with a knowing look and pulled out his phone.

After a few hours, the duo ended up on the dirty carpet of the library. It was their usual place to discuss things privately. They leaned against a bookcase and stretched their legs across the aisle. Their feet lightly touched the bookcase that faced them. The books muted their hushed conversations.

"Would it *really* be that bad if he knew? He's so nice!"

"I can't risk it."

"Risk what?"

"You *know* what," she gave him a hard stare.

She must've been rubbing off on him, because for once, Owen was the one to quirk up an eyebrow. Adelie sighed.

"Even if he did accept me, what if he blabbed to someone without meaning to? The kid couldn't lie if his life depended on it. Plus, the more I'm around him, the less time I have in this body."

"You've got a point, I'll admit it. Still, though, you shouldn't just leave him hanging like this."

"You think I want to be doing this? I don't want any of this! I can't even be around them, or else I'll expose myself!"

"I was just—"

"I'd rather him hate me and move on. It'd save both of us a ton of trouble. His friendship means so much to me, though."

"I know, and it can still be saved!"

"NO IT CAN'T!"

Adelie's whisper broke into a sudden yell. Owen winced while shrinking into the textbooks at his back. She quickly recoiled, shocked at the anger that had overtaken her.

"There's just no winning," her flames melted into puddles of sorrow.

She looked away from Owen, not wanting to see his pity, when the boy jumped to his feet.

"S-Sorry but my dad is here. I've gotta go. I'll text you later," he stuttered out.

Adelie was confused about his sudden exit but could only watch as he quickly turned away.

"Oh, alright, see ya."

He had sped off before the words had even rolled off her tongue.

❖

8:23 PM

Jeremy: Were you at school today? I didn't see you. Hope you are okay.

It was amazing how much effort Jeremy always put into his texts. He always had proper wording, capitalization, and punctuation. This simple, yet very powerful fact, sent Adelie into a tailspin. Why did he have to be so thoughtful?

8:35 PM

Adelie: i wasnt feeling well. im sorry. i meant to tell u.

Adelie was about to start on homework to get her mind off things when a loud, crashing noise spooked her from her thoughts. Tentatively, she crept to her window. It was just a giant glob of snow that had slid off the roof. Her eyes scanned the sparkling snow. Something shone, glowed, in the already dark evening.

Eyes. Animal eyes. She squinted to try to see the outline against winter's cascade of powder. Its ears were pricked, and it had a fluffed, curly tail. Adelie tapped the glass to get its attention. It worked, the animal turning in her direction.

It was the husky she'd encountered before. Ace, he was called. His paws were hidden under a few inches of fresh snow. Snowflakes clung to the dark saddle of fur on his back. The weather threatened to bleach him entirely as he froze to the spot. He sniffed the air before allowing his nose to dip down to the ground, seemingly on the trail of something. Adelie thumped down the stairs to throw on her coat and boots. Her mother frowned at her, a phone to her ear, as she motioned for her to be quiet. Paying her no mind, Adelie quickly opened the door.

She was met with frigid air, but no dog. He'd already moved on. Still, she took a couple steps off the porch and into the powder. Pawprints gave away his trail but became messy and erratic just a few feet farther down the lawn. Adelie sighed, her breath consuming her face in unsatisfying warmth. Her phone buzzed in her pocket.

Mid-December blew in like a banshee, screaming down snow and wind as it traveled across the area. The kits were starting to resemble their adult forms— Adelie thanked any God out there for their survival—as their thick winter coats supplied extra protection from the elements. Prey was scarce, but Adelie's love was not. She brought them meat every few days, weather depending. Sometimes, if the coast was clear, she would bound around in the snow with them for a while. They were always so happy to get to spend time with their mother. All three of them turned into jumping, squealing messes whenever she drew near.

Seeing the kits always lightened Adelie's spirits, especially on days where her guilt about Jeremy threatened to swallow her whole.

She hoped that he would move on sooner than later. However, she couldn't blame him. After all, it was her own fault that this was happening.

One particularly snowy weekend, when her mother was away at work, Adelie decided to make the long trek to the kits' den by foot. She made sure to wear her thickest coat and her trusty boots. Her pockets were insulated with both wool and fresh cuts of meat.

The trees were becoming crystalized, twinkling and swaying in the winter wind. It was incredibly quiet. The flattening of snow by human boots was basically the only sound. Tracks of various animals riddled the snowy ground. The blue sky spread its color onto the land, everything covered with a pale blue tint.

Once at the den, she hurriedly dug snow away from the entrance with her cold, human hands. She could hear them yapping in excitement. She shushed them, urging them to be quiet as she handed them the food through the entrance.

Snow crunched behind her.

Adelie's heart sprang from her chest as she leapt to her feet. She turned swiftly, back to the rocks, and faced the unexpected guest. Ready for anything, she hardened herself.

"H-Hey, it's okay, it's just me!"

A familiar blue-eyed boy stepped into view. Adelie deflated like a balloon.

"Jesus. Owen. You *cannot* do that."

"Listen, there's no good way to approach you, so you can't get mad at me."

The boy had a rifle strapped around his torso and a bag that hung heavy with trapping gear. He was no doubt playing the role of "perfect son" today.

"Whatever. Let's just get away from here."

Owen nodded. The duo walked together in the opposite direction of the kits' location. They were silent a while, that is, until Owen spoke up again.

"How are they doing? The kits, I mean," he whispered.

"They're doing well. This is their first winter, though, so I've been bringing them food," she replied, a little pleased to hear him ask about them.

"Good, good. No one else on this Earth knows about them. They're safe."

"It needs to stay that way."

"I know. You can trust me," his eyes were desperate.

Adelie returned his look with a nod of approval. She was about to speak again when someone else came upon them. The teenagers froze. It was a man with all the same gear that Owen had. However, he was the real deal.

"Hey, what the hell's she doin' out here?"

Luckily, Owen was quick-witted when he needed to be.

"Sir, I don't know, but I'm escorting her home," he roughly grabbed hold of one of her arms.

If the stakes weren't so high, she would've smacked his hand away. The hunter raised an eyebrow before smirking.

"She should know better than to go in the woods alone. Good thing you are here."

Of course, this was code for something more like: "We know who you are and you need to get the fuck away from our hunting grounds before we gut you, too."

Adelie played her part, acting limp and pathetic. She dared not look either of them in the eyes.

"Looks like she's sorry. Best be off," the hunter stepped aside to let them through.

"Yeah, let's go," Owen shoved Adelie ahead of him and placed his hands on her shoulders to guide her forward.

Once they'd gotten a fair distance away, he leaned forward.

"I'm so, so sorry," his voice was quieter than a falling feather, but held its weight in humility.

"They must think you're so macho," Adelie snorted.

"Shut *up,*" his voice came out louder than expected.

He looked over his shoulder and was spooked to see the hunter staring at him from afar. Owen gulped, cleared his throat, and then began to yell.

"Shut up! I don't wanna hear another word! This isn't the place for you!"

At that, the hunter wandered away into the woods. Now Owen was the one to sigh in relief. He continued to speak in whispers to be safe.

"That was Jace's dad. He's pretty much my dad but version two. Don't worry though, things will be fine."

"Okay," she replied, though she didn't really mean it.

"Also, I still don't have any leads on finding your dad. I'll keep trying."

"We've gotta keep looking! We can't just give up!"

The tween raised her voice and fists to her mother. She retaliated by grabbing her daughter's hands and holding them above her head.

"He's gone, Addie, okay? He's not coming back! He left us!"

"How can you say that? Daddy needs help!"

"We are the ones that need help now, not him!"

The tween ripped her hands free as her eyes bubbled with hot tears.

"I wish he was here instead of you."

Adelie stopped and stared at the fresh powder. Owen bumped into her from the abrupt stop.

"It's fine. It was a stupid idea. You don't need to," her breath came out in clouds.

"Huh? No way! We're just getting started!"

"So? I was being stupidly hopeful."

"Sometimes you *need* to be stupidly hopeful. Also, you're not stupid, so stop saying that stupid word."

Adelie looked over her shoulder at Owen's stupid face before cracking up a little. He grinned in response but quickly cleared his throat and guided her by the shoulders to keep walking.

"We need to get you out of here now, though, so that jackass won't chew you out again. I dunno what else he could do, and I don't wanna find out."

They walked through the forest in silence, save for the crumbling of ice and snow beneath their boots. There was the occasional flicker of a squirrel or rabbit, but the woods felt like an empty husk. Owen's bike was soon within view. Without turning around, Adelie spoke again.

"Hey Owen?"

"Yeah?"

"Thanks."

❖

As Owen dropped Adelie off at her house, a familiar voice made him think twice before riding off. There were two silhouettes behind the living room window instead of one. Something was off. The teens glanced at each other before hesitantly walking toward the front door. Adelie reached for the doorknob but was interrupted when it spun on its own and opened. She looked up and her heart lurched for the second time that day.

Owen's father towered above her, thick-browed and lips curled in a snarl. Her mother, who stood beside him, was somehow even more intimidating. She glared down at her daughter.

"Where on *Earth* have you been? I got home from work, and you were gone! You cannot be doing that!"

It was almost comical how long it had taken her mother to figure out that she'd been sneaking out. To be fair, Adelie had been careful of when she did so, only leaving when it was good to assume her mother wouldn't notice. Mostly after school or when her mother was working. Today wasn't a lucky day.

Owen's father looked past Adelie and caught sight of his son. She could feel Owen's fear in waves. Instinctively, Adelie moved in front of the man's view to block his threatening gaze from her friend. Now, even more angered, the father turned his attention to Adelie instead.

"Better question—Where on Earth have you been with my *son*? How *dare* you push him to break my rules?"

Owen interjected.

"Sir, she didn't do anything, I—"

"Oh, save your lies. I find that hard to believe with the way she has been sneaking about. She's been nothing but trouble since she got here."

Adelie stood her ground and sent the man a hard stare. Her mother blinked, a bit dumbfounded at the previous statement.

"You have something you need to tell us?"

How Adelie wished she were her father at that moment. She could've ripped them to ribbons.

"No—and 'us?' He's not my fucking dad," she hissed.

"You watch your language. We just moved here, and you want to ruin things? Don't you know Mr. Smit is the only reason this town is still around? I called him when I saw you weren't home, and he was kind enough to come here and wait with me to see if Owen would show up, too. There's no doubt that you made Owen join you in your little game."

Head exploding with all the false accusations, Adelie stormed past the two adults and slammed the door behind her.

"You need to discipline that girl. Looks like she thinks she can get whatever she wants, whenever she wants," Mr. Smit growled to Mrs. Henderson.

"Y'know, you're right. Without a father around, there hasn't been enough of that. I'll handle it."

When the parents looked up, Owen had already begun pedaling to his house down the street. His father took it upon himself to leave. As he loaded up into his truck, he called out to Adelie's mother.

"See ya, Marianne."

"See ya, Richard."

Once the Smits had gone, Adelie's mother turned to her daughter like a ghost— quiet and menacing— before making her presence truly known.

"What are you hiding from me?"

"Really? What are *you* hiding from *me*? Why the *fuck* was *he* here?"

The mother's palm met harshly with the fair skin of the daughter's face.

"I TOLD YOU TO WATCH YOUR LANGUAGE!"

Adelie nearly fell to the floor. She cupped her sore cheek. Ah, this again. Her mother's trump card.

"Seriously? He doesn't care about you," she spat back.

The mother's face twisted in disgust. She bent down to Adelie's level, just inches from her face.

"He cares about me more than you have in the past four years. You are young and ungrateful. I am tired of it," she reached toward her daughter.

Adelie jumped back and arched her back, perhaps in the hopes that she would look bigger than she was.

"Don't touch me."

That same hand continued to reach for Adelie, who smacked it away. The mother gritted her teeth as she retaliated, grabbing a hold of her daughter's hood and yanking up. Adelie snarled, scratched, and kicked, but the hold was final. She was dragged up the rickety stairs and practically thrown into her bedroom. As soon as she was free of her grip, Adelie thrust herself toward the door, but it had been locked from the outside. The lock must've been a new addition, courtesy of Mr. Smit.

Again and again, she smashed herself into the door like a wild animal caught in a cage. She screamed insults, accusations, and grief through the floorboards. The mother did not bother to respond. Adelie only gave up when pain began to sear through her arms. As she slid onto the floor, she found herself in the same spot that she'd been when they'd last fought. A few red strands of hair still decorated the wood around her. She added some more to the pile.

The floor was a familiar place. It was hard, unmoving, unchangeable. Something predictable. She wanted to melt into it. Everything was too much. Still, she had a calling, and she couldn't give up yet.

There were walls of snow pelting down against her window.

Sharp rasps at the young girl's window woke her from her deep slumber. She rubbed her eyes, still sleepy, when the noise grew louder. Though shaken, she dared to go toward it. It was cold out and ice had framed the glass. The heat from the house had created a layer of fog on the inside. She used her hand to smudge it away. What she saw sent her stumbling back, legs giving out from under her.

Her father stood on the other side. His hand pressed against the glass, long claws glittering from his fingertips. The daughter shook as if the winter had kissed her. It'd been three months since the incident.

"Addie! It's me! C'mere, listen!"

His voice was muffled. She could barely understand him. Part of her didn't even want to. Yet, her body crept closer.

"That's it, that's my girl. Look," his dark eyes focused on her frightened ones.

"I can't stay. You know I can't. I wanted to say I love you, okay? Don't you forget that."

For some reason, this supposedly reassuring statement made her shake even more. She nodded.

He gave a grin. His teeth looked pointed, unhuman. He hurriedly ducked his head and disappeared. The young girl, stunned, ran to her window and opened it. The deathly cold engulfed her. She screamed, hot steam rising into the wind. Her mother showed up a moment later. Her father did not.

Adelie closed her window behind her as she slid down the roof of her house. There was enough snow to cushion her fall, so she decided to take a straight shot down. Though a little fearful, she landed in a giant snowfall and escaped with only a cold face. Something called to her. It grasped her ankles and pulled her through the icy streets. It paused for a moment, beckoning for her to glance at Owen's home. It stood solemnly, its windows darker than the night sky. The entire house seemed to sag under the weight of snowdrifts. It cried icicles.

She continued her journey, the invisible force keeping a steady hold of her feet. It warmed her body against the elements. Her breath melted away the coldness of her mother's words. It caressed the scratch on her cheek. In what seemed like no time at all, she was in front of the kits' den again. She just couldn't stay away.

Her thoughts flashed to Jeremy.

She wished things were different. She wished she hadn't been born like this. She wished her dad had been around. She wished she could stop herself from caring for these kits, but she couldn't. No matter how many days, months, or years, it took from her human life to raise them, she didn't care. Adelie was their only mother now. Their only family, mentor, and friend. After being deprived of those things herself, she couldn't bring herself to do the same thing to these innocent beings. Jeremy was just as innocent, but maybe a small part of her knew he could move on. He deserved better than her for a friend. Even if Adelie had been the same age and loved him in the same way he loved her, it could never work out for either of them. The only thing that could be done now was to get rid of the attachments.

Forget. Move on. Live.

Adelie entered the rocky den and made her bushy tail into a scarf, wrapping it around her children. She could show them that she loved them. She could stay. She would.

She climbed back into her room in the early morning, mere moments before her mother unlocked the door. At least luck was on her side this time.

<u>Chapter 10</u>

The day before winter break was especially chilling. Adelie wore three layers but could not get warm. Each time she caught a glimpse of curly blond hair, she felt even colder. It was never Jeremy, but it could've been.

At lunch, Owen and his pals gave her a crudely wrapped gift.

"No, no, I don't do gifts. C'mon, I don't have anything for you guys."

"Don't sweat it! There's not much. Just open it," Damien's eyes gleamed.

Adelie sent them a playful smirk before tearing the thing open. First, there was some candy. It usually wasn't her thing, but it looked appetizing right about now.

Next, there was a gift card. Flipping it over, she gulped. It was for the ice cream parlor they used to frequent. Her lips forced a smile.

"We should really go back there when it's not ass-crack cold," Jace snorted.

The last item shocked her the most, though. There was a piece of wire. Her fingers slid over it. It was a piece of one of the fox traps in the woods. Her face flung up, eyes wide. They all shared a moment of understanding. Owen had finally told them.

"You guys--?"

"We wanna end this too. We wanna help," Damien announced.

Adelie could've broken down into tears, right then and there. Instead, she gave them a big smile—perhaps the biggest smile she'd mustered in the past month. All the boys grinned right back, and soon she was in the midst of a group hug. It felt wrong when they pulled away as the bell rang. Before everyone scattered, Adelie spotted Owen placing something in her backpack.

"Open it later," he whispered as he walked past her.

She certainly would. Zipping her backpack closed, she slung it around her shoulder and stood up.

Jeremy's face met hers. Dozens of teens wandered around them, yet everything fell silent. His face was tight, confused, concerned. Adelie's heart thumped in time with the hair that stood at the back of her neck.

"Adelie, I—"

"Jeremy," she huffed out.

"Y-Yeah, can we please talk?"

Her entire soul felt torn and feathered. She needed to leave. She needed to talk to him. She needed to save herself. She needed to save him. Jeremy spoke again without her answer.

"Is it Owen?"

Adelie's cacophony of thought quieted.

"What?"

"Owen. Are you guys together? I promise I won't mess things up for you guys. I just miss you and want to know what's going on," his eyebrows came together in desperation.

Breath escaped her lungs. This poor boy. This sweet boy. This lonely boy.

"Oh, no, we're not. I promise."

"Then what is it? Did I do something to upset you? I want to make things right."

Adelie's blood pumped harder, nearly drowning Jeremy's words. The lunchroom began to empty.

"No, it's me."

"It can't possibly be you. It must've been me. You're wonderful," a glimmer of light shone through his gray eyes.

A wave of absorbism passed over her, nearly knocking her over. She grabbed onto a nearby chair to steady herself. Jeremy lurched forward to catch her.

"Are you okay?"

No. Not at all. This is so terrible. Everything feels so bad.

"I-I'm so sorry Jeremy. I can't say. You haven't done anything wrong. You need to just stay away from me."

Adelie could just hear his entire heart shatter from the sigh that left his lips.

"Why?"

"You need to just stay away, okay? Please?"

She couldn't look at him.

"Anything for you, Miss Adelie."

❖

As soon as Adelie got home and into her room, she dug through her backpack to pluck out Owen's gift to her. She ripped apart the wrapping with fervor to discover a hand-carved figurine of a fox. It was in a sitting position with its tail curled around itself at the base. It seemed he *did* end up making her something after all. She wished to display it proudly on her windowsill but feared being questioned by her mother. What if Mr.Smit came back over and saw it? Adelie wistfully placed it in the small drawer of her vanity.

Empty candy wrappers accompanied her in bed that night. They tasted better than her mother's dinner.

❖

Warm colors. Silver and gold. Fluorescent lights. Sugary air. Christmas was swept into existence. So was a letter in the mailbox.

Adelie's mother stole the card from her hands and skimmed over it quickly.

"Hm, that's right. Poor boy," she sighed.

"I don't really have a choice," Adelie argued.

"I know. I'm sorry, love."

The pet name made Adelie nauseous. If her love for her daughter was so unbridled, how come Adelie never changed forms when around her? How could she hit her own creation? How could she be working against her every single day? Not that it was really a surprise, anyway, but a small part of her wished that she would change form because of her mother's love again. The child in her truly wanted to have a mother to lean on.

Her mother placed Jeremy's card on the kitchen counter before opening another envelope that had come in. It was from the Smits. Adelie turned around and sat by their Christmas tree. She didn't want to see the card. She didn't want to hear it.

The tree was only a few feet high and ornaments were hung sparingly. It didn't even have a topper. It also didn't have any gifts underneath it. She laid down on her back and took in the warmth from the fireplace. Melting into the carpet felt like a nice idea right now. She dozed off to the visions of shapes in the flames.

The burly man led the way as his wife and daughter followed behind him. The daughter had to hop over the high mounds of snow. Her mother held her hand so she wouldn't lose her to Winter's quicksand.

"How 'bout this one, Addie?"

The father pointed his saw to an evergreen.

"Not tall enough! It has to be as tall as you, or taller," the redhead giggled.

The three of them continued their search for the perfect Christmas tree. Eventually, the little girl let go of her mother's hand and trudged ahead of her parents. The mother began to panic, urging her husband to catch her. He disagreed.

"Let her explore! She gets to pick!"

It didn't take long for the girl to settle on an exceptionally tall spruce. She bounced up and down with glee.

"This one! I want this one!"

"Your wish is my command," her father smiled.

"You're sure you want this one? It's a bit big," the mother worried.

Her husband frowned and whispered words to his wife. The wind blew them away from the daughter. His face soon snapped back to its jolly self.

"Let's do this, then!"

He began to saw away at the trunk while his daughter became his own personal cheerleader. The mother stood a few feet away, face scrunched with concern.

"Ok, Addie, when I say 'timber,' you've gotta go stand by your mama!"

"But I wanna stay over here with you!"

He kept slicing away at the wood.

"I know, but the tree's gotta fall, sometime!"

As the girl pouted, the tree began to sway violently.

"Honey, come here," the mom called.

Snap. The spruce was falling.

"ADDIE! TIMBER! TIMBER!"

"Wha—"

The trunk collided with bone. The child yelped in pain. The mother screeched with anger at her husband. He screamed right back.

A pain in her legs woke Adelie up from her snooze. Her hands went to the sore spots, only to find that nothing was there. Nothing was broken. She looked around. No one was there, not even her mother. Her phone buzzed in her pocket.

__2:46 PM__

__Owen__: ur moms here w cookies?

Of course she was. How nice of her.

__2:48 PM__

__Adelie__: xmas blows

__2:50 PM__

__Owen__: did u like my present? B-)

__2:52 PM__

__Adelie__: i did! thanks!

__2:55 PM__

__Owen__: npppppp :-) :-) :-)

❖

After a long and boring winter break, Adelie came back feeling a bit rejuvenated. She hadn't heard from Jeremy in two weeks and Owen's friends were now joining the fight against Owen's father. Most of her felt the need to be guilty about Jeremy, but she had to keep reminding herself to forget, move on, and live however long her body allowed her to.

Finally back at school, Adelie sat with her friends as they all discussed how their breaks were. Her eyes wandered around the cafeteria, their voices meshing with the dozens of others. She spotted Jeremy at a different table. He had a couple of boys his age with him. There was a small smile on his face. It looked like he'd made a couple of companions. Half of Adelie cried while the other half cheered. It

100

was bittersweet. It was even more bittersweet to see their old table uninhabited. It was almost ghostly.

"Hello, Earth to Adelie," Owen snapped his fingers in front of her face.

Adelie blinked several times.

"Sorry. A little spacey today."

Sadly, for them, Adelie was in another world for the remainder of the lunch period. Her mind was a compass, and its four points were Maple, Birch, Aspen, and her father. Even the bell's ring didn't wake her up.

"Hey, hey," Owen shook her by the shoulders.

"H-Hey. Sorry."

"You alright?"

"Yeah, I'm fine," she forced out.

"Hm. Walk with me," he nudged her to stand up.

The two of them exited the building and walked under the outside awning. There was a covered pathway that led them back to the main class building.

"Somethin' new eatin' ya?"

"Nothing new, no."

"Hey, you know that gift I gave you? I carved it myself," he smiled a goofy smile.

She let out a small chuckle at his sudden enthusiasm.

"I figured. Something about it looked just like Maple," she lowered her voice to a whisper.

"Maple?"

"Shh, keep your voice down. Maple is one of the kits."

"Oh. You hadn't told me their names before."

Shit. She should stop talking, stop blabbing.

"Hey, uh, don't worry. No one knows about them, not even the guys. Even *I* didn't know their names until just now," he reassured.

He could see her thoughts zig-zagging behind her eyes.

"Right. Thank you."

"You can trust me, remember?"

She remembered, no matter how much her brain wanted her to forget. Trust was still so foreign.

"Yeah. Speaking of, did you find anything on my dad? I haven't seen anything."

Owen's gait changed slightly, and his hands went in his pockets.

"Nothing really. I saw a few bear paw prints a few miles out of town, though."

Adelie stopped walking. She wanted to scream but they were surrounded by students. Instead, she scream-whispered.

"You call that nothing!?! Did you try to track 'em?"

"Listen, with all the snow we keep getting, it's impossible to follow a trail. Everything gets covered or blown away."

He was right. She didn't want him to be, but he was. Adelie let out a frustrated sigh. Maybe they would have more luck when the snow melted.

Who knows when that would happen, though. This winter already felt like forever.

<u>Chapter 11</u>

Maple hopped through the snow, her short legs barely carrying her above all the white. Aspen followed behind her, poking her with his muzzle to tease her. Birch was third, and Adelie was the caboose. The four foxes walked single file through the forest. It was getting harder and harder to keep them fed through the heart of winter, especially when Adelie's mother was down her throat whenever she wanted to leave the house. Owen had offered to buy meat from the store for her, but his dad was just as bad. Today, she supervised as they foraged.

The snow moved up ahead. There was a rabbit. It was barely visible, but it was there. She signaled for the kits to stop with a quick click of her jaws. All three looked at her curiously, so she pointed the prey out to them. There was no way of having the element of surprise with how much they stood out against the scenery. They'd have to just go for it and use teamwork.

Their three, furry bodies burst toward the rabbit. It quickly shot off, ears pricked and nose twitching. Maple and Aspen chased it around a tree as Birch rounded it off from the other side. Sadly, Adelie saw the quick little thing leap right over Birch's head. It was bounding towards her now. She growled and persuaded it to turn back around. Birch's jaws were waiting. Dinner was served.

As they dug in, something caught Adelie's eye. She swiftly passed the kits, promising to only be away for a moment. Her paws brought her to the top of a nearby hill. A few yards away stood Ace, the husky. He was also standing atop a slippery slope. His eyes were scanning the landscape. Adelie decided to return to the kits and led them back to the den.

Though their coats had grown long and silky, Adelie could see their ribs beginning to poke out. She groomed them earnestly to make up for lost time. Maple curled up exceptionally close. Her eyes had grown so bright. They were all growing up way too fast. Yet, they needed to.

Adelie wondered if her mother ever wished her daughter had stayed a happy little girl. Had she ever been? She couldn't even remember anymore.

❖

"We found four traps yesterday. Ripped 'em up and threw 'em out in pieces. No one saw us," Damien reported, dark eyes glimmering with pride.

Adelie and Owen now shared their library hiding place with the rest of their pack of friends.

"Good, thank you," Adelie replied.

Owen cleared his throat.

"I saw my dad gathering some supplies together. It looks like he might start using poison to get easier kills," he sighed.

"He's such a coward," Adelie growled.

"I'll look out for them. Anything on Adelie's dad?"

The rest of the gang hung their heads low. That was a big, fat no.

"Guys, Owen and I will handle the search for my dad. Just keep doing what you're doing with the traps, okay?"

"You sure? We really wanna help with that, too," Jace insisted.

Adelie felt a strange fear bubble up in her throat. She didn't want her own years of disappointment to spread to them, too. More than anything, she wanted the remaining wild foxes to be safe. This area continued to grow thin of them. Though her father also continued to remain scarce, it was nothing new. Finding him would probably turn out to be a pipe dream. It always had been.

"Yeah, I'm sure."

When Colby, Damien, and Jace left to go home, Owen and Adelie stayed to chat for a bit.

"Jeremy came up to me right before winter break. It was after you put your gift in my backpack," she informed him.

"Shit, really?"

"Yeah, it was terrible. Y'know he thought you and I were dating?"

"Oh, god, *no*. Never."

Adelie punched him in the shoulder, which he promptly rubbed.

"Shut up. You're right, though. Gross."

"*Very* gross."

"Anyway, I ended up telling him that he needed to stay away from me," her eyes dragged along the floor.

"I'm sorry. What did he say, then?"

"That he would do anything I said."

"Ouch."

"Yeah. I've been avoiding talking about it, sorry."

"It's fine, I get it. I hope he does leave you alone, though. Poor dude."

"You don't need to remind me."

Both of their phones vibrated.

"My dad's outside."

"My mom's outside, too."

They shared a look of horror. This didn't seem good.

"I'll go out first and see what's up," Owen offered.

"You sure? I don't want your dad killing you on my watch," Adelie insisted.

"Don't worry," he sent her a small smile before making his way to the front doors.

Adelie didn't dare move from her spot. A few minutes later, her phone started ringing, sending a shrill tune through the quiet library. Her fingers fumbled to flip it open.

"Addie, I'm outside. Let's go," her mother's voice cooed.

Adelie simply grunted before snapping the phone shut. Once outside, she was relieved to see Owen and his father in their own vehicle. Their truck held Owen's bike in the back, its handles poking over the sides. She went ahead and hopped into her mother's much smaller vehicle. The moment the door clicked shut, her mother spoke again.

"Addie, I'm sorry I hit you."

"It's fine," she halfheartedly replied.

If she was so sorry, then she wouldn't continue to do it to her, she wouldn't try to bring it up nearly a week later as if nothing had really happened.

The car was put into drive. Both women were silent.

"Richard and I closed up the shop early so we could pick you two up," the mother explained.

"'Richard'?"

"Mr. Smit," the mother clarified.

"Ah."

More driving. More silence.

"Addie, I cannot keep picking you up. You need to use the bus *correctly*."

"Stop calling me that," the girl growled.

"Excuse me?"

"Just stop trying to make it seem like we're best friends. We're not. Only dad ever called me that," she snapped back.

The mother's hands clenched the steering wheel, hard.

"You're my daughter. We have always called you that," the mother spoke through gritted teeth.

"Whatever," Adelie sighed and glanced at her phone.

3:48 PM

***Owen**: false alarm. U ok? :-O*

11:48 PM

***Adelie**: yea :P*

"If you don't take the bus straight home, I will know, so don't even try anything."

❖

A few hours passed with no texts from Owen. It was unusual. It worried Adelie, so she sent him a few of her own. She thought he would surely respond when he saw his friend actually *worrying* about him. She figured she would be teased, but she didn't care. His father was unpredictable at best.

The moon sat in the highest branches of the sky. Its thin body was just a sliver of its full self. Sometimes Adelie wondered if Owen was this way—an iceberg with an upside-down mountain of secrets. However, it did not plague her mind. Everyone had secrets. She really wasn't one to talk. What mattered was that he cared about her. He was loyal above all else. It was hard for Adelie to trust anyone anymore, but Owen continuously proved his devotion to their cause.

It was close to midnight when she sent him another text. A couple minutes later, her phone blew up with more than just a reply. It was ringing with the promise of a voice on the other end. This immediately spiked suspicion in her. They only texted because no one could hear them talk, because the words could be erased, deleted. Something was very off about this. Though her hands ached to answer the call, her brain stood firm. After a few moments, the ringing stopped. She looked at the device anxiously as something popped up on the screen.

There was a voicemail. She quickly opened it and let it play. Mr. Smit's voice flowed from the speaker.

"I know this is you, Adelie Henderson. My son's phone is being disconnected. You need to stay away from him. I don't know what you guys are doing or planning, but I am putting an end to it. Remember, everyone knows everyone around here. Good night."

She immediately called back. Straight to voicemail. Again, still voicemail.

It wouldn't be deactivated until tomorrow, but he was keeping the phone under lock and key, now. It had been turned off along with her and Owen's line of communication. She threw her device across the bed in frustration.

Shit.

❖

Everything was black, nothing to see or hear. Adelie stood, her senses defenseless. A hand grabbed hers. She jumped at the touch, but a voice soon quieted her.

"Shh, just follow me," it said.

It was Owen. She could trust him to be her eyes, her ears. Her feet found footing as his hand pulled her through the thick darkness. Everything remained quiet for a while. It was almost pleasant. A crunching noise awoke her panic again.

"I see you. Do you see me?"

The voice sent chills down her skin, her spine prickling. The voice was familiar, but she couldn't put her finger on it.

"Shhhh," Owen's voice continued to pull her along just as much as his hand did.

"Please see me," the voice crackled.

Static suddenly overpowered the silence. It hurt. She let go of Owen's hand to cover her ears.

"SEE ME!"

This wasn't the first time that Adelie had been tormented in her sleep. She sat up slowly, noting that it was still dark outside. It made her dream feel even more real. Nightmare, rather. Whose voice was that?

To shake it off, she checked her phone for anything from Owen. Still nothing. It looked like his dad was serious about what he had said. Adelie felt foolish for believing that he might not be. That got her thinking about what Owen had told her many months ago.

"I'll just come out and say this. My mom died when she had me. It was twelve years after my big brother. I wasn't expected. Andres—my brother—said that my dad was never the same after that. Always drinking and yelling."

At some point in time, this man must've had a heart beating underneath that heavy chest. Those lips must've genuinely smiled, genuinely laughed, genuinely kissed. That was all gone now, the only witness of it being Owen's brother. Owen had never had a true and loving dad. Never had a mother, either. Adelie couldn't decide on what was worse— having that love and losing it, or never having it at all. It was all bad, she supposed.

Her thoughts kept her awake until the first dull rays of winter sunshine washed into the sky. Right, one more day of school until the weekend. Owen would surely be there.

❖

Adelie's bus ride was as unpleasant as always until her phone went off. She'd never picked it up so fast.

6:48 AM

Jace: hey its owen. dads a dick. using jaces phone

Her excitement fell to the muddy floor. She was happy to have heard from him but was sad to have noticed his demeanor simply from the way he was texting. No smileys or silly words, no "hey" with eighteen y's. Maybe some humor was needed right now.

That was more like it.

When the bus arrived, the first bell was already ringing. Figures it would be late today! She'd wanted to try to find Owen before first period, but it looked like it would have to wait until lunch time. Her boots squeaked as she jogged through the wet hallways—the worst part of winter, in her opinion. She hastily flung her locker open to grab her textbooks, not noticing a card on the floor until she had finished. Picking it up, she realized that it must've fallen right out of her locker. It was pink, covered in hearts, and read "Happy Valentine's Day."

It was obvious who it was from. Her brain screamed to not open it while her heart thumped in anticipation. Temptation won, and she stole away to the bathroom to open it in private.

Dear Ms. Adelie,

I know I had agreed to not contact you, but I just had to give you a card. You know how I am with formalities. I hope you are doing alright. I miss you dearly. Should you ever need an ear to listen or a shoulder to cry on, I am here. Your friendship means the world to me. May we hang out again sometime soon.

Love, Jeremy Rider

Her brain was right. She shouldn't have read it. It quickly became crumpled and buried under the contents of her backpack. Her eyes couldn't bear to see it again.

The sorrow she felt hadn't lessened by the time lunch time came around. However, she put on a brave face to avoid speculation from the boys. Plus, Owen had way more reasons to be upset today. Instead, though, he was playing games on Jace's phone while Jace watched. Damien and Colby were doing last minute homework problems. It was a normal day. Why didn't Adelie feel normal, too? Today felt off. Dread drilled into her forehead, leaving an ache.

Things would be fine. There was no need to talk about it. Owen knew everything about the situation. There was nothing that anyone could do about it. Time would heal this wound. It would have to.

<u>Chapter 12</u>

A month later, the snow began to melt. Spring's warm soul emerged from the frostbitten earth to spread its seeds. Oceans of slush covered the land, painting it brown and gray. Birds returned to their homes as they filled the air with color. Though the ground paled in comparison, small specs of green could be found where the sun's hands reached far enough into the soil to pluck them out. Little buds were scooped to the surface, where they grew with glee. Hibernating rivers started to trickle back to life. They shed their icy skins.

Adelie's "Jeremy" wound had begun to slowly scab up. She sometimes saw him in the hallways, busy with his new little group of friends. He was never alone at lunch, either. Happiness, relief, and a tinge of guilt blossomed in her chest. Happy that he seemed to be moving on. Relieved that she didn't have to worry about her absorbism with him. Guilty that he still wished her all the best. Guilty that he still had feelings for her. Guilty that he would never know why he had to be dropped from her life. Guilty that part of his own wound may never heal because of it.

She shook off the thoughts as she shook snow from her muzzle. Her kits danced around in front of her. They were real, they were here, they weren't leaving. They wouldn't have to imagine a world without her.

Their coats were beginning to shed into sleeker, lighter pelts. All three were currently playing in a large melted-snow mud puddle. Aspen enjoyed crashing through it, spraying his siblings and mother. Birch toppled on top of him to wrestle. Maple sniffed at the mud cautiously before deciding to dig at it, ignoring her brothers. Adelie wished she could stay here forever. At least she had some human friends, too.

Adelie and the gang continued their mission of plucking out traps and poisoned bait. Owen and Adelie had to be extra careful due to Owen losing his phone. They kept their meetings short and sweet to hopefully avoid being caught by his father or the other hunters. At one point, Jace's father showed up while everyone was in the woods, but the other boys were able to convince him that they were cleaning up old traps to set in new ones. This man definitely wasn't as bright as Owen's father, but he was just as nasty, so it was a relief to see him leave in peace.

On an especially warm day, the five of them crossed the river that ran through the heart of the forest. It was slow-moving, but steady as ice continued to lose against the rage of the sun. She urged them all to stay still for a moment to watch the nature that surrounded them. So they did. A few ducks dared to poke their webbed feet into the water. A chipmunk was seen drinking from the river while digging up its old stash. Some fish splashed around. This watery aorta was truly life-giving.

They continued uphill from there. Most of the snow in the higher hills still clung to the earth, refusing to melt. Large boulders and fallen trees remained peppered with Winter. Adelie quickly realized that they would be passing by the kits' den. Owen did too, sparing her a small, knowing glance.

"Woah, guys, get over here," Damien sounded, disbelief in his voice.

Everyone was horrified when they did. There were traps and bait galore. The ground was littered with man-made objects, and they all surrounded one outcrop. Adelie felt her heart fall into her stomach. The kits.

"God, *fuck* them," Owen snarled.

It was weird for him to be the first to be upset. Usually, it was Adelie. However, her mind swam with all the possibilities of disaster that had been laid out for Maple, Birch, and Aspen. Before she could even say anything, Owen was already ripping traps apart and throwing the bait into garbage bags. His anger was clear. The rest of the boys joined in, soon becoming just as angry. Only Owen knew of the kits' whereabouts, yet here were these boys getting passionate for a cause they didn't even know the half of. It snapped Adelie awake.

"Fucking bastards," she grumbled as she cut apart a wire trap.

Thankfully, when she crouched down and rested her hand against the rock, she could feel the three foxes stirring behind it. She longed to see them but was glad to know that they had learned well from her. They weren't coming out. They probably didn't have any of the poisoned prey. Just as she began to feel the beginnings of absorbism pulse through her body, Colby stood up.

"I'm gonna personally beat the shit out of your father one of these days," Colby said to Owen.

Everything was picked up. The land was clean. No death today.

❖

Spring break. Freedom, choice, fun. Birds, flowers, and morning showers.

The gang headed to the ice cream parlor when they were done with their duties. Adelie used the gift card she'd gotten from Jace before winter break. The dessert tasted bittersweet. The boys, though happily munching, seemed to feel the same way. This belief was confirmed when Damien spoke up.

"Man, I miss Jeremy. Did something happen?"

Adelie froze up, suddenly unaware of how to answer the question. She'd forgotten that they didn't know why the curly-headed boy didn't frequent them anymore.

"Nah, he's just been busy with school and stuff," Owen lied.

"Too busy to hang with us? I've seen him around with some other guys at school," Colby objected.

"Really? Huh," Owen lied again, his eyes frantically flicking to Adelie's face.

She wanted to scream. To flip over the tables. To dump all the ice cream out onto the street. To let it melt with the snow into a giant, ugly puddle. To let all the lies escape from her throat. To replace the lies with honesty. To replace the absorbism with something, anything. Instead, her tongue rattled off on its own.

"He probably just feels weird about hanging with seniors. It's better that he has friends his age."

"You're the one that brought him into the circle, though," Damien replied skeptically.

"Yeah. I'm not gonna bully him or nothin', but you'd think he would've said something to us. This doesn't add up," Colby agreed.

"It *does* seem out of character for him. Does it have to do with Thanksgiving? That night was weird," Jace added.

Adelie stood up and swiftly made her way to the restroom. Their eyes followed. She stood in front of the sink and splashed her face with warm water. The mirror stared at her. It saw her pale skin, now reddened. Her equally red hair hung limply from the sides of her face. Her black coat hugged her frame while her grey scarf tightened around her throat.

She splashed herself again. Now the mirror showed Jeremy's face. It was covered in chocolate and vanilla. His eyes cried milk. There was a cherry in his hair. It leaked crimson down his nose. She blinked, and he was gone.

In truth, nothing added up anymore.

After tidying herself up, she dared to go back out and face them. The walk to her seat felt like hours. They'd all finished their treats and were waiting for her to come back. Now, more than ever, their eyes were glued to her. Owen looked worried.

"Listen. Here's the deal, okay? Jeremy told me he liked me. I told him that I didn't like him the same way. He's just bummed out," she sighed.

There. It wasn't a total lie. Owen's face lightened. Damien erupted.

"I knew it! I knew it!"

"Damn, that sucks. I'm sorry," Jace grabbed Damien back down to his seat while he apologized to Adelie.

"Oh, yeah, sorry," Damien said sheepishly.

"Should've known," Colby scratched his chin.

Now everyone was looking at Owen.

"I knew about it. Sorry guys," he answered their suspicions.

"What the hell? If I didn't know any better, I'd say you and Adelie were *dating*," Jace teased.

"No way, man. You know you're my number one," Owen teased right back.

"Jeremy actually thought the same thing after I told him that I didn't have feelings for him. It's not happening, though. Trust me," Adelie clarified.

Everyone shared a collective "phew."

Since everyone had finished up, they all piled onto the outside sidewalk. Flower baskets were beginning to be hung up around the shops. Dirt and debris were being cleaned up. The sun jumped out from behind the clouds. A bit distracted, Adelie didn't notice the boys going into a nearby comic book shop. She sat down on a bench and soaked up the early days of Spring. Her eyes slowly squeezed shut.

"Adelie?"

They flew open again. It had been faint, but someone had called her name. Her amber eyes danced around in her skull. The sidewalk. The stores. The cars. The street. Across the street.

Across the street. Jeremy was there. He was squinting. He waved when he noticed her eyes on his, and then mouthed "hold on." She gave a small wave back. The rest of her felt paralyzed.

Traffic lights turned red. People began to use the crosswalk. He used it too, his friends in front of him. She got to her feet. Sirens went off in her head. To run, or to stay? To be a jerk, or to be exposed? Jeremy continued to get closer. The sun felt like an oven.

"Are you coming?"

Adelie's head snapped to the right. Owen was there, one foot on the sidewalk, one foot in the store. He was holding the door for her. Adelie looked forward again. Jeremy had stopped in the middle of the street. He'd noticed Owen, too. His face had fallen into the asphalt. Confusion melted into a dejected frown.

"Adelie?"

Owen's voice called again. Adelie didn't answer. The crosswalk signal began to count down as Jeremy's friends urged him to hurry up. Instead, he seemed to be just as frozen as Adelie was.

A semi-truck horn blew. Everyone's heads turned. A semi was rolling toward the intersection, skidding and slipping. The wet roads were making it impossible for it to brake. Slush was built up around its tires. Tree trunks swung around on its back. A few fell onto the ground as the vehicle fish tailed.

"Oh my god," she heard Owen gasp.

More horns honked at Jeremy. Some people jumped from their cars. The boy had barely moved, transfixed on Adelie.

Move.

She tried to run to him. She tried to scream. She couldn't.

MOVE!

After an eternity, Jeremy finally came back to his senses. He looked to his right. Everything happened so quickly, yet the world slowed down enough for Adelie to take in every detail.

The screams. The crash of metal. The squawks of birds.

Owen's footsteps. His yells. His hands covering her eyes.

Jeremy's quiet. Jeremy's soul leaving his ruined body.

Owen running from the scene.

Part II

UBI AMOR, UBI DOLOR

"Death is not the greatest loss in life. The greatest loss is what dies inside us while we live."

\- Norman Cousins

<u>Chapter 1</u>

My fault.

Bells rang from the church to beckon the mourners to its entrance. Their pale faces stood out amongst the black attire. Everyone had stained cheeks.

My fault.

Some guests were familiar, and some were not. Jeremy's family was there, most of the members having that unmistakable curly, dirty blonde hair. The mother and father were there. She was a puddle of tears that her husband kept trying to soak up. Though stoic, his eyes were red.

My fault.

Damien, Colby, and Jace were sniveling as they sat in a row. The seat next to them was empty, so Adelie took it. It looked like Owen wasn't coming.

He left me on that bench and now I'm sitting on this bench without him, too.

Adelie's mother tried to help console Jeremy's mother, but her efforts grew futile. The women clung to each other. They both knew of loss.

The funeral felt like forever. The eulogies, acknowledgements, apologies—the tears. Adelie couldn't bring herself to go up to the podium. She didn't deserve to talk so fondly of someone who was dead because of her. Someone who died with the sense of betrayal on his face. Someone who *died* trying to tell *her* something. It should've been the other way around. None of this should've happened.

At the end of it all, Adelie went up to his casket. It was closed, sealed in white, and covered in flowers. A large portrait of Jeremy hung to the side, his smile once contagious. Not today, though. She traced her fingers along the wood, a small part of her hoping that it would pop open and reveal that everything was, in fact, okay. Jeremy would jump down and laugh at everyone. It would've been the perfect prank. The other boys would chime in, laughing along with him. Sadly, life was the only one playing pranks.

A hand touched her shoulder. Adelie jumped, spooked out of her daydream. For a moment, she thought it might've been Jeremy's hand. Her eyes threatened to spill but were interrupted by Jeremy's mother's voice.

"He really liked you, y'know. You really opened up doors for him."

I closed them, too.

There were so many things that she wanted to say, but they died on her tongue.

"I know," she mumbled back.

"I just wanted to thank you for all the kindness you gave to our Jeremy. You showed him how to make friends, how to laugh—"

Her words caught in her throat.

"How to love. You will always be welcome in our home," she pulled Adelie into a crushing hug.

It all felt so wrong. She wished this hug would kill her, squeeze her lungs from her chest. Maybe then things would feel justified. Instead, it just left her feeling even more guilty.

"Thank you," was all she could mutter as the hug broke.

Adelie quickly shuffled past her to get to her own mother. It was time to leave.

❖

The minute the car was parked in the driveway, Adelie bolted out, not sparing anyone or anything a second glance. It was hard to run in the fancy black flats that her mom had made her wear. She tugged them off her feet. Her black dress billowed out behind her and her hair fought with the wind. The mother's calls couldn't even begin to break down her daughter's barriers of grief. She let her go for now.

So Adelie ran. The cool, early Spring air mingled with the sweat upon her freckled skin. She didn't know whether to feel cold or hot. She passed a few street signs. Almost all of them had directions to funerals around town. Jeremy wasn't the only one to have died that day. Adelie wished she could've experienced all their deaths for them. She deserved it.

As she rounded a corner, Owen came speeding by on his bike. The two made eye contact. The boy gasped, swerving and pumping on his brakes, his tires screeching. The girl also stopped, her body unsettlingly still.

"Where were you?"

Her stern face stared straight ahead, the question dropping from firm lips.

"Adelie, I—"

"You left me *twice*. On that street, and on his casket."

"Look, I couldn't do it, okay? I couldn't."

Her head immediately snapped in his direction.

"*You* couldn't do it? How do you think *I'm* feeling?"

Owen's hands gripped his bike handles in newfound anger.

"*Everyone* is hurting, okay? We all handle it differently. He was my friend, too," he spit from clenched teeth.

"You were the only one who didn't come. A friend would've been there."

Her scathing remark turned to poison upon Owen's ears. It infected him.

"You weren't there for him, though, *were* you?"

Owen seemed to immediately regret his rebuttal. Adelie went quiet again. Her hands clenched into fists at her sides.

"Go."

Owen put his kickstand down and stood up from his seat.

"I didn't mean that, I—"

"I said *go*," her voice refused to waver.

He started to reach out his hand to her, but soon realized that it would be a bad idea.

"Okay," he complied as he hopped back up on his seat.

Adelie watched him ride away. He was heading toward his house when he took a sharp turn onto a side street. Once he was out of sight, she turned away and started running again.

How dare he say that to me? Who does he think he is?

She tripped and landed on her knee. A sharp scream flew from her as both her skin and dress ripped. Blood streamed down her leg as she got back up. Though in pain, she kept going, albeit with a slight limp. Red droplets left a bread crumb trail behind her. All her self-esteem drained out with it.

I deserved that. I deserved what Owen said. He's right. I wasn't there.
Now I can never be.

The forest welcomed her with open branches. Melted snow was giving way to beds of dead grass and flowers. Her tired body fell into them.

I should've figured something out. I'm a fool, a coward. I should be dead.

All at once, the dam broke behind her eyes. She cried openly, loudly, sincerely. Her shrill sobs echoed all around her. Now on her hands and knees, her tears fed the soil beneath her, which quickly became caked within her fingers. The pain inside her ribs was unbearable. It crushed her lungs, her stomach, her heart. Her entire body was alight with agony.

Is this how Jeremy felt? Was this how he lived? Did he die like this?

Adelie went to sit up but fell onto her side when her knee struck a spiky twig. She cradled it close, seeing splinters within the scrapes. Though she squeezed her eyelids shut, the water continued to flow. Darkness was all she saw. Her fingers acted on their own as they crawled up to her scalp. They went to work at plucking out the weak locks. Threads of red joined the leaves on the forest floor.

Stupid, stupid, stupid!

A soft rustling noise in front of her pulled her back to Earth. Opening her eyes, she was met with Ace's furred face. He was staring at her inquisitively. Adelie sometimes doubted if this dog was even real—he was like a ghost, a spirit. The husky would always disappear as quickly as he came. Was he just a folktale or vision seen by the residents of this town?

All her confused thoughts were put on hold when Ace stepped forward and licked at her cheek.

Okay, that was real.

Still, Adelie was so set aback. So much so, that she began to cry again. She didn't know why she did, but she did. Nothing felt real anymore, if she was being honest, except this small moment. The dog crept closer before laying down and placing its head on her bad knee.

"Hi," she hiccupped between sobs.

Adelie stopped pulling at her own hair so that she could pet Ace's. His fur was soft and warm. It'd been a long time since she'd been comforted by an animal while in her human form. For some reason, it made the connection even stronger.

"What're you doin' out here, huh? All alone?"

He's probably wondering the same thing about me.

Ace whined a little and shifted to lay next to her. Some of Adelie's blood had stained the white parts of his coat.

"Don't you have a home to go back to? An owner?"

She reached out to see if he had a collar, but he veered away, suddenly getting back on his feet.

"I guess you don't need one. That's okay."

His tail wagged a little as he trotted off farther into the woods. Like always, he was gone in seconds. As Adelie watched him go, she somehow felt a sense of peace come over her. The encounter had proved to be therapeutic. Though her body still ached, her emotions had subsided for now. Her attention returned to her wounded knee, which she wrapped with the torn scraps of her dress. It's not like she would've worn it again, anyway.

Since she was already in the forest, and had a valid excuse to be, Adelie decided to go see the kits. She limped through the trees while keeping eyes and ears alert for hunters. Last thing was to be literally caught red-handed. Though injured, her stealth was just as effective. She reached the den with ease and slipped right in as a fox. The kits yapped with joy as they cascaded upon their mother. It made it hard to believe that there was a big, sad world outside.

Her cuts were still existent on her matching hindleg. Maple soon began to lick at the wound. Birch and Aspen engulfed her as they groomed her messy fur. Sleep came naturally, and she spent most of the rest of the day in and out of it.

Adelie stretched her languid limbs as the first beams of light dusted over the land. Still in her fox form, she yawned and shook out her coat. Her stomach grumbled just as a mouse scrambled out from the undergrowth. She barely had to lift a paw to catch it. Breakfast.

After her meal, she trotted along the dirt path in front of her. A strong scent hit her nostrils, urging her to follow it. Nose to the ground, she now hunted for the source of the smell. The ground began to wither away from under her the farther she walked. Now afraid, she darted forward, running as fast as she could to not fall into the abyss. Something new showed up in front of her, causing her body to screech to a halt.

Bear paw prints. Fresh, deliberate, menacing. There were spots of blood in the soil. The scent bombarded her senses. Everything turned black.

Adelie's body twitched in her sleep, her frame rocking back and forth. The kits cuddled closer.

Adelie startled awake in the kits' den while still in her human form. It was cramped, uncomfortable, and unnatural. She was able to wiggle her body out from the rocks by sheer luck but was soon struck by a familiar face. Jeremy stood just outside, his eyes wide.

"I need to tell you something."

Before Adelie could reply, his form started to fade.

"No, please, please tell me!"

His head hung low, tears dripping from his closed eyes.

"PLEASE TELL ME!"

All at once, Jeremy's body fell apart, limbs chunking off and breaking into crumbling heaps.

Fear gripped her body as she jolted awake, for real this time. Looking down at herself, she was relieved to see that she was still in her fox form. The presence of the kits must've kept her absorbism from wearing off. Maple licked her mother's shoulder lazily. The sun was beginning to burst into flame outside. She gave her daughter and sons farewell licks before dragging herself outside. Half of her wondered if Jeremy would be there.

Her sore legs carried her to the street, where she remembered that her phone was in the pocket of the dress she was wearing. She pulled it out, but not without noticing the condition of both her knee and her black dress. The bleeding had ceased. Giant brown stains and scabs covered her skin. To her surprise, her phone rang only once before being answered.

"Adelie? You okay?"

For now, she ignored the fact that he had somehow gotten his phone back.

"Yeah. Can we talk?"

"Yeah. Where are you?"

❖

Owen slowed down and veered off the side of the road, coming to a stop next to the mangled heap that was Adelie's figure. He hopped off and let his bike rest across the grass before sitting down beside her.

"I'm sorry."

"I'm sorry."

The two teens stared at each other in shock at their matching apologies.

"No, really, what I said was way out of turn," Owen insisted.

"I was out of turn, too. We're all hurting. It wasn't fair of me to accuse you like that," she fidgeted with the growing grass around them.

Owen sighed and rested back on the palms of his hands.

"It's fine. I was the coward who couldn't bring myself to show up."

"You're not a coward," Adelie whispered.

"I am. I was a coward when I bullied him, and I'm a coward now. I should've become his friend from the start," his face grew tired.

"It's not your fault that you were raised by a bully. We can't help what we've learned from our parents, but you made it right in the end," she reassured him.

"I guess," he was unconvinced.

"You're already more tolerable than when I first met you, at least."

"Is that a compliment? Did you—Adelie—just give me a compliment?"

"I did, and don't expect another one."

They let out a couple small laughs.

"I'm glad I met you."

Adelie looked up from the grass to gaze his way.

"I already feel so much freer. My dad is still terrible, but, I dunno, knowing that your mom is terrible too somehow makes me feel better."

Adelie blinked, a bit lost in thought.

"Sorry, that came out really wrong. What I mean is, well, it's nice to not be alone. You've helped me to express and change myself."

When Owen met her eyes again, they were filled with tears. His own face filled with panic, until he realized that she was smiling. It might've been the smallest smile in the world, but it was a smile, nonetheless.

As Adelie wiped at her face, she felt the hairs on her neck stand up. So, this was what true friendship was. They both appreciated each other so much.

"Thank you, Owen."

Owen grew even more startled when his friend leaned over and pulled him into a hug. He made sure to take a million mental snapshots of this moment— it might never happen again. Adelie, though warm on the inside, was covered in a cold, glass exterior. He felt it crack against his chest. Not wanting to chase her away, he reciprocated, wrapping his arms around her.

"Thank *you*, Adelie."

Her weight shifted, and a second later, when Owen looked down, there was a fox in his lap. Instinctually, he held her close and looked around to make sure that no one was around. Once the coast was declared clear, he returned his focus to Adelie. He'd never held a fox before, much less *Adelie* as a fox. He'd only seen her transform on one occasion. She curled up in a content ball. Her fur felt like satin on his fingertips. Owen's brain took another mental snapshot. Her golden eyes flicked up to his as they reflected the rising moon.

"I should get you home."

He stood up and Adelie jumped back down to the earth. Within seconds she changed back to her human form, hair a bit disheveled. They both climbed on the bike. Owen spoke after he gained some steady pedaling.

"I'll tell you about what happened with my dad, with my phone. I'm sure you're wondering how I even answered at all," his voice was low, almost low enough for the wind to snatch it away.

"I'm listening."

He picked up the pace of his pedaling.

"I feel nasty even saying it."

"You already said you would tell me. C'mon."

"Okay," he sighed, revving himself up.

"I made him believe that I was pretending to date you to keep you distracted. To have you wrapped around my finger, so to speak," he visibly shuttered in disgust.

"Just like he's doing with your mom, which he proudly announced to me."

"Okay, I hate this, but why would he believe you and approve of it enough for him to give you your phone back?"

"It's all about keeping tabs. Before, he thought that you were brainwashing me. Now, he thinks I'm brainwashing *you*."

"Ugh," she threw her head back and groaned.

"I'm sorry. I hate it too, but I needed my phone back."

"It's fine, I get it. Just no hand holding."

"Don't worry about that, Ms. Murder."

❖

When she'd arrived home, her mother had looked relieved that she was in Owen's presence. She thanked Owen for taking care of her daughter before ushering her inside to get a look at her knee. Adelie watched Owen leave as the front door swung shut.

"He's a nice boy," her mother had uttered, hands busy disinfecting the wound.

Adelie grunted in agreement. She remained silent as her mother pretended to act like a mom. It felt wrong. Adelie could've done this herself. She didn't need her to do this. She was used to taking care of herself.

"How are you feeling? I know today was hard," she probed.

"I'm fine," was Adelie's curt answer.

I'm fucking miserable and you're making it worse. Stop talking to me.

"You can talk to me, you know," the mother had replied, now wrapping the knee in gauze.

No, I can't.

She didn't answer. The silence afterward lasted only a few seconds.

"So, I heard from Mr. Smit that you and Owen are an item."

Adelie groaned and wanted to kick her mom and blame it on a knee-jerk reaction. She lied instead but was still angry.

"I didn't know how to tell you yet, but, seriously? Today of all days?"

Her mother finished up with her knee and gave a look of innocence curled with a knowing smile.

"Well, I know, but I just can't believe it! So much makes sense now!"

Adelie didn't really understand what she meant by that, but she didn't have time to think about it. She was pulled into a hug-- much more unpleasant than her hug with Owen-- and smooched on the cheek. Her body fought to contain the urge to shove her away.

"Yeah, uh, it's great. I want to go lay down, though," Adelie resorted to patting her mom's back in protest instead of shoving.

Her mother pulled away and nodded.

"Of course, take all the time you need."

It was funny that she said this when she could have waited to talk about this on a day that Adelie wasn't *grieving*. Either way, she took her opportunity to leave and head upstairs.

Her own bed felt like a doormat. The room around her was cornered with shadows that wished to swallow her up in black. Shapes danced along the floorboards to haunt her sleep. Was she lucid dreaming? She couldn't tell, but then again, nothing, except Owen and Ace, had felt real today. Maybe the funeral had never even happened. Maybe Jeremy would be waiting for her at school tomorrow.

Maybe her dad had never really left. Maybe he was standing at the front door, right now, hand poised to knock.

Adelie sighed and turned over to lay on her side. She now faced the window. The tree outside began to morph into a human-like figure. The moon turned into two staring, yellow orbs. Something warm created fog against the glass.

She immediately shot up and rubbed her eyes. The figure was still there, a constant stream of warmth flowing in and out from just below its two glowing moons. Adelie raked her nails down her sides, wincing in pain as she did so. This was happening. This was real. There was something watching her.

A piercing scream flew from her throat, threatening to shatter the glass and let the unknown visitor in. However, the being did not waver. It continued staring. Panic swept Adelie under her sheets for protection. A moment later, her bedroom door opened.

"Adelie? What the hell? What's wrong?"

Adelie shakily removed the sheets from her head to speak when she noticed the thing was gone.

"Th-there was someone outside. On the roof. Outside my window."

"What? That's impossible," the mother scoffed.

"I *swear* there was something watching me," Adelie's voice grew dark.

"You're probably just tired," the mother walked over to the window to investigate.

"There's nothing but that old tree. You're fine," she now walked to her daughter's bedside.

"You're safe, okay?"

Her hand began to cradle Adelie's cheek when it was slapped away.

"How many times have I told you not to touch me?"

Before the mother could even reply, Adelie had already started flinching. She was expecting a slap of her own. Fortunately, it never came.

"I'm your mother and I'm just trying to comfort you, can't you see that?"

You never have before, so don't start trying now.

Adelie turned away from her and attempted to make herself comfortable.

"I just want to sleep now."

The mom, unsure of what to do, almost put her hand on Adelie's shoulder, before rethinking it. She left the room, softly closing the door behind her. As she walked down the stairs, she glanced at an old family portrait, her eyes pinpointing her missing husband. Adelie could just make out the words she said as she reached the first floor.

"Things were bad before, but with you gone, it's even worse now."

Chapter 2

School was back in session. At the very start of the day, everyone held a moment of silence for the people who had died in the truck accident. Two other people had died along with Jeremy. Not students, but humans all the same. Guilt clogged her throat.

Why couldn't it have been me instead?

The fog outside wasn't the only thing that made Adelie's day hazy. Everyone was abuzz with the tragic news. Each time she heard his name, her brain seemed to just shut down altogether. Passing by his locker seemed to snap her spine in two. She didn't want to see, to feel, to think. Yet, here she was, about to attend her next class.

During a lecture, her phone buzzed. She snuck a peek at the screen.

11:33 AM

Colby: we r gonna sit outside 2day.

Adelie noticed Jace, Colby, and Damien sitting at an outdoor table under the overhang that covered the pathway to the cafeteria. Though she was relieved that she wouldn't have to be near Jeremy's old table, she was a little surprised to see the guys not wanting to be near it, either. She questioned them as she set her things down.

"Everything alright?"

"We'd overheard people saying that flowers were gonna be put at the table that Jeremy shared with those newer friends of his. I don't think any of us want to have to go through that," Damien sighed.

Fair enough.

"Thank you. Also, where's Owen?"

"He's sick," Jace replied.

"Bullshit. I bet he's just playin' hookey," Colby retorted

"Nah, he seemed actually sick when he called me this morning," Jace shrugged.

"Listen, we're all going through this shit too. What makes him think he's so special? I don't get it," Colby began to look visibly irritated.

"Dude, I'm just telling you what he told me," Jace put his hands up.

"Not just today. I mean at the accident, the funeral. He just straight up disappeared."

Adelie could see where Colby was coming from. Hell, she had thought these exact same things until she'd sat down and talked with Owen. Now Colby's words sent a flare of annoyance through her.

"He already hates himself for both of those things. He was scared and sad, like anyone else would be. He's taking it really hard because he's blaming himself," Adelie corrected.

So am I.

Colby looked as if he'd seen a ghost. The words struck him, and abruptly so. His tense demeanor soon relaxed as he leaned back against the plastic seat.

"Idiot. We're all blaming ourselves. He doesn't have to do it alone."

A bolt of pain shot through Adelie. They didn't deserve to hurt, too.

I should be the one doing it alone.

❖

Spring felt just as long, quiet, and cold as the winter before it. Even though the world was becoming colorful again, Adelie couldn't see it. Everything still looked grey. The only thing that distracted her were dashes of red—the kits. Owen had been hard to get a hold of lately, but she didn't push it. She wasn't exactly great company right now, either. Her dreams continued to worsen along with the feeling of someone watching her. Was she being paranoid, or just more observant than everyone else?

Each time she visited the forest, the more off it felt. Less prey was showing up, and instead, poisoned bodies continued to litter the dirt. She narrowly stopped Aspen from picking one up out of sheer hunger. As she did, something sounded from a few yards away. She flicked a furred ear at the noise. It was familiar.

Mr. Smit was walking about the woods. She couldn't see him yet, but twigs were snapping. The air had changed. Scuttling squirrels and chipmunks dashed by her. Crows screeched. The kits' tails slowly wagged with worry. The four of them froze while waiting to get a clear sense of where he was. A closer snap of twigs was detected by a flicked ear.

That was when she saw him between some far trees, hands sported with a trap and what was most likely poisoned prey.

Fearfully, she rushed the kits to hide them behind a nearby fallen evergreen. She mused at the irony but kept watch through the needles. He crept close to their den before stuffing more poisoned bait just under the entrance. Adelie knew that the den had been noticed but had been too lost in grief to properly move the kits out. That was selfish of her. It had to happen *today*.

The sad sound of a mourning dove cried out just above the foxes in a nearby tree branch. Mr. Smit turned his head at the sound.

He looked at the bird and slowly dragged his eyes down before resting them on the fallen evergreen. An uncaring face seemed to stare directly at the foxes now. The kits shook with fear, rustling the branches slightly. Adelie stood her ground.

He took a step toward them. Then another. Adelie prepared for the worst, sharp teeth gritted and her tail beginning to lash behind her. The hunter was about to reach the evergreen when a human voice called out from somewhere in the woods. A fellow hunter yelling for Mr. Smit to come and look at something. He hesitated but decided to turn around and head toward his colleague. The fur on Adelie's back flattened again.

Once a few minutes had passed since Mr. Smit had paid his visit, she signaled for the kits to follow her. She didn't know where she was going, but anywhere was better than here. The three seemed to know that the move was happening, too. They constantly looked over their shoulders, no doubt saying goodbye to their second home. Their muscles bunched beneath them as they moved. Swift tails bushed out behind them. They were nearly full-grown.

At this point in the season, there wasn't any more snow on the ground, which would make it much easier to burrow a proper den. It meant the soil would be soft instead of frozen. Adelie sniffed around to check for possible dangers such as badgers, coyotes, or other foxes. Both luckily, and sadly, she didn't find a trace of anything. In fact, since she'd moved here, there'd been a very low number of carnivorous animals around. She guessed that came from the overhunting. That could also explain the subtle decline of prey around—the plant life was being eaten faster than it could regenerate.

Getting back to the task at hand, she spotted a hole on the incline of the forest floor. As they got nearer, she noticed that it was an abandoned rabbit den. Hardly any prey scent greeted her when she took a big whiff. She dug at it a little with her front paws.

Soft, easy to dig. The inside looks like it can be expanded upon too.

She let out a little yip to the kits to bring them to the spot. Her paws continued to dig as she beckoned for them to help her. They did, and excitedly so. Pausing for a moment, she realized that one of them would need to keep a lookout. Maple quickly took that position while Adelie and the boys created their new home.

After a little while, their work was done. From the front entrance led three tunnels: one to a second exit at the back of the hill, one to food storage, and one to a den. As the mother and sons clambered out into the sunlight, they shook off their dusty pelts and invited Maple inside. It was a bit of a squeeze in parts, but it would do. Adelie could already tell that, despite being nostalgic of their old home, the kits would settle in quickly and comfortably. This den would keep them warm during the cold months and cool during the hottest days of summer. All four of them made sure to cover both entrances with leafy branches and sticks to make it more inconspicuous.

Before saying her goodbyes, Adelie decided to accompany them to find some food. She climbed up a slanted tree and sat with her tail curled around her paws. Her eyes flitted back and forth between the kits and their surroundings. Maple pursued a mouse while Birch and Aspen chased after some crickets. The food was meager, but it would sustain them until she could get her hands on some store-bought meat for them.

A bush stirred, and a black and white face appeared. Hackles raised, Adelie prepared herself to strike, but was set aback when she realized that it was Ace. The kits scattered and hissed. Maple, now with said mouse in her jaws, let out a muffled growl. Surprisingly, Ace did not snarl or bare his teeth. Instead, he set down an offering—a freshly killed rabbit. Before any of them could move, Adelie bounded over to her children. Though Ace didn't seem like a threat, he was still an enigma, and therefore could not be trusted. She leaned down and gave the dead rabbit a good whiff. There was no smell of chemicals, poison, or Man's interference.

Once she had determined the food to be safe, she dipped her head to the canine.

Thank you.

The husky's tail wagged in just the slightest. A moment later, he began to trot away. Adelie gave the kits swift licks on their ears as she left them for the day. Aspen, Birch, and Maple dragged the rabbit and mouse to their new den, where they would stay for the remainder of the day. Their mother trotted after Ace.

Adelie's vixen body swiftly cut through the forest in pursuit of the fluffy beacon in front of her. She hoped to observe him. A few yards in front of her, Ace stopped in his tracks and flicked one of his ears in her direction. Adelie froze before flattening herself to the ground. To her disappointment, he turned around and pinpointed her location quickly, his ice-blue eyes locking with her amber ones. She stood up straight and pricked her ears.

Ace opened his mouth and let out a bark that bounced off the trees. Adelie's fur stood on end. Was he challenging her? Was he playing? What did he want? Why was he here?

Just like he usually does, he turned around again and resumed his running. Adelie followed him with an even more intense sense of curiosity. As he gained distance on her, he jumped down a small hill and went out of sight. She pushed herself to move faster and propelled her body over the gap. When she landed, he was gone. Both her nose and eyes failed her.

Maybe he really is just a ghost. Still, he's a ghost that brought us a rabbit.

The following week, as Adelie exited the bus at school, she quickly spotted Owen walking through the crowd of students. This was the first time he'd been back since Jeremy's funeral almost two weeks ago. Her feet felt spring-loaded as she rushed through the bodies around her. When she found her target, she latched onto him with a big hug. Owen froze, unsure of what to do with their grand total of two hugs under his belt. Adelie pulled back and scowled at him.

"You said that you were here for me, but you know that me and the guys are here for you too, right?"

The boy blinked, still a bit stunned from the physical contact. Adelie patted his shoulder.

"Stop carrying all this shit by yourself," she commanded, feeling a bit hypocritical.

As if on cue, the three other boys bounced from the buses and found their exchange. Colby, Damien, and Jace proceeded to tackle Owen to the ground, to the annoyance and confusion of the surrounding students.

"Idiot! Welcome back!"

"I missed you man!"

"Don't disappear on us again, okay?"

Adelie felt the hairs on the back of her neck stand up, but she pushed it back for the moment. She then saw Owen's face soften—a lone ice cube melting under warm light.

"I love you guys. Thank you."

The absorbism begged to take over, thickening her hair and making her teeth chatter. Thankfully, she was literally saved by the bell as the moment was broken by the sound of classes starting. The other boys split up to go to their respective classes. However, as she walked away, she soon felt a tug on her right hand.

"Hey, you're not getting away so easily after all that," Owen teased.

Fear crept over Adelie at the thought of shifting in front of so many people, out in the open, with no escape. A finger in her face brought her back to the boy in front of her.

"I know what you're thinking, but don't worry, it'll only be a second," he led the two of them to a nook in a nearby school building. The other boys split up to go to their respective classes.

"I'm sorry I haven't been very talkative. I'm sure you know why," his face looked a bit solemn.

"It's fine. I know what you mean," she glanced around before continuing, her voice now a whisper.

"I moved the kits to a different spot because your dad wouldn't let up on leaving that poisoned bait."

"God, I'm sorry about that, too. I've been doing my best to try to make him stop without looking suspicious. Still, the good news is that he hasn't been getting nearly as much fur lately. Looks like we're working faster than he can get the supplies out," he gleamed a snaggle toothed grin.

"That's really good to hear. Any luck on my dad?"

The final bell rang. They were both late.

"Shit, I'll get back to you on that," he sighed as they parted.

❖

Adelie thanked whatever Gods were out there that the school year was almost over. She didn't know what would happen after graduation, but constantly being reminded of Jeremy's absence seemed to have put her in a never-ending spiral. The stress of the safety of the kits combined with Owen's quiet had really put a damper on her hopes in the last week. However, she now found herself antsy with anticipation. What information did Owen have?

Could this day go any slower? I need to know!

Thankfully for Adelie, she and Owen shared their last class together along with Damien and Jace. They finished up their classwork quickly and were revving to go by the time the final bell rang. Adelie and Owen wandered out the door together but were stopped when Damien tugged on the hood of Owen's jacket.

"Hey, we usually have meetings all together, don't we? Can't Jace and I come?"

The boy's brown eyes swirled with frustration, but also worry. Jace stared with his own pleading look.

"Uh, it's just boring 'our parents are terrible' stuff, guys. Don't sweat it," Owen replied, as he began to sweat instead.

"We wanna be there for you guys, too. We've said that a million times," Damien pushed.

Jace put a hand on Damien's shoulder to gently move him aside.

"Owen, I can *always* tell when you're lying. Is this about Adelie's dad?"

Owen's face jittered a moment longer before sagging. He'd been caught.

"You know me too well. Yes, it is. That's why we can't take you guys."

Jace's green eyes burned into Owen's blue ones.

"Well, I hope it's good news. Let us know if there's anything we can do. We'd like to help, if you'll let us," his last words were edged with desperation.

Owen turned away and sped off before either he or Adelie could put another sentence in.

"I'm sorry, guys," Adelie quickly patched up the situation before trailing behind Owen.

"What's up with you?"

Owen swiveled on his heel to quickly face Adelie. They were near the library now.

"I just don't have great news, okay? I wanna get this over with," he growled out.

Adelie took a moment to respond, a bit stunned by her friend's sudden mood change. She also allowed herself a moment of panic about the "bad news."

"Okay, but don't take it out on me or the guys. Maybe we should let them in on everything, even me being—"

She cut herself off, remembering that they weren't in a safe space yet. Owen filled in the blanks for her.

"There's no point. C'mon."

"Owen, wait," she grasped his wrist gently.

Owen turned around and blinked with surprise. As much as she had been waiting all day to hear this news-- and was now extremely worried that it was "bad"-- she figured it would actually be better to talk somewhere more private.

"Maybe... we could talk somewhere else? I'm not keen on being told secret bad news at the library," she explained.

Owen glanced up at the sky, which had begun to form gray clouds and water droplets. He looked back at her and nodded.

"That makes sense. I agree. We could go to the duck pond. My father and the others don't go out when it's raining," he answered, keeping his voice low.

It only took one look between them to declare an agreement.

"I'll take the bus."

"I'll take my bike."

❖

Unlike the first time, *both* teens were ready with umbrellas. They sat just outside of the pond on the same rocky outcrop as before. There weren't any ducks out today.

"Alright, tell me what's going on."

Owen had been staring at the ripples on the pond for a few moments. He lifted his face up, slicked back his hair, and exhaled heavily.

"Adelie, I'm so sorry."

His words were blank, deadpan, somber.

She sucked in a shaky breath. Somehow, she knew what he was going to say, but she didn't want to admit that she knew. It was as if a lump of coal had landed into her stomach. It started to corrode her insides.

"Please just tell me what's happened. Don't hold back."

Owen gripped the sides of his jeans earnestly.

"He's dead. Some of my dad's buddies upstate scored a bear, but something about it seemed off. They found it dead but with no injuries or signs of disease. When they had its DNA tested, it came back stating that it was of human origin. Its inner organs were human, too. They did more testing and found that everything belonged to a Mr. Henderson. There's no way it could've been anyone else."

Adelie felt numb as her eyes glued themselves to the pitter patter of rain against the outcrop.

"I haven't been around much because I've been dealing with this information. I didn't know how to begin to tell you. I felt so guilty this morning when you hugged me. I didn't deserve it. Between Jeremy, and now this—"

"It's not your fault. You don't have to be sorry. *I'm* sorry. I should've just handled this mess on my own."

"You never would've found out, though."

"Even if I had been left wondering, it would've spared you a bit of pain. I should've trusted my gut a long time ago."

All these years of wondering, wanting, and searching, boiled down to something she should've accepted for herself long ago. Her father was dead. In her heart, she knew he couldn't have lived long from how bad his absorbism was, but still a foolish part of her clung on to any shred of hope. She felt his presence all the time, saw him in her dreams, and had even started to invest herself into the plan of having him help them with legal action against Owen's father. Maybe if they'd found him alive, they'd be a family again, too. Maybe her mom would've been better. Maybe Adelie would've been better, too— but then again, God, he was so sick.

Owen's hand nudged her side. She'd been so entranced in her thoughts that the rest of her had fallen silent.

"You okay?"

Adelie offered him a slow nod. She wasn't entirely okay, but she wasn't about to display all of her pain to him. No. She would take it home with her. Fall into bed and let it pour onto her sheets. Owen had gone through enough already.

Maybe she was a little more okay than she thought she would be. All those wishes and desperate cries within her could calm down now. She would grieve but perhaps not as intensely as she had with

Jeremy. At least this wasn't totally unexpected. It still hurt all the same, though.

"Yeah, I'm okay. Thanks for telling me,"she finally turned her gaze to the boy next to her.

Though his face still looked pained, he put his hand over hers in comfort.

❖

Shockingly, Adelie was able to go about her night well, save for having to deal with her mom. Not one tear drop littered her face, her bed. No dreams—or nightmares—interrupted her sleep. When she closed her eyes, only darkness greeted her for once. No visions of Jeremy or beastly forms of her dad. Her body fell further and further into the cold, damp, quiet. It felt so different from the pain she sustained from Jeremy's death, which had been like falling into a pit of boiling lava. Now she just felt, well... *nothing*.

Was this how people always slept? Free of pain? Free of clammy skin? She didn't know, but she quite liked the nothingness. Even if there was no joy, there was no sadness, either. It brought a sort of comfort that she had never felt before. Maybe "carefree" was the word she was thinking of?

Yeah, "carefree." Carefree grief.

<u>Chapter 3</u>

Graduation was quickly approaching. Tempers were short, the essays long. It'd been a couple weeks since Owen had shared his news of her father's fate. Sometimes she felt completely fine. Other days, the guilt crippled her and brought up the still-fresh wounds from Jeremy's death, too. Life had just assigned her to rip off two band aids as quickly as she could. Whether she liked it or not, she tended to dwell on things, overanalyze, wonder if things would've turned out better if she'd done one little thing differently.

Her brain buzzed as her pencil carved patterns into her scantron sheet. She couldn't think of these things right now. She needed to stay focused. Sure, she knew she wouldn't be going to college, but it was always harder to not try at something than to give it her all.

Colby sat across the room from her with his tongue sticking out from concentration. He was doing his best to be eligible for a full-ride scholarship due to his football excellence. Though he usually acted as the dopey, jockey friend, he was very intelligent when it came down to it. Adelie wondered how Owen and the others were doing on their tests. She wondered how Jeremy would've done in a few years' time. He probably could've gotten into any college he wanted.

"Time! Pencils down!"

Adelie tensed, the pencil dropping from her fingers. A few more rounds of scribbling and alarm clocks later, it was all done. Colby wiped at the sweat on his brow as all the students exited the building.

"I think I did good enough. I hope I did," the tall boy worried.

They walked side by side. Adelie had to tilt her head up to speak to him.

"Hey, it's over now. It's done. I'm sure you did just fine," she reassured him.

He let out a long, exasperated sigh before replying.

"Thanks."

They soon reached the curb of the carpool lane. Other students were still catching up.

"Hey, um, I kinda ended up hearing about your dad. I know you didn't want us to be involved, but I'm really sorry."

Adelie wasn't sure what he had heard from the others. She didn't know if Owen had fabricated a story for them or had simply told them that his body had been found. Either way, the sentiment was felt.

"Thank you, Colb."

"Hey, we interruptin' somethin'?"

Adelie and Colby turned around at the sound of Damien's voice. He stood with his arms crossed, lips smiling, and his dark brown eyes glittering. Jace and Owen leaned in from just behind the shorter boy.

"Actually, yeah. We've been together in secret," Adelie quipped.

Well, what the hell. Might as well tell them about the *real* hidden relationship.

"This reminds me. Owen, don't we have something *else* hidden to share with the boys?"

She laughed internally at the panic and confusion on all of her friends' faces. Owen quivered out a reply.

"We... do?"

Jace stared at Owen with intent.

"Wait, are you guys dating?"

"*No!*"

Owen looked like he'd smelled something bad as he exclaimed his answer. The other boys looked especially confused now.

"You act like Adelie is the worst person to be in a relationship with," Damien snorted.

"It's not that. I mean, I personally would never actually do that-- sorry, Adelie— but," exasperated breath left him as he struggled to explain the situation.

She took the lead from there.

"We're faking a relationship to get our parents off our backs. They seem a little more... *tame* this way. Plus, it made Owen's dad give him his phone back."

Everyone looked a bit shocked. Colby shrugged.

"Well, if it works, it works!"

"Damn, I was wondering how you'd gotten your phone back. You *lied*. The absolute betrayal," Damien kidded and bumped Owen's elbow.

Owen still looked nervous. Jace patted his shoulder.

"I see both your parents are stupid enough to believe it, so why not fuck with 'em, right?"

A car chirped in the distance. Jace held a key high in the air, a smirk on his face.

"Anyway, I can drive us home."

Jace's father had given him a brand-new car for his recent birthday and soon-to-be graduation. It was blood-money for sure, but if it meant more freedom, he'd take it—especially for the sake of his friends, too.

"SHOTGUN!"

Damien exclaimed and pushed himself past his pals. The boys zoomed ahead of Owen and Adelie, who were looking at each other with relieved smiles. After a moment, they ran after the others. It made her wonder how she ever lived without friends before.

Oh, Jeremy, how I wish things had been different.

The five of them cruised through the small town, windows down to let the warm air mingle with the new-car smell. Adelie sat squished between Owen and Colby.

"I was thinking of asking my dad if we could all hit up his lake house this summer. Y'know, sometime after graduation," Jace suggested, hands on the wheel.

Adelie whispered to Owen.

"What's a 'lake house'?"

"Oh, some of the richer folk around here own more than one house. Jace's dad has another one farther upstate. It has its own private little lake. It's pretty rad," he grinned.

The others whooped in excitement. Adelie felt apprehensive.

"Is it pretty safe?"

While Jace, Damien, and Colby chatted, Owen leaned in closer to her.

"Yeah! It's basically in the middle of nowhere. No one would bother us."

"You think our parents are gonna let us?"

"Oh, for sure. It'll promote the idea that we're getting *closer*," he pursed his lips with the last word.

Adelie shoved his face away with a scoff.

"Okay, seriously, what would we be doing?"

"Stupid stuff. Swimming, making campfires, running around naked, maybe," Owen joked.

Colby heard the tail-end of Owen's sentence, upon which he pointed at Jace.

"This guy will get naked for literally anything. Streaking, skinny-dipping, you name it."

Adelie's face twisted with horror. Owen couldn't stifle a laugh.

"Don't ask, I have no idea why he's like this."

❖

Jace slowly pulled his car into Adelie's driveway. Besides the driver, just she and Owen remained. The other two friends had already gotten dropped off.

Owen hopped out of the vehicle and held the door open for his "girlfriend."

"Ladies, first."

"Well, I'll be damned! Chivalry isn't dead," she joked as she climbed out alongside him.

Something caught her eye. The blinds on the front window had moved. Her mother must've realized they were home. Adelie's hand shot out on its own and grabbed Owen's. They both nearly jumped out of their skin.

"Just follow my lead. We need to lay it on thick," she urged through clenched teeth.

Though he was initially unsettled, Owen quickly settled into character.

"Gotcha," he replied, taking a step toward the door, hand sweating against Adelie's palm.

Owen's free hand knocked at the rickety wood.

Mother Henderson was upon them in seconds, and with a smile, at that. Adelie had never seen her so happy. Figures.

"Oh, what a pleasant surprise! Thank you so much for bringing her home safely," the mother put on her airs.

It looked like both parties were involved in their own kind of act.

"It was my pleasure, Ms. Henderson," Owen responded politely.

Adelie forced a smile and held Owen's hand tighter. He squeezed hers back supportively.

"Now, I won't keep you. Have a good night, ladies," Owen swooped in and placed a quick kiss to Adelie's cheek as he let her free of his grip.

It took everything in her not to flinch away. Instead, she let out a girlish giggle and followed her mom into the house. Owen took his leave shortly after. Adelie spotted the two boys driving off, Owen's head lowered and his lips moving. Facing forward again, Adelie closed the front door and locked it.

"Honey, I've never seen you so happy!"

I could say the same to you.

Adelie shrugged whilst putting down her backpack.

"Owen's just, really cool, y'know?"

"He *is* quite the gentleman. I guess things are going well?"

"Very. I actually need to ask you something," Adelie admitted.

The mother and daughter now sat on the couch.

"Owen and his friends are going to Jace's dad's lake house sometime this summer. It seems like fun. Could I go?"

Bile built in the girl's throat. She despised acting like a distressed dame.

"Adelie, I didn't think you even knew what 'fun' meant anymore," the mother laughed, hand stapling itself to her daughter's shoulder.

The redhead's face twitched.

"Of course you can go. I'm sure Owen and Mr. Smit will be thrilled! Let me know when you guys are planning to go," her hand moved to Adelie's face now, fingers caressing her cheek.

Adelie's mind flashed to the many times that those fingers had caressed her cheek in a different way.

"Sure thing. Thank you, mom."

The last word made her mouth dry.

❖

Adelie slipped her phone open as she slipped comfortably into her bedsheets.

While she waited for Owen's reply, her mind flew into the ceiling. It hurt to know how easily she could pull a "yes" from her mother at the drop of a boy. A lot of things about her life hurt—her father, Jeremy, constantly being a different person depending on who she was with—but what hurt most was the constant up-and-down waves of her mother. Riding the highs felt easy, but they would quickly fall into the sand webbed beneath. Adelie choked there, continuously tossed like small fry, always unsure of when she'd get a gulp of air. Should she keep her lungs, or evolve and grow gills? Her cuts oozed salt.

The buzz of her cellphone pulled her from the depths.

❖

Every day the sun crept closer and closer to the small town. It promised summer, blowing in both rain and shine. The last bits of snow evaporated under its breath. Birch, Aspen, and Maple found solace in the slight increase of prey available. It allowed them to nap with full bellies inside their spacious den, cool dirt beneath their paws.

Along with the sun's power growing stronger, so, too, did the power of Adelie's absorbism. The more time she spent with the kits, the more time she chipped away from herself. Thoughts of Jeremy reared their ugly heads from time to time, calling hypocrisy and bursting through her scabs. Why hadn't she just told him? Why did she value the kits over him? She would've been losing human years anyway. Why didn't she take a chance on him? She avoided him to conserve herself, yet now she spends most of her days alongside the beings that drain her humanity the most. What was it all for?

Stop thinking. Hindsight is twenty-twenty.

Though she rationally found this to be true, she often snowballed into a pit of regret. It was getting easier, but there were still bad days. The same could be said about the fate of her father. The relief was there, but it still hurt—not to mention that she'd come to a standstill on what to do about Owen's dad and the hunters.

Instead of stopping my thoughts, I need to put them to good use.

Adelie lay on her bed, eyes staring blankly at the angled ceiling. Perhaps the foolish part of her hoped that the answers she needed would be weaved into the wood.

Her saving grace would be graduation. She'd be free of the strain of school, and since she had no college plans, she'd have plenty of time to figure things out. Maybe she'd allow herself to have fun, too.

<u>Chapter 4</u>

Not even a month later, it was finally graduation day. Adelie arrived with time to spare, her hair slightly curled and her body adorned in a forest green gown and cap. The tassel hung with gold threads. Her mother snapped a few photos with her clunky camera.

Kindergarten graduation. Hobbles of little children clustered together. Some faces smiled, some cried, and some screamed. The one redhead of the class stood rather silent, face blank and eyes wandering. The kids were supposed to be lining up for roll call, but she was in another world. A woman snapped her fingers irritably.

"Adelie, hon, get with the others! C'mon! They're waiting!"

It was undoubtedly her mother. Still, the girl couldn't focus.

"Addie girl, you're gonna do great! You've got this," a much deeper voice called out.

It got the girl's attention, her focus shifting to the voice's source. Her dad. She nodded, offering a small smile, before shuffling into the line of toddlers.

"Mom, quit it," Adelie purposely waved a hand in front of her face to ruin the photo.

Before her mother could respond, Colby, Damien, and Jace walked up the sidewalk. All three boys wore the same garb along with giant grins. Their parents separated from them and headed inside.

"Adelie! Green truly is your color," Jace flirted.

"Hey, wouldn't want to let Owen catch you guys flirting," Colby joked.

Forgetting about her mother's presence, Adelie joined in the banter.

"Boys there is *plenty* to go around!"

All of them laughed and hugged, only separating when said mother interrupted them.

"Speaking of, where's Owen?"

Damien glanced at his watch and sighed.

"Dunno, but he better get here soon. We need to head inside in a few minutes."

So, they waited, leaning expectedly when a car would show up, only to droop again when it was someone else. Adelie's mother's foot tapped impatiently. The ceremony would be starting in the gymnasium any minute. All four teens checked their phones but got nothing.

Suddenly, Colby, being the tallest, squinted and started pointing.

"I think that's him! He's on his bike."

On his bike? Is his father not even coming to his graduation?

Adelie didn't know why she felt surprised. Still, it physically hurt to watch Owen roll up to the bike-stands, no parent in tow. Small bits of his black hair poked out from his cap and his gown was a size too big— yet he waltzed over with the utmost confidence in his step.

"Hello, fine people. Let's do this," he flashed his slight snaggletooth and led the way.

He held the door open for everyone, and as Adelie stepped in, she hung back for a moment.

"You alright?"

Owen's grip on the door slipped and then went back into place.

"Yeah, thanks," his tone felt grateful.

The auditorium was teeming with young adults. The school only had 200 students at the very most, but all the echoing voices made the crowd seem bigger. Adelie's mother took her place in the parent section as the graduates took their assigned seats for their line-up.

For Adelie, the rest was a giant blur. A giant, two-hour long blur. There were speeches, one by Damien, the valedictorian. Then students claiming their awards. Last but not least was when everyone received their diplomas. Adelie made sure to walk on and off the stage as quickly as possible. Her friends did the same and were civil until hats were flying into the air.

Once everything finally concluded, Adelie met back up with her mom outside. The sun was setting. Dozens of newly inaugurated young adults were departing to graduation parties and the like, loud laughing and revving engines echoing through the parking lot. Adelie repressed a sigh. Though she wasn't the biggest social butterfly, she envied the wild youth around her. She'd had to grow up so fast.

All at once, the sidewalk disappeared from beneath her feet. The humid air thickened. Fog filled her vision. She was floating above everything, looking at her mother, the school, her own body, the green of her gown, the lone ant crawling across the concrete.

A lone ant.

First grade recess. One of the girls sat alone with her back to a chain-link fence. Her face was starkly stoic compared to the joyous faces of the other children. There was a reason—other kids avoided her, or maybe it was the other way around? Either way, she didn't seem to be easy company. As her eyes wandered, she came upon the crying souls of two baby birds. They were fresh, naked, pink against the woodchips of the playground. Newly hatched and newly fallen. The redhead remained where she was, determined to watch over the chicks without bringing attention to them.

A boy ran by, a stick in hand, no doubt playing a game of tag. Sadly, he stopped dead in his tracks when he heard the wailing chicks. The girl tensed as he got closer to them, eyes filled with curiosity. He soon called his friends over too. For a few moments, all the boys stared at the hatchlings in wonder. She gripped the fence tightly, hoping they were simply looking.

One of them jabbed the baby birds with a piece of mulch. The first boy poked them with the stick he'd been holding. It soon became a frenzy. A mauling.

The girl sat in shock, her body refusing to move. Weren't kids supposed to be as innocent as these defenseless beings? Weren't kids supposed to see the good in the world when others couldn't?

Breaking out of her frozen state, she flew to their aid, kicking, punching, and screaming at the marauding boys. Even as a child, she felt her mind float above her own body, watching the scene unfold from a third person's view. Her fists acted on their own, striking hard blows as her throat screamed indignity.

When the teacher intervened, she was the first one to get in trouble. No good deed goes unpunished. As she sat in time-out, a small black ant stumbled upon her pale skin. A large ant pile sat just a few feet from here, yet this one particular insect was alone. It was the only company she had for the next twenty-two minutes. They were more alike than they thought.

She cried when they had to part.

"Addie?"

The nickname woke her up.

"Dad?"

She blinked. No. Her dad wasn't here. Why did she say that out loud? It was just her mother calling her something she'd told her not to. Said mother stared at her in shock.

"Sorry. I was zoning out. What is it?"

"Owen and his friends said they're having a graduation party at one of their houses. You can go, if you'd like," her last words were phrased as a guilt trip.

It didn't faze Adelie. She raised an eyebrow in response.

"Well, alright, sure."

Her mother almost looked disappointed. Again, it didn't faze the daughter. Adelie quickly separated from her to dash off to her companions. After relishing in their post-graduation glow, they all piled into Jace's car. Between the laughter and gossip, she spotted a flash of her mother's solemn face leaving the parking lot in her own, lonely vehicle. It tugged at her insides.

Why am I feeling guilty now? Whatever. She can deal.

❖

Adelie quickly became comfortable in Colby's home, his parents away and accepting of this party– as long as it didn't get *too* crazy. The home was a little bigger than Adelie's and did not have a second floor. There was a kitchen, and a large living/dining room area accompanied by three bedrooms and two bathrooms; the quintessential American home.

The island in the middle of the kitchen was covered in dozens of drinks and solo cups. There was also a mess of snacks. A ping-pong table was set up in the garage, its door open to all who dared to enter.

Hoots and hollers hovered above the howling music. The scent of beer pong and sweat coated the house in a perfume of adolescence. Faces both familiar and foreign swirled about the room, making Adelie dizzier than the alcohol in her hand. Still, it wasn't bad. She'd never drank before, but she was enjoying it. Everything felt so fuzzy, so warm. Anxiety eroded with each sip of her drink. Nothing clouded her mind except a passive, pleasant buzz. She sank languidly into the plush couch beneath her while still holding her cup.

Colby's house is so nice. This couch is so nice.

Someone plopped down beside her, making the cushions push her into a sitting position. She nearly lost her solo cup.

"Hey, you okay?"

Blinking heavily, she looked up at the source of the sound.

"Oh, Owen. Yeah, I'm good," her words slurred in the slightest.

"I don't think I've ever seen you so relaxed," he laughed.

She simply shrugged, took a sip, and got comfortable again.

"N'you?"

"I've been doing beer pong. I just take alcohol well. I guess that's the bright side of my dad's shitty genetics."

A mighty roar interrupted them, followed by a teenage body slamming between them. It was Jace, absolutely plastered.

"GUUUYYSS. I THINK 'M DRUNK!"

"No shit," Adelie blurted out.

Jace just laughed hysterically and fell directly on their laps. He was shirtless and his face was red from the warmth of the beer. It matched Owen's. Colby and Damien were soon upon the scene, grabbing the intoxicated boy by the ankles to drag him away.

"Fuckin' idiot," they muttered, grins on their faces.

Jace's limp, happy body dragged across the floor. His pants began to fall down. Adelie watched with amusement.

"So, he gets naked when he's drunk?"

"S-sometimes," Owen cracked a can open and took a long swig.

"Why are you guys like this? I have no idea why I'm friends with you," she playfully pushed him, causing him to choke and sputter.

"Because you *love* us. We are IRRESISTABLE," Colby suddenly butted in, his voice loud and his breath smelly.

❖

The party died down a few hours later. Everyone but the original group of five had already left, Colby sobering up enough to usher them out and get them rides home. Damien was splayed out on the couch, drool hanging from his lips as he snored. Adelie looked around, suddenly aware that not only had she fallen asleep on the floor, but that Owen and Jace were missing.

Damn, did I black out?

Shaking her head to get the grogginess out, she slowly got to her feet. The room immediately spun, her eyes swimming with the drinks she'd consumed. Before she could say anything, Colby rushed over and steadied her.

"You need food and water. Wait here."

He quickly dashed to the kitchen. Honestly, this kid never ceased to amaze Adelie. He was the biggest jock they knew—he sometimes had the brains of one too—but could also be incredibly sweet.

"O-Okay. 'M just gonna find a bathroom," she called out.

Without his approval, she proceeded to stumble around the house in search of a toilet. All that water was coming fast. She was met with a couple empty rooms and a closet.

How many rooms does this damn house have? I just want a bathroom!

Her palms found another door as they ghosted along the walls. With a heavy sigh, she shoved the door open, hoping to find relief.

Another bedroom. It wasn't empty. Owen and Jace were there. Jace held Owen in his arms as they leaned against a small desk. Their movements were slow, but there was no denying what was happening. They were kissing, touching, embracing. Owen's fingers were in Jace's hair. They wore lazy smiles.

Adelie suddenly didn't have to pee anymore.

Damn, are they just drunk, or did they get liquid courage?

Though she really wanted an answer, she went to turn around and leave them in peace. She'd ask Owen about it later. Unfortunately, she waddled directly into the door frame and fell on her back.

The boys bolted up from their positions, shame and shock coloring Owen's face as their bodies instinctually peeled apart.

"Fuck, no, sorry, sorry," she rambled, the pain quickly sobering her back to a bit of normalcy.

"Are you okay? You fell pretty hard," Jace knelt down to help her up.

Owen shoved past Jace and Adelie to quickly and quietly shut the bedroom door. He pressed his back against it until it clicked close, a loud exhale leaving him. Jace sat himself at the edge of the bed in the center of the room after helping Adelie up. She blinked her eyes intensely as she came back to her senses. This must've been Colby's room. Sports paraphernalia covered the walls and a few trophies were scattered on various shelves.

"You guys--- and in here," she found herself rattling off words without realizing it.

Owen vigorously shushed her.

"Shhh!"

"It defeats the point if you're loud," she noted.

"Just—don't tell anyone, okay?"

Adelie looked back and forth between the two boys. They kept sending each other knowing glances. Jace nodded in agreement. Still, there was an undeniable warmth between them. She felt the hairs on her neck stand on end.

Oh my god. How did I never notice this? Have they just been hiding it so well that it got past my absorbism?

A lot of things started to make sense now. The constant horseplay, the one-on-one conversations and outings, the excessive closeness compared to Damien and Colby.

"Are you guys together, then?"

"N-No. It's complicated."

Jace finally spoke up, he, too, now fully losing his intoxication.

"It is?"

"Not between us! Just—ugh. I don't really know how to put this," Owen scratched his neck anxiously.

Jace took Adelie by the hands and looked at her with a seriousness she had never seen before.

"He sucks at talking, so I guess I'll do it. Adelie, we've liked each other a long time. I'm bi, he's gay. The world's just not ready for us yet."

"Oh my *god*," Owen just about combusted on the spot.

"It's the truth! God, it feels good to say it," Jace's face lit up like a starry sky.

Owen kept muttering "oh my god's" as Adelie broke out in laughter. He slapped his palm over her mouth, but the amusement in her eyes still showed.

"It's not funny!"

"It kinda is. Another secret added to my collection," her voice was muffled by his sweaty hand.

A knock on the door made them all jump.

"Adelie! I made you some food! Also, that's not a bathroom!"

She'd forgotten all about Colby doting on her. She'd also forgotten about the dam that was about to burst. Grabbing Owen's hand and setting it to the side, she faced the now-lovers.

"Don't worry. I won't tell," she promised.

She stood tall, wiped herself off, and stepped toward the door. Looking over her shoulder, she threw them a last set of words.

"Stay happy, you guys."

Her last image of them that night was them sitting side-by-side, hands intertwined, and their bodies awash with relief.

<u>Chapter 5</u>

The summer equinox; the longest day of the year. Adelie and the kits stalked through the lush, green undergrowth. Still, several areas were void of vegetation, so they had to choose their steps carefully. The overhunting had left the forest without enough large predators to keep the herbivores in check. Though it was still beautiful, it must've paled in comparison to how it was years ago. Adelie also wondered if the kits' bodies paled in comparison to how they would be with more food. She hoped the warm months ahead would somehow prepare them for their second winter.

Though they were a bit thin, their coats and eyes shined as bright as the midday sun. Muscles rippled beneath auburn fur. Long legs moved with the wind. Skilled noses guided their path. They were fully grown, accomplished adults, now, so not really kits any longer, but they were *her* kits.

I hope their true mother thinks I've done right by them.

The four of them pushed on, grateful for the shade on such a hot day. Eventually, they came upon the small river that zig-zagged its way through the land. The kits lapped at the cool water while their mother stood guard. After a few moments, Maple nudged her with a wet chin. She took over while Adelie got a drink for herself. Small fish glittered in front of her whiskers.

Snap!

One of the fish now wriggled between her teeth, tail flapping across her muzzle. A quick bite finished the job, and she laid the prey at her children's feet. While they ate, Adelie stood alert again, a clearing of yellowed grass catching her eye up ahead. It was an area they hadn't ventured to due to lack of cover. Squinting, she could just make out the shapes of a herd of white-tailed deer. They grazed leisurely. She envied them.

Her envious thoughts soon withered under the sound of a doe bleating in alert. All the foxes shot up, their bodies stilling with tension. Fish bones fell from Aspen's mouth, his attention turning to the deer-filled meadow. A bellow rang out and was followed by thunderous thumping. Adelie's hackles rose with fright.

The spooked animals were headed straight for them—straight for the safety of bushes and branches. Their hooves dug up earth in their frantic attempt to escape whatever rare predator had spooked them. Even the fawns were giving it their all, weak limbs going in all directions. Adelie and the kits got out of the way just in time, their bodies dashing to the side as the stampede came splashing through the river. They watched the frenzy with awe.

A few moments later, another furry figure flashed from the ferns. At first, it seemed to just be another deer. That is, until they saw its ears and tail. The creature stopped abruptly at the river's edge. Its paws teetered, debating if it wanted to take a dip or not.

It was another fox, albeit a gray one. It might've been what scared the herd. It looked to them with a start. It must've been just as surprised as they were to see another one of their kind. Adelie had not seen another fox since the one she had taken pictures of several months before. It took a drink from the river and gave them a curt nod. Just as Adelie was going to attempt communication, the gray fox slithered away into the flora. It felt bittersweet. She hoped it would survive in this place.

On the way back to the den, they managed to catch a squirrel and mouse between the four of them. The air instantly turned cool as they padded down the tunnels of the burrow. It was amazing—and refreshing—to feel the difference. Adelie made sure the kits were settled down and eating before leaving for the day. She also made sure to cover the entrance with more branches and leaves once she was in human form.

Eat and sleep well, my dear ones.

When Adelie reached her human residence, the air turned cold in a different way.

The house stood empty, her mother still finishing up at work. The good thing was that there was always food to eat, now. The bad thing was just about everything else. Coming home to the kits was always filled with excitement and joy. Coming home to the house meant silence and shadow. Gathering herself up, she soon stood directly in front of their old family portrait on the way up the stairs to her room. Her mother's words echoed between her ears.

"Things were bad before, but with you gone, it's even worse now."

The statement felt so double-sided. A dual-edged sword, a word with two meanings. Knowing that the words spoke truth hurt in any interpretation. It hurt even more to see a smile on her own childhood face. When did she lose that smile? Were things really that bad before?

She didn't want to try to remember. She didn't want to think about it.

<u>*3:28 PM*</u>

<u>*Adelie*</u>*: hey. u free?*

<u>*3:33 PM*</u>

<u>*Owen*</u>*: yea wats up? :-O*

<u>*3:36 PM*</u>

<u>*Adelie*</u>*: idk. bored*

<u>*3:39 PM*</u>

<u>*Owen*</u>*: can i come over? :-D*

The question caught Adelie off-guard. He'd never asked to come over before. She figured that, with their situation, they just shouldn't visit each other's houses. However, it would be a good opportunity to make their "relationship" seem more real.

164

**Adelie**: sure. come whenever. mom's not home.

**Owen**: dads not home either :-P omw! :-DDD

The doorbell rang mere minutes later. Owen stood at the door, a giant grin on his face.

"Never thought I'd see this day. Can I come in?"

She hesitated for a moment before fully opening the door.

"Welcome to my abode, I guess," she gestured for him to walk ahead of her.

Owen immediately shook off his shoes before entering. He didn't speak again until the front door was shut.

"Honestly, though. Are you okay? You've never asked for me to come over before."

Adelie locked the front door and sighed.

"I guess I just didn't want to be alone," she confessed.

"Well, you could start by showing me around the place, maybe," he waggled an eyebrow at her as he spoke.

"There's really not much to see, but sure."

The two of them went up the stairs to her room, passing the pictures on the wall as they went. Owen stopped at the old family portrait.

"Woah, is this you and your parents?"

"Yep. Can you believe it?"

"Man, I almost can't. That's your dad, then?"

"Yeah," her voice was a whisper.

"He looked like a really cool dude."

They continued to her room.

"Have you been doing okay? About your dad, I mean."

"I think so. I dunno. I feel okay but part of me feels like I shouldn't feel okay."

"We all take things differently. I'm sorry I had to bear the bad news."

Owen went quiet for a moment as he realized what he'd just said.

"Oh my god, no pun intended. I'm sorry—"

Adelie broke out in a laughter that Owen had never heard before. The tension both lightened and strengthened. The laugh felt like a shield against the repressed emotions inside her.

"It's okay, it's okay. That was a good one," she barely got the words out between giggles.

"You sure you're alright?"

Wiping at her eyes, she nodded and changed the subject. She had no idea how to answer that question.

"Anyway, here's my room. It's really not much."

Owen's eyes ran over her bed, her dresser, the arched ceiling, and finally, her windows. He then walked up to the largest one, peering through it curiously.

"I can see my house from here. Is this where you saw me and my dad that night, a long time ago?"

She joined him at the window to reminisce.

"Yeah. I heard something, so I looked. I saw your dad throw you out. Then you rode away on your bike."

"Sounds like us," he exhaled.

Since there were no chairs, they both sat down at the edge of Adelie's bed. The silence wasn't exactly awkward, but it was still filled with a questioning air.

"I've gotta ask. When were you gonna tell me about you and Jace?"

Owen immediately stiffened; his face flushed.

"Uh, probably never! It's not really something you talk about these days, especially not here," he replied, hand rubbing at his neck nervously.

"I-I don't know why we even have to talk about it. It's not serious. It's nothing. I'm not even gay. We were drunk a-and—"

"Owen. I've got absorbism, remember? You can't lie about love to me."

Owen proceeded to groan and throw himself back against the sheets in anguish. He watched the ceiling for a while, his mind lost in thought.

"Sorry. I know. Just a habit."

Adelie decided to lay back beside him, a small smile on her face.

"Tell me more about Jace. How did you guys meet?"

The heat radiating off Owen was undeniable.

"W-Well, uh, we were kids. Really young—like 6 or 7. My dad had just gotten done yelling at me for something when I slipped into the woods and ran into him—Jace, I mean. He was an explorer, much braver than I was. Maybe he still is," his voice trailed off as a calm warmth filled his features.

Adelie felt the hairs on her neck start to rise.

"Anyway, I tagged along with him and his adventures. We kinda ran away for the day. He told me about his dad, and I told him about mine. We didn't want to go back home, but we had to. When we *did* get back, our dads acted as if we'd never even been gone. We realized that they didn't really care if we were around or not. So, we kept playing together and exploring."

A cicada broke out into song outside.

"Maybe two years into our friendship, we, uh, kinda kissed. A little kiss, y'know? A child's curiosity," he chuckled bashfully.

"Don't be embarrassed. That's sweet," she reassured him.

"Our dads caught us and were super pissed. They kept us separated for a long time, and even *they* didn't speak for a while. They each thought the other's kid was a bad influence on their own. A few years later, my brother moved away," Owen's tone took a more resentful tone at the mention of his kin.

"I'm sorry. That must've been hard."

"It was. He basically raised me. Still, what I'm getting to is that, after Andres—my brother—left, my dad put more responsibility on me. He got the idea for the fur business and had me put out most of the traps. I saw Jace again around then since his dad was making him do the same thing. We were reunited, in a way," he huffed out another small laugh.

Another wave of absorbism shook Adelie to her core, pushing her hard enough to cause her to transform. Owen looked over and blushed up to his ears when he realized what he'd done. The vixen motioned her head as if to say, *"continue your story!"* Owen turned to look at the ceiling again.

"From then on, we've been inseparable. We're older now and more careful about keeping things hidden. I don't think Damien or Colby even know. Sometimes I even deny that anything is happening because it's so ingrained in me. Thanks, Dad," his tone then shifted to sarcasm, complete with a middle finger to the ceiling.

Adelie shifted back into her human form. She laid back on the bed beside her friend.

"I'm sorry you've had to be so secretive. I really didn't mean to intrude, though," Adelie apologized.

The boy turned to her, now laying on his side, his hand holding up his head.

"Y'know what? I'm glad you did. If you hadn't, I never would've realized that at least one person was okay with us," he grinned.

"Well, I guess getting drunk was a good thing, then, huh?"

"Yeah, for sure. That was a fun night. Speaking of which," he hoisted himself into a sitting position as he spoke.

"I think we're planning on doing the lake house for the Fourth of July. We're all gonna ride in Jace's car. Sound good?"

"Oh, yeah, right, I'd forgotten," Adelie quickly straightened up alongside him.

"Don't worry about bringing anything. We've got it handled. Fireworks, snacks—"

"Booze?"

"Adelie, you are getting more and more adventurous by the day!"

"Well, it *is* summer."

"Touché."

A familiar voice sounded from downstairs along with the slamming of a door.

"Hello? Adelie?"

Mom's home.

"Yeah, just a sec!"

"Is someone here? I heard another voice and saw a bike outside!"

Adelie rolled her eyes and looked to Owen for guidance.

"We'll just walk down together like any other couple," he suggested.

"Ugh. Okay," she obliged.

"Adelie!?!"

"Yes, Owen's here! Coming!"

The two teens then started to descend the stairs, the mother's prying eyes watching them with every step. She looked suspicious, but happy, too.

"What a pleasant surprise! Nice to see you, Owen!"

"You too, Ms. Henderson. I hope it was okay to come over unannounced?"

"Absolutely. This girl is never social," the mother playfully elbowed her daughter, who did not reciprocate the banter.

"Well, I'll be off, then. My father should be home soon. Thank you."

Owen nodded at Adelie's mother before swiftly leaving the home. After he'd left, the mother turned to her daughter, excitement painted across her forehead.

"Adelie, I can't believe you actually brought a boy home."

Yeah, you would be happy about that, wouldn't you?

❖

The rest of the day was long, not only because of the equinox, but because of the restless energy in Adelie's heart. Since her mother had come home, she'd become cooped up in the house. Though the summer days meant that the sun would hang around longer, she found herself wishing that it would just set already.

She wanted it to be the Fourth of July as soon as possible.

<u>Chapter 6</u>

Jace's car's trunk thumped as it was filled with sleeping bags, food, clothes, and dozens of other lake house necessities such as floaties, fireworks, and, of course, alcohol. The sweltering heat was unrelenting as the morning went on. Adelie felt light-headed.

She was excited, but apprehensive, too. Would they truly be safe there?

"Adelie, you okay?"

Damien had stopped packing to tap her on the shoulder.

"Oh, uh, yeah. Just a little warm, is all," she wasn't exactly lying.

Colby showed up right on cue with a water bottle in hand.

"This heat can be killer—trust me, I practice football in it every day. Have some of this! You'll feel better," the tall boy smiled and handed the water to her.

"Still being the mom of the group, I see," she teased and took a sip.

"Am I *really* that motherly?"

"Dude, you made everyone eat the eggs you made at 2 AM during the party because you didn't want any of us to be hungover," Damien chimed in.

"You weren't hungover, though, were you?"

Adelie walked to the front of the car, leaving the jock and math whizz to their own devices. Owen sat in the passenger seat, openly relishing in the A.C. Jace sat in the driver's seat. He lowered his sunglasses as she approached.

"Ready to go?"

"Just about. Owen, can we talk for a minute?"

Jace turned to Owen, an impish smile on his face.

"Ooooh, mama miaaaa, you're in trouubbbllee!"

"Shut up," Owen retaliated, shoving Jace away with a smile of his own.

The raven-haired boy stepped out of the car and beckoned for Adelie to come over. He looked concerned about her.

"What's up?"

"I just—this is safe, right? No one else will be there?"

"Well, probably some ducks and squirrels will keep us company."

"I'm *serious*."

"So am I! We're gonna be *fine*," he lowered his voice to a whisper before continuing.

"Jace even said that he heard his dad saying that he was about ready to quit doing the trapping business since my dad's not delivering like he used to. Looks like those two are gonna have a meeting while we're gone. If they're here, they won't be *there*."

"Shouldn't we be trying to sneak in on that meeting, though?"

"Definitely not. I'm not kidding when I say that they'd probably shoot us if they found us."

Adelie went quiet, eyes drifting to the side.

"I've been looking forward to this, but now I'm so worried about a million things," she admitted.

"Look, the kits are gonna be fine for just one day. I know destroying the traps and learning more information is important to you, but remember that we're kind of at a standstill right now with your dad unable to help us. You need time for yourself, too," he put a hand on her shoulder, blue eyes stretched with sympathy.

Adelie let out a long, deep sigh. He was right. She needed to just relax for once.

"Okay. Thank you."

"Just try to have fun, will ya?"

❖

The drive was long—about an hour or so—but scenic. Though Adelie found herself sandwiched between Damien and Colby in the backseat, she was still able to enjoy the view out the windows. This was a truly "middle of nowhere" kind of place. The trees and plants were even thicker here, perhaps to shade the various ponds and lakes that dotted the land. As they got closer, the roads turned to gravel, the car bouncing and kicking up dust to the tune of the blasting radio.

Jace turned around a bend and they were soon facing the lake house itself. It sat at the bottom of a dead-end road, no other houses to keep it company. The house wasn't as big as Adelie had imagined, but she kind of liked that. It was a quaint and quiet little cabin. It was surprising that someone like Jace's dad owned this place. There was even a tire swing on one of the trees, the old rubber swaying with the wind. It almost looked lonely, like it was calling for a young Jace to come back to its embrace.

Was his dad always so bad?

Beside the cabin rolled the expanse of a decently sized lake, a small dock floating in the middle of it. The wood was worn and rickety, but it still looked strong enough to hold weight. Another dock sat at the shore. On the other side of the house stood miles and miles of untouched woods.

"Well, we're here," Jace announced, his car pulling up to the front porch.

The boys shouted excitedly and burst from the vehicle, taking in the freedom and fresh air. Adelie had to remind herself that she was safe and had been looking forward to this trip. She needed to remember that she trusted Owen. She trusted her friends. Trust was always a hard thing to hold onto. However, she pushed through the doubt and exited the car just as everything was unloaded.

Owen winked at her and handed her the backpack she had brought.

"Trying to skimp out on the labor, huh?"

"Exactly. Thanks boys," she sneered.

As soon as Jace had unlocked the cabin's front door, all the walls creaked, and the house almost seemed to expand. It took a huge breath through dusty lungs to welcome its guests. Said guests quickly made themselves at home, filling the living room with their array of items. As everyone set up their things, Jace cleared his throat.

"Okay, so, obviously, don't trash this place or else my dad will never let me hear the end of it. Second, there's no running water here, so you'll have to shit and piss in the outhouse or in the woods," he announced.

Adelie leaned over to whisper to Damien.

"I wanted to go rustic, but damn."

He giggled in return. Jace interrupted them.

"That's about it. Let's go!"

His yell was immediately followed by the removal of his shirt, revealing that his shorts were actually swim trunks. A unanimous "yeah!" followed, and the teens headed outside to the lake. Everyone seemed to get the memo to wear their swimsuits under their clothes, everyone except Adelie. The pleasantness of the sun soon felt like flaming pokers. Without another word, she shuffled back into the house, hoping no one had noticed. She dug through her backpack and quickly located her purple one-piece. Though she'd had it for years, it looked practically brand new.

Because I don't know how to swim.

Her face burned with shame as she changed clothes. She hoped that she could get away with just sitting at the shore. Muffled voices from outside caught her attention.

"Hey, where'd Adelie go?"

She'd just finished getting dressed when Colby barged in. He took one look at her and swiftly hid behind the door.

"Oh! You're changing! Sorry!"

"It's alright. I'm done."

He dared to peek around the corner and give her a smile.

"Oh, okay. You look nice!"

"Thanks, Colb," she relaxed at the compliment while applying sunscreen to herself.

The two of them went down to the shore where Damien was still taking his first few steps in.

"Guys, it's cold!"

Adelie blinked and Colby had belly flopped in, showering Damien in the process.

"C'mon, *seriously?*"

The blond boy popped back up and shook off the chills, further dowsing the other.

"Yeah, seriously," he replied smugly.

Adelie sat herself on the dock, toes touching the water, to watch the show unfolding before her. Jace was already on the floating dock with Owen, who was being thrown back into the lake's waves. Colby and Damien began a splash fight. She quickly found herself laughing at their foolish displays.

Owen called to her, head bobbing just above the surface.

"Join us, Adelie!"

When she didn't respond, he swam over and hoisted himself onto the deck next to her. Lake water dripped everywhere. His hair was flat against his skull.

"Is something wrong?"

She sighed deeply at his inquiry.

"I really didn't want to have to say this out loud, but... I can't swim. I can hang out with you guys when you're on land again."

"You can't swim? What? *Adelie*!"

"*Owen*!"

The pair stared at each other a moment before bursting into laughter.

"Okay, well, I think I know a solution," he offered before dashing toward the cabin.

Adelie sat in confused anticipation for a few minutes. The others didn't seem to notice his absence as they continued with their shenanigans. Before she knew it, the house door flew open with a mighty crack. There stood Owen, a blow-up tube in his hand and a triumphant expression on his face. She'd never seen him run so fast.

"Look! Now you can go in without fear," he pushed the ring excitedly into her lap.

She had to hand it to him, it was a pretty good solution. Colby, a few feet away, stopped his splashing.

"Wait, Adelie, can you not swim?"

She hid herself behind the tube.

"Look what you did," she hissed to Owen, only half-joking.

"We could teach you," Damien chimed in, swimming closer.

"No, it's fine, I'll just float around."

Owen leaned down and whispered to Damien and Colby, though it was very easily heard by the redhead.

"Just don't let her drown, alright?"

Adelie rolled her eyes.

"Oh, Owen, my hero—"

She pushed Owen square on the back and into the surf. He fell straight down, his body making a loud *plap* noise. Colby and Damien laughed to high heaven when he came back up, coughing, hacking, and adorned with a lily pad hat. With that, Adelie set the tube into the water and let herself lean back into it. She used her feet to push herself away from the dock, and off she went. Using her hands, she slowly paddled herself farther out, appreciating the calm and quiet of nature. Her head lay on the back of the tube and her eyes eventually closed.

So, she did. The sounds of her friends were distant, now, and covered with the trickling of water. Birds called out from the trees. Though the water was chilly, the sun was not, and it blanketed her in peace. It was like she was back in the den with her kits, away from all the bad things in the world.

Something bumped into her tube, abruptly waking her from her reverie. She was met with the edge of the floating dock, Jace gazing down at her curiously.

"You good?"

"Yeah, I am. Help me up?"

Once he did, they stood together on the dock and watched as Colby made his way toward them.

"Colby, don't throw this one off the dock," Jace motioned toward Adelie with an upturned chin.

"Trust me, I know a death sentence when I see one."

Adelie simply flipped her hair behind her shoulder in triumph.

"Adelie, if you wanna swim, you could hang onto my back! It'd be just like the turtles in *Finding Nemo*," Colby offered excitedly.

She blinked, momentarily set aback. She actually hadn't seen the movie yet, but she got the implications—he'd swim around while she held onto him from above. It was enticing, but also scary, and maybe a little weird.

"Uh, I dunno, Colb. I don't wanna put that on you."

"It's nothing! I need a workout, anyway. How 'bout it?"

When she looked at Jace, he simply crossed his arms and raised an eyebrow. It was a challenge, now.

"Alright, alright. Just don't go under or I'll kill you," she threatened as she lowered herself into the lake.

Colby was quickly there with open arms. It was strange to be held like this—strangely intimate—but nothing was awkward about it. She'd grown very close with her friends and it felt like nothing. He then flipped over and let her clutch onto his shoulders. As he took off, she lost her grip, sending a stone of fear into her stomach. However, she quickly caught hold of him again, and they were soon zooming toward the shoreline.

When they got close to Owen and Damien, the two boys made chase, pretending to be sharks after a two-headed mermaid. Adelie screamed playfully and kicked her legs, spraying the deadly predators in their human faces.

By the time they all got out of the water, skin pruned and chafing, Adelie's cheeks hurt from smiling so much.

❖

Afternoon turned to evening as the group started up a campfire and grill. By now, everyone was starving. It was good that they had come prepared. They had enough food to feed an army, and yet, it seemed to be munched down in minutes. Between hot dogs, burgers, soda, and s'mores, everyone was soon satisfied. Even Adelie had her fill and was now comfortably lounging against a log to digest. Everyone had changed into comfortable evening attire. They told ghost stories for a while, one in particular about a devil-possessed goat making everyone shiver. The subject changed after that.

"Listen, when we all leave for college, we *have* to keep in touch. I don't want us to be another one of those 'disbanded friend group' clichés," Damien urged in the fire light.

"Agreed. That shit is so stupid. We've been bros for so long," Jace agreed, chewing on yet another s'more.

"I think I'm gonna major in sports science. Could be cool to be a personal trainer some day. Y'know, after football," Colby spoke after finishing his fourth s'more.

"I wanna be a teacher. A trigonometry teacher, in fact," Damien added.

"We get it, we get it, you're smart. I'm not really sure what I'm gonna major in yet," Jace said with a sigh.

"Me neither," Owen agreed.

Adelie hadn't even thought about college. The only thing she knew was that she wasn't doing it. The thought of her friends all moving away soon sent a jolt of terror through her, enough for her to sit up and catch the others' attention.

"You guys are all leaving town then?"

"Uh, yeah. I thought we had talked about that," Colby answered, his words unsure.

"I guess it hadn't really hit me until now."

"Yeah, my mom put aside college money for me before she had me. That's pretty much the only reason my dad is even doing it," Owen scoffed.

"Oh, I must've forgotten. Sorry," her voice turned mournful.

"Hey! No tears! Today's a fun day! I know—let's get the fireworks set up," Damien hopped up from his respective log, lighter in hand.

While the boys got things set up, Adelie sat quietly to stew in her thoughts. It was a bad idea, but she couldn't help it. She exhaled and got up to help when something appeared in the corner of her vision. Throwing her head in the same direction, she found herself paralyzed with shock.

There was a bear. It was standing at the edge of the trees. The flickering fire made its eyes glow in the darkness. It stared at her, unblinking.

A shrill, terrified scream tore itself from her mouth. One of the boys fumbled with the fireworks at the sound, accidentally causing one to go and fly out across the lake. Luckily, it exploded before it could reach dry land, its bright lights descending into the depths. The sound further scared the girl, causing her to jump and slip into the sand. When she looked at the line of trees again, the creature was gone.

Was that real? Was that my dad? Is he still alive? Was it all in my head?

"Adelie! Are you okay!?!"

Owen's shout was soon followed by his hands on her shoulders. The others followed suit.

"I-I don't know, I don't know," she mumbled, index finger pointing to the forest.

"Did you see something? What happened?"

"I saw a bear. A bear. Standing right over there."

Owen turned his attention to the trees and squinted.

"Well, if there was a bear, it's gone now and won't come back. Here, sit down," he guided her back down onto the log seat.

Colby draped a towel across her shoulders, which she clutched onto until her knuckles turned white.

"I'm sorry, I-I really thought I saw something."

"It's okay! We're just glad that Damien didn't blow us up," Jace tried to lighten the mood.

"Not funny, dude," Damien play-punched him in the ribs.

"Okay, okay, let's all just chill out and hold off on the fireworks for now," Owen instructed whilst sitting next to his shaken friend.

"I don't know if that was real. I don't know if my head made that up," Adelie's voice shook.

"Even if it did, it's okay. You've been through a lot," he comforted her.

That was when it hit her. The guys didn't even know about her dad's identity. They didn't know about her absorbism. They didn't know about the kits. Guilt hit her like a wayward wind—but so did courage. It was time her *friends* knew the truth.

We're safe out here. No one will hear. No one will tell. I trust them.

In a single motion, Adelie got to her feet and let the towel drop. The fire illuminated the even stronger flame burning in her chestnut eyes.

"Guys, I'm sorry, but I haven't been completely honest with you. I'd like to fix that, now, if you'd let me."

When she snuck a glance at Owen, he looked mortified. He even mouthed the words "are you sure?"

Yeah, I'm sure.

Her voice caught everyone's attention.

"I don't know if you guys remember what happened on the news a few years back, about a lawyer turning into a bear, but that was... my dad. He was an Absorber and so am I."

The confession fell from her lips just how sand falls from an hourglass. It left her feeling weightless, empty, but also relieved to have it pour from her system. She drew a long intake of breath before continuing.

"I wanted to find him so badly because I thought he could help us legally fight Owen's dad and the other hunters. I thought he could stop it, once and for all, and help bring the forest back to its former glory. But he can't. He's dead."

Surprise painted the faces of her audience. They looked at one another with incredulousness.

"That's not all. As an Absorber, my emotion is love, and my animal is a fox. That night, at Thanksgiving dinner, I discovered that Jeremy was falling in love with me. I had to cut ties with him to keep myself from being exposed—from ending up like my dad. It's my biggest regret," her words cracked under the weight of her wounds.

"My mom was never the same after my dad left. She treats me like shit. I've lost Jeremy. I've lost my dad for good. All I have left is you guys and three foxes who I've mothered since their real mother was killed. Owen's the only one who has known all this. I'm so sorry I didn't tell you this sooner. I didn't know how."

There was a gap of silence that was big enough for doubt to creep up her shoulders and whisper worries in her ear. Her hands balled into fists. She shut her eyes, expecting the worst to follow. However, it remained silent.

Suddenly, there was a weight on her back, then her sides, then her front. It was a foreign feeling. It spurred her to finally open her eyes, and when she did, she felt as if she might faint. Her friends now surrounded her and had their arms wrapped around her body in a tight embrace. A group hug.

"Wh-What, I don't—"

"We forgive you, Adelie," Colby stated from behind her.

"Why? You don't have to. I've been a shitty friend," she argued.

The boys only hugged her tighter. Tears started to form under her lashes. It wasn't sadness, but rather a landslide of a hundred emotions crashing into her at once. Relief. Doubt. Guilt. Appreciation. Happiness. Love.

Love. These friends loved her enough to forgive her without hesitation, without resentment or contemplation. Negative thoughts tugged at her brain, willing her to think that she didn't deserve this display of affection. The love around her grew all the while, not only from the boys and from herself, but *for* herself, too. If they could forgive her, maybe she could forgive herself, too.

"I think we all had a feeling something was going on, we just didn't want to push it. Thanks for trusting us. It's really okay. We get it," Damien encouraged.

Adelie couldn't even thank them before her absorbism took over. Her body rapidly changed form, now a fox dangling off the ground, torso held up by the others' arms. Everyone jumped back, spooked by the sudden transformation. She plopped to the ground and shook herself off before scratching sand from behind her ears.

The boys' eyes were wide, and the three in shock soon locked their sights on Owen.

"Yeah, that happens," Owen shrugged.

They then looked back at their *now* furry friend, who was looking up at them expectedly. Jace scratched his chin.

"Is she okay?"

"Yeah. She *did* just tell you that she's an Absorber," Owen answered.

"I know, I know, but, damn, I didn't think it would happen so quickly," Jace laughed.

"Oh, Adelie, you're so cute!"

Colby gushed over the fox, petting her soft fur and watching her thick, fluffy tail wag in just the slightest. She proceeded to hop around the campfire, legs spry and free. Her eyes shone radiantly. Fireflies danced in the night air. Crickets chirped happily. They played chase with her a while before settling down onto the logs again. It took a bit, but she finally transformed back once the atmosphere had cooled back down to normal.

"Thank you, guys. I don't know what else to say. Also, this probably goes without saying, but don't tell anyone about this. Absorbism isn't well-accepted. It doesn't help that there's so little of us and so little research done."

"Scouts honor," Colby put his hand over his heart.

"As for the kits, their names are Maple, Birch, and Aspen. They're about fully grown now. They used to live in those boulders where all those traps were set out. The hunters must've spotted them one day and caught on to their den. I've since moved them."

"Smart move," Jace pointed out.

It was quiet for a few moments when Owen quickly stood up. His mouth opened and then closed again. His fists clenched at his sides. Finally, the boy spoke, hair disheveled from drying after his swim.

"Okay, well, since it seems to be the night of sharing secrets—"

The boys crowded closer, their eyes moons.

"I'm—I'm gay. There, I said it."

Crickets filled the silence before being taken over by a mixture of laughs. Owen stood frozen in place.

"Dude, we've *been* known that," Damien said between laughing fits.

Owen shook and slicked back hair from his eyes. Disbelief. Complete disbelief took over his body. Adelie could understand. She didn't think they would forgive or understand her own secrets. Yet they did. This was something she knew he'd stressed over for a long time. Jace couldn't have looked more proud. Owen couldn't help but shout in confusion.

"What!?!"

"Yeah, man! It's all good," Colby rushed over and pulled him into a hug.

Owen's frozen face melted into a smile. He battered his hands against Colby's back.

"Thank you-- alright-- I can't breathe," he coughed out.

Jace followed and politely peeled Owen from the taller boy. He laced his fingers with his. Everyone gasped.

"I'm bi. We're together," Jace announced.

Damien and Colby broke out into loud fits of excited screaming.

"I *KNEW* IT. I TOLD YOU!"

"THERE WERE SO MANY SIGNS! HOW DID I MISS IT?"

"You guys are idiots," Adelie teased.

Owen's face was as red as the glowing embers at the bottom of the firepit. Yet, he didn't shy away from Jace or the attention of the group. In fact, he relaxed rather quickly, soaking in his new reality. He wasn't the only one to be freed from a burden tonight.

"Yeah. We're together," he affirmed.

His words had barely left his lips before Jace had smothered them from existence. The two kissed fully and openly in front of their friends. It gained them extra whoops and hollers. Even Adelie joined in. When the two lovers pulled apart, Owen smiled at Jace with so much love that Adelie felt as if she may change form again.

Owen let go of Jace to grab from their collection of alcohol.

"Anyone want a drink?"

Of course everyone did. A couple of rowdy, drunken hours later, Jace, Damien, and Colby found themselves passed out in their sleeping bags. Owen and Adelie had gathered them up and put them safely in the house. They snored like hogs. Instead of joining them, the two friends went back outside to sit on the dock. It was windy and felt nice on their warm, tingly skin. It seemed to sober them up.

"I can't believe we said those things *before* getting drunk," Owen laughed.

"I know. What a relief, though, right?"

"Yeah. I don't regret it."

"Me neither," Adelie agreed.

They sat side by side and let the water lap at their feet. It was then that Adelie noticed the sky. It was coated in blue and purple, complete with a sprinkling of white.

"I've never seen the Milky Way like this before," she stated, jaw agape.

"Yeah, it's cool to see the stars like this."

Owen laid back, using his hands as a cushion, to stargaze. Adelie copied his movements.

There were still some questions on Adelie's mind, but she tried to quiet them in order to gawk at the splendor of such a beautiful night.

"Adelie, even though I'm going away soon, I still really wanna be friends."

He read my mind.

"Me too."

"I'm sorry."

"Don't be. You deserve to get out of this town the most. At least you'll be away from your dad."

Though she meant what she'd said, a small bite of sadness still sank into her chest.

"I'll be away from you, too, though. I'm really only going because, like I said, my mom set aside money for me while she was pregnant, specifically for my education. That's probably the only reason my dad hasn't spent it, too."

"That was kind of her. I wish she were still around for you."

"Yeah, me too."

A loon called out somewhere in the deep, dark void.

"What about your brother? Will you see him?"

It took Owen a few moments to respond.

"Probably not. We're not very close anymore. He got out when he could, even though I couldn't. I guess I don't really blame him anymore, but I just don't even know how to face him at this point."

"I understand."

"I'd rather not talk about it anymore, if that's okay?"

"Sure," she kindly obliged.

They remained quiet for a long while after that, their eyes focused on the night sky. Adelie felt her eyelids getting heavy, so she sat up and rubbed at them.

"I think I'm gonna call it a night. Wanna come with?"

"I think I'll sit out here a little bit longer. It's nice," Owen replied, his eyes a bit distant.

"Alright, just be safe."

"I will, *mom.*"

Adelie gave his shoulder a little shove as she got walking back to the house. Inside, the boys were still heavy as rocks. She chuckled at their sleepy expressions as she got comfortable. Once she did, sleep came easily. Unfortunately, so did the morning, and deep down, she didn't ever want to leave the comfort of this little cabin.

<u>Chapter 7</u>

Adelie was halfway home when she realized that she hadn't thought of Jeremy even once in the last 24 hours. Not an inkling of his spirit had ghosted over her brain to make her eyes mist with regret. It was an entirely nebulous feeling. Did she even deserve to begin to feel relief? Is she a horrible person for having fun and feeling joy, even after being the cause of the death of a friend? Would he be glad that she was moving on, or would he be resentful?

"Adelieeeee you're zonin' out again."

Owen's finger planted itself on Adelie's cheek to pull her down from the clouds and into Jace's car. It worked. She really needed to stop doing that.

"You caught me. Are we home yet?"

"Getting there. We just dropped off Damien. You're up next. Somethin' buggin' you?"

She was tempted to mention her returned guilt, but she decided to swallow it down. There was no point in dampening the end of their good weekend.

"Nah, just kinda tired still. I'll probably nap when I get home."

"Oh, that's a big fat lie. I *know* you're gonna go and check on the kits," Owen replied matter-of-factly.

"Ooh, could we meet them, Adelie? They sound so cool," Colby begged.

Jace snapped at Colby from the driver's seat."

"No, idiot, we gotta keep 'em on the downlow, remember?"

"Right, sorry! I promise, my lips are sealed," he replied, hand imitating a zipper over his lips.

"Could you guys actually drop me off somewhere else? I'll show you where to go."

A few minutes and turns later, they arrived at a weirdly specific spot on the side of a backroad. Adelie hopped out before the car had even hit a complete stop.

"Thanks guys. See ya later?"

All three boys turned her way and nodded.

"You know it," Jace winked.

A second later, Adelie and her friends found themselves speeding off in opposite directions. Her heart guided her footsteps, which soon turned to paw steps and brought her to the hill that the den was embedded in. She brushed the branches aside and crawled down to the main den. Aspen and Maple were already on high alert, but they soon relaxed at the sight of their mother. Adelie was happy, too, but that happiness sparked into worried confusion.

Birch wasn't there. They were always together. She told them to never go out alone.

Where is he? Is he okay? Oh, God, what if he's hurt– or worse? I never should've left town!

The other two kits soon picked up on her anxiety and let out soft whimpers to communicate their own apprehension. They didn't seem to know where their brother had gone, either. His scent still lingered in the den, but it was staler than usual. He must've been out since last night. It wasn't like any of them to wander out on their own, even to find food. Besides, there was a strong smell of prey in the other den, leading Adelie to believe that they were fine in that department.

She swung her body around and stared out the tunnel entrance in thought. Maple and Aspen squeezed themselves beside her, offering to leave with her and help find their brother. She nudged them affectionately but also firmly as if to say, *"Thank you, but you must stay here where it is safe."* Without another twitch of her whiskers, she exited their home and re-covered the hole with vegetation.

The ground was damp. It must've rained last night. His scent trail was fading fast, but the fox quickly caught onto it and followed it through the woods. Along the way, she nearly walked straight into a bear trap since all her senses were homed in on finding the missing kit. However, it had a stick through it, rendering it useless, the iron jaws clamped around the wood. Birch might've kicked it in there at some point? She hoped he had. That hope carried her paws onward just as her motherly instincts kept her absorbism on display.

Soon, the fox's nose met the edge of the canal instead of the scent of her lost one. The trail ended here. She searched high and low for any pocket of smell, any trace of fur—even for the sight of a body—but had no luck. The vixen paced along the shoreline, her tail flicking with frustration. Her paw flicked a stone into the water, reflecting the equally heavy one that had just settled at the bottom of her chest. It made it hard to breathe. None of this made any sense.

This is what I get for letting my guard down.

She glanced at her fox reflection in the churning water, somehow hoping his form would appear beside her and everything would be how it was.

He might've come down here for some water in the middle of the night, but then what? Birch, where are you?

❖

"Gone? What do you mean?"

Adelie had called Jace to get a ride home. Owen, now incredulous, had tagged along.

"I don't know. Just, gone. His scent led to nowhere. The kits couldn't find him, either," Adelie adamantly answered.

"Okay, well, I can definitely tell you that there's no new bodies or pelts where my dad keeps all his stuff. He has me count everything every morning and night and he had me do it when I got back home. Insurance for him, I guess. So, that doesn't really give us a lead, but we know he didn't nab him," Owen offered.

"My dad didn't get anything new, either. We'll find him," Jace added while he drove.

"I just don't understand. None of them would just wander away for no reason. I've taught them better than that."

"Is it possible he's sick and trying to not get the others sick? Maybe that would explain you losing his scent since maybe he would smell different," Owen guessed.

"It's possible. God, I should've just stayed home. None of this would have happened. I'm so selfish," Adelie mumbled, turning her head away from the boys.

"You don't know that. It probably would've happened even if you were home. Try not to beat yourself up," Jace tried to reassure his friend.

"I can't help it. He's practically my son and I wasn't there for him."

Owen argued her statement.

"Well, you needed some time for you, too! Plus, you've got us to help. We'll keep our eyes peeled. Is there anything about him that physically sets him apart from other foxes?"

"Well, he's kind of large for a red fox, and his coat is more brownish. Oh, and he has a tear in his right ear from always play-fighting with Aspen," Adelie informed them.

"Noted," Owen and Jace replied in unison.

Adelie's house rolled into view sooner than she'd hoped. To everyone's dismay, her mother was standing on the front lawn and chatting with Mr. Smit. Irritation scratched at her insides.

"Just got home and I already have to deal with this bullshit," she growled from the backseat as she exited the vehicle.

Mr. Smit's head turned in their direction and immediately spotted his son's presence. He waved them down. Owen cringed and cranked his window open slowly.

"Sir?"

"You and Adelie come on out," he flashed a well-rehearsed smile while Adelie's mother looked on.

The two in question looked at each other in confusion before hopping out of the vehicle. Jace watched them anxiously. The minute Adelie's feet hit the asphalt, her mother was all over her with an over-the-top, lavish hug—kisses on the cheek and all.

"Oh, you're back! Did you have fun?"

Adelie swiftly escaped her grip and grunted as a way of saying "yes." Mr. Smit took Owen by the shoulder, positioned him next to him, and shook him lightly. Owen's teeth seemed to rattle in his head as he did so, fright lighting his features.

"It's about time you lovebirds got back. We were startin' to worry," Owen's father remarked.

The remark seemed like a veil, hiding the monstrous anger underneath.

Adelie wasted no time in trying to get to the bottom of things.

"What's going on?"

"Nothing, we were just waiting for you guys to come home! Richard—Mr. Smit kept me company," her mother replied, putting a hand on Adelie's shoulder.

Adelie noted something odd sparking in Mr. Smit's eyes. A mutual act between him and her mom? Some kind of stereotypical, diabolical plan? She didn't know, but she didn't like it. She shrugged her mother's hand off.

"Well, I'm gonna go inside now. I'm tired," Adelie announced.

"I'm tired, too. Could we head home, sir?"

Owen looked up at his father like a dog anticipating a swift kick in the ribs. His hand held his son's shoulder tighter. Said son winced.

"Yes, we must not keep the Hendersons all day. See you, Marianne," Mr. Smit waved before turning to head for home.

Jace watched the interaction for a few moments longer before backing away and heading to his own home. Before Adelie entered her house, she glanced back at Owen, whose form had grown extremely stiff under the control of his father. Those powerful fingers gripped Owen's shirt ever tighter. Adelie hoped his night would be okay. After the door was shut, she faced her mother.

"You really need to stop letting him around here. Do you not see what he's doing?"

"If you mean he's being a good, kind neighbor and boss, then yes, I do see what he's doing."

"Mom, he's using you."

"Okay, let's say he *was* using me. *What* is he using me for, then?"

"He's doing some shady stuff in his hunting and he's trying to keep tabs on us to stop me from fighting it. Also, can you not see the way he treats Owen?"

Her mother burst out laughing. Adelie's chest burst with frustration.

"Addie, honey, you really need to lighten up. Richard hunts responsibly and runs his own shop, that I work at, mind you. As for Owen, he has created a deep sense of respect in him for his parent figure, which I applaud, since you do not show even an *ounce* of that same respect towards *me*," the mother's tone suddenly shifted to anger.

"I'm his girlfriend. I know him better than anyone. Who are you to say I'm wrong? You don't have a clue about anything happening around you," Adelie snarled back, playing the "girlfriend" role.

"Who are *you* to be talking back to your mother this way? Go to your room. Now."

Adelie walked past her. She had ultimately wanted to go to her room, anyway. However, the rest of her anger slipped through her lips in a whisper.

"You're no mother."

A sharp hand dug into Adelie's arm to spin her around. It stung like an animal's claws. She half-expected to come face to face with a beast. In a way, she did.

"You are such an ungrateful, spoiled little child. I'm all you've got left, so you better start liking it," the mother hissed.

Adelie's face twitched in both hurt and disgust. She fought the urge to spit. Instead, she tore herself away from her oppressor and hurried up the stairs to her room, slamming the door shut. After locking it, she threw herself onto her bed. She kicked and screamed into the blankets. She punched her pillows. She tore out pieces of her hair. Catharsis never came. Eventually, she wore herself out enough to fall asleep.

❖

Adelie awoke many hours later, her body scrunched up and her throat sore. She glanced at the window through her bedhead to see that the sun was beginning to set. Stiffly, she gathered herself into a sitting position, her face wet in her hands.

Just yesterday everything was so good and right. I wish each day could be like that. I'm a fool for thinking things would be better when I got back. Everything is so much worse.

Taking a deep breath, she pushed the hair from her eyes and stood up. She hadn't even taken off her boots earlier. They thumped on the hardwood as she neared her window.

I need to find Birch. Even if my own mother can't love me the way I need her to, I can still love him in the way that he needs me to.

Adelie's hands worked the window open in seconds. Carefully, she climbed out and shut it quietly behind her. She skittered down the slanted roof, kicking up dirt and a shingle. Sadly, there was no snow to cushion her fall now, so she had to make-do with a nearby bush. She sucked in another deep breath as she lowered herself off the edge, arms swinging her in place for a moment before dropping down into the plants. The branches and leaves stung a bit, but it was better than a broken leg. She'd get over a few itchy scratches. Her mother had done more damage than this before. A quick dust-off and she was setting down the road on quick feet.

Despite the summer days lasting longer, the night did eventually creep in. At least the fireflies gave her comfort. In all honesty, she felt safer out here on these back roads than in her own house. Her mind wandered to Birch again, and she felt that familiar tug of absorbism. However, something was off. The tug was much stronger than usual. It was like a fist yanking violently at her hair. It made her sprawl backwards. When she fell, things went black.

Unbeknownst to her, she'd transformed, but her mind was not present. She was a fox and a fox only. The creature flicked its ears and sniffed at the ground, eyes glowing faintly in the darkness. It trotted along the road for a few moments before falling to its side and turning back into a human.

Adelie awoke as if from a deep sleep and found herself laying on the gravel. With a gasp, she sat up and looked down at herself.

What just happened? Did I lose myself for a second? That's never happened before.

Though she knew this day would come, the surprise that accompanied it was eminent. The disease was spreading and growing stronger.

I did this to myself, didn't I?

Admitting it hurt, but she knew it was the truth. Between the trauma of Jeremy, getting closer to friends, and continuing to care for the kits, she'd put herself into situations that had aggravated her absorbed emotion.

The road was long, but it eventually met its mark near the kits'
den. Adelie took a moment to clear her head and remind herself of
the ones she loved: Owen. Jace. Damien. Colby. Birch. Aspen. Maple.
Dad? Jeremy?

The last individuals distracted her, but she grasped onto the
others and soon became a fox again—this time with her psyche still
intact. The fox shook off her coat as she did so, hoping to brush the
rest of the bad thoughts away. Birch needed her. He was more
important right now.

Her muzzle glued itself to the Earth as she vacuumed about the
woods, sniffing for any and every scent available. Most times she
would end up with a nose full of dust or dirt. Other times she caught
faint hints of Birch, but they would disappear in seconds due to their
staleness. Doubt coursed through her, but still, she pushed on.

A colony of bats burst into the night air, slightly startling the
vixen. Adelie raised her head to see their dark wings blanketing the
forest canopy. Their ruckus and movement momentarily distracted
her, and it took her a moment to get back to business. When she
turned back around, a new scent overcame her. Moments later, she
spotted Ace just a few yards away, sniffing at some ferns. Her spirits
lifted in the slightest.

It's nice to see him again, even if he's such a mystery

The husky swiftly lifted his leg and peed on the nearest tree.
Adelie suddenly regretted ever missing the dog. Afterward, he caught
sight of her. Instead of greeting her, though, he immediately took off
running in the opposite direction. This confused her and led her to
follow him. Though her legs were shorter than his, she was quick—as
all foxes were—and succeeded in keeping up with him from a
distance. After a minute of full-blown sprinting, Ace slowed down to a
trot and stopped at the canal to get a drink. The fox watched from
behind a nearby tree. The dog got his fill of water, circled three times,
and laid down in the grass near the bank, his face melancholy.

Her mission now on hold, the fox slowly turned back to being a
human. Adelie cautiously made herself over to the canine, who barely
moved upon her approach. She sat down next to him and planted her
feet in the gravel of the stream bank. Slowly, she moved her hand to

pet his fur. She got close, hesitated, but then followed through. A large sigh left Ace when she made the contact. He seemed content to have his neck and back pet just as Adelie was content to sit still for a moment. The husky curled up tighter and laid his tail over his nose.

Crickets and the squeaks of distant bats echoed around them as they sat in silence. A few minutes later, Ace began to uncurl himself. He stood up, stretched, and looked her directly in the face, his eyes just inches from her own. Something about this experience brought her back to when she was looking at her dad through the playroom window. It had the same feeling of twine threatening to snap. Time felt stretched beyond its limits. Seconds later, it was over when Ace decided to carry himself back through the trees.

When Adelie snuck back in her house that night, she couldn't stop thinking about that feeling.

<u>Chapter 8</u>

A week passed without head or tail of Birch. Adelie was beside herself. Something was clearly wrong, but she was powerless to stop it. All she could do was continue searching. Aspen and Maple helped but to no avail. None of the boys, as far as they knew, had seen him, either. Mr. Smit had caught a fox, but Owen had confirmed that it wasn't him.

Things at home remained the same. Adelie's mother had Mr. Smit over for dinner one night. She didn't say what she was thinking but she glared at her mother like looks could kill.

"Join us, Adelie. You must be hungry," her mother graciously suggested.

"No thanks."

"Your mother took the time to make this meal. It would be ungrateful to turn it down," Mr. Smit's voice was like thunder before a storm.

Adelie hated that she felt afraid. Mostly irritated, but also afraid. She couldn't imagine living with a man like him. Being related to him. Poor Owen. She looked up at Mr. Smit with unwavering brown eyes.

"I'm not hungry."

He stepped closer. He smelled like sweat. His blue eyes weren't kind like Owen's. They were hard and piercing. She wouldn't let them hurt her. She couldn't. He didn't get another word in due to her mother cutting them off.

"Oh, stop it you two. Let's just eat."

Adelie turned right around and walked the steps to her room. The man climbed behind her in seconds. Her heart beat faster, that fear now taking over. Was he about to grab her? Hurt her? Would her mother just watch? She didn't dare to turn around. His voice growled like the noises she'd hear from her dad at night.

"It is unacceptable to be this rude to your mother. Get down here and *eat.*"

The redhead's body shook with the force of his demand. She imagined this was only the half of his anger. If she were Owen, she'd be done for. She replied without turning around.

"You're not my dad."

"I don't care. I won't just stand by and let you treat your mother like this."

Adelie's nose wrinkled with rage and disgust. Not let her treat her *mother* like this? Someone who took her physical and mental abuse daily? Someone who had to take care of herself for years due to the absence of a true mom? Someone who got over her dad's disappearance faster than healing from pain caused by her mother?

She finally looked over her shoulder. Her eyes glanced at the family portrait, then at Mr. Smit.

"It's none of your business."

A coarse hand reached out to her. Slipping away into her bedroom allowed her to avoid it. She locked the door. The sound of thumping feet descended away from her. It sounded like the two parents acted like nothing had happened.

They ate and talked loudly for hours. Adelie couldn't stomach going down there again. It felt like keeping away from a wolf's den. She went hungry and fell into a starved stupor. Familiar nightmares plagued her sleep. Again and again she wished she could go back to that night at the lake house. Things weren't great then, but for that pocket of time, she was happy. She wondered if she'd ever feel like that again. The vibration of her phone woke her the next morning.

<u>10:22 AM</u>

<u>Owen:</u> wake up!!!!!

Adelie groaned and thought of just shutting the damn thing off. Instead, she rolled onto her back and replied to him.

Against her best wishes, Adelie soon found herself clothed and standing at the front of her house. It was just starting to get warm out and felt pretty nice. It wasn't long before Jace's vehicle was pulling up the driveway, all her friends in tow. Adelie's mother came out to see what the commotion was.

"Just stealing her for a bit, Ms. Henderson! Adelie can explain everything to you later," Colby grinned out the open backseat window.

She gave Adelie a questioning look all the same. Adelie simply shrugged.

"Just don't be out too late, okay? I think it's supposed to storm," the mother informed them.

All the boys gave her a thumbs up while Adelie climbed into the backseat with Colby and Damien. She waited until her mom was out of sight to interrogate them on what was happening.

"You'll see, you'll see," Jace waved at her from the driver's seat.

Adelie huffed in annoyance and sank back into her seat. To her dismay, the car pulled into their once-popular spot downtown—the ice cream parlor. They had all stopped coming to this part of town due to the bad feelings associated with it since springtime. Panic began to rise within her.

Why are we here?

"You guys should've just left me at home if you were going to bring me here," she growled.

"No, there's something you've gotta see, first," Damien insisted.

"I'm not sure I want to see it."

Owen unbuckled and turned around in the passenger seat to look at his distressed friend.

"Trust us. Please?"

Though apprehension pricked at her heart, she nodded and stepped out of the car with the others. They led her down the sidewalk, all of them walking at her sides. She followed numbly. When they got to the ice cream shop, there was something new in front of it.

A plaque. A plaque dedicated to the lives lost that day. A plaque that included all their names. A plaque that showcased Jeremy's name. A plaque that was adorned in flower bouquets from top to bottom.

Several feelings declared war inside her, ranging from elation to disgust. The former was for Jeremy. The latter was for herself. In the end, she remained physically stoic, her face perfectly poised to prevent an emotional slip. The boys looked at her expectantly. Even though she didn't know how to feel, she knew that she was grateful to have them as friends.

"Thank you for showing me, guys. I never would've known. It's really beautiful."

"We thought you'd like it. They even posted about it in the paper," Owen smiled.

"He'll live on, then," she answered quietly.

"As if there was ever any doubt," Colby rubbed her shoulder comfortingly.

Adelie took a deep breath, her eyes now closed, and let it out of her mouth in a steady rush of air. She surprised herself with what she said next.

"Should we get ice cream to commemorate it?"

❖

An hour of laughs and sweets later, Adelie had them drop her off on the road near the kits' den. Even though the experience was bittersweet, it thankfully left her feeling light and confident. She hoped the improved mood would help with her current quest. Instead of seeking out Maple and Aspen so she could transform, she decided to go human for a bit to see if she saw anything she hadn't seen before. Though fox noses were keen, human eyesight was a thing to behold, too. She was also able to dismantle two fox traps along the way.

The farther she walked, the more she saw the consequences of overhunting. Most plants were stripped bare and stood on the verge of dying. Hardly any creatures stirred, save for a bird call or two. The quiet hung like ghostly curtains across the landscape. Maybe the prey animals were beginning to move on. That, or disease was spreading.

A crunching noise up ahead shook Adelie from her contemplative state. It sounded like a pair of boots stepping on twigs. She quickly ducked behind a clump of thick trees just as she heard a man's voice speak.

"Yeah I'm out there now. I'm puttin' in some more of the new traps."

It sounded like Jace's father was on the phone with Mr. Smit or another hunter to give them his progress report.

"No, I haven't found any yet. Might have to start catching some damn squirrels to make commission," he cursed.

Just as he finished his sentence, a horrid, guttural screech tore its way through the forest. It sounded like a fox, but also *not* a fox at all. It didn't seem very far away, either.

"Spoke too soon! I hear one out there! Lemme go get 'em and get back to ya."

Adelie heard the snap of his cell phone shutting followed by the rustle of hustling feet. Every muscle screamed for her to follow him, but she had to play it safe. She couldn't get caught or she'd risk punishment from both Mr. Smit and her mother. Instead, she remained anxiously crouched behind the pines around her. The seconds ticked on, feeling like hours against the summer heat.

Her resolve was about to break when she heard yet another screech. This time, it was human. She saw Jace's father tear back the way he'd come, terror on his face as he continued to scream. He tripped over a bulging tree root and scrambled clumsily back onto his feet, only to run again. It wasn't long until he had left the woods completely. As soon as the coast was clear, she ran from her hiding place and followed his trail of boot prints. She could hear more noises now. There were high-pitched yelps and growls accompanied by wheezy panting. Whatever animal was in trouble, she had to help it— even if it was a giant wolf or bear that had scared Jace's father away.

Unfortunately, her discovery was much, much worse. Beyond a large boulder lay a red fox caught in one of the hunters' new traps. The strap was wrapped tightly around its neck, blood beginning to seep out from its skin. Its mouth was laced with foam, flecks of it scattered on the ground around it. Its body and head twitched erratically as it paced in circles around the steel bar buried in the dirt. Dark eyes stared ahead at seemingly nothing. That is, until it caught sight of Adelie.

It was Birch. A rabid, trap-caught Birch.

Adelie felt all the air leave her lungs when he lurched toward her, teeth snapping at the space between them. She stumbled back and fell into a prickly bush but barely felt the pain. Shock flooded her system, and everything felt like it was in slow motion. Surprisingly, her mind was strangely clear. Everything seemed to piece together all at once.

He must've gotten bit by something a while ago— a bat, maybe— and started to act strange the day I went to the lake house. That's why he disappeared and didn't come back. That's why we couldn't sniff him out very well. His scent had totally changed. He had totally changed.

The more Birch moved, the tighter the trap got, and the more blood spilled onto the soil. He continuously jumped in his mother's direction, but not for the right reasons. His eyes were bloodshot, and his coat was filthy. His snarls and cries were soul-sucking. Adelie couldn't bring herself to move. She was transfixed to the spot, unable to get on her feet again. A single tear rolled down her chin.

What can I do? How can I help him? He can't die!

Seconds later, Maple and Aspen arrived on the scene, most likely beckoned by the sounds of their brother. This only angered Birch more, causing him to choke himself against the hold of the trap. The siblings stood stark still, save for the lashing of their tails. Adelie's motherly instinct forced her to crawl forward.

There must be something I can do. I can save him. I can try! I have to try!

Just before she'd reached the point of no return, she turned to see Maple and Aspen tugging on the bottom of her jeans to stop her. They pulled and pulled until they succeeded in doing so. Now flat on her face, Adelie looked at her kits, tears dripping onto the dry earth. Their eyes were just as sorrowful.

They know. They know and they don't want to lose me, too.

When she looked back to Birch, he'd begun to sputter and cough against the forces of Man, front legs reaching into the air. A wail of woe came from Adelie, a wail mournful enough to droop the forest ferns. A wail mournful enough to shake the pinecones from their branches. Mournful enough to make Birch go quiet.

Adelie squeezed her eyes shut to escape from the tragic scene. Maple and Aspen kept their eyes on Birch as they curled into a shield around her. She morphed into a fox without even noticing. What she did notice, though, was the thump of Birch's body as it hit the ground. Her ears quickly flattened against her skull at the sound. She cried again in anguish. Maple and Aspen huddled closer.

Birch died on his side, mouth agape, blood pooling from his throat and mouth in one last desperate cry of release. It was unclear as to whether rabies or asphyxiation had killed him first. Perhaps it was both. Either way, he was no longer with them. His absence was immediately felt, even with his form lying just a few feet away. Perhaps the last week had prepared them for this. It hurt all the same.

The pain in Adelie's chest was even worse than learning about her dad's death or when she'd lost Jeremy. It was a weed sprouting from her ribs and weaving itself through her entire body. The tendrils curled and pulled against every organ, every tissue, every cell. It pricked everything it touched and showed no sign of stopping. It coiled around her like a boa until she had no oxygen left in her lungs. Emptiness hit. Everything was blurry and white.

Is this how he died just now? Did he feel like this? Am I doomed to relive everyone's deaths for them?

Though the world did not feel real to Adelie, it continued to exist without her. Maple shot up suddenly at a nearby noise, eyes diligent. In the distance, Jace's father was returning with some others to take care of the contagious body. Maple and Aspen nosed at their mother desperately. They needed to get moving or they'd risk joining their deceased brother. Adelie still wouldn't move.

I still have Aspen and Maple. They need me. Get up.

Adelie awoke as if from a ten-minute coma. Maple and Aspen were now dragging her in a feeble attempt to get her to safety with them. A shake of her head and a kick of her legs and she was on her paws again, even if she couldn't even feel the ground beneath her. The sound of the oncoming hunters met her ears while she took one last glance at her fallen son. She regretted doing so when she saw the state of his body. Shriveling at the sight, she took a deep breath and bounded away with her remaining children. That boa continued to squeeze around Adelie's tired body as she moved. Aspen took the lead and Maple ran just behind her to encourage her to keep going. All three of them were physically and emotionally spent, but it wasn't over until they were safe inside their den.

Just when their hearts were ready to burst, the den was upon them, and they were feverishly digging at the entrance to get in. Branches and dirt were thrown aside just enough for them to fit inside. Adelie rushed in, all the way to their resting area, while Aspen and Maple covered the entrance back up. That was when she felt her body collapse, not only physically, but inwardly, too. She lost consciousness for a few fleeting moments, returning to that span of black she had experienced the week before. When she came to, Aspen and Maple were right beside her once again, pupils dilated with worry. All Adelie could do was whimper and close her eyes.

Everything is so painful. I don't want to feel anything at all. I want to return to that blackness, even for just a few minutes.

All three foxes proceeded to fall asleep for a long while. The only thing that woke them was the crack of thunder that came from overhead. They cuddled closer.

Mom did say it was going to rain, didn't she? I guess she was right for once. I should probably call Jace to get a ride home.

Reluctantly, Adelie stood and licked Maple and Aspen on the ears before heading up to the surface. She stared down the tunnel for a few seconds before sealing it back up.

Please stay safe. I love you both so much.

Her head hung low as she trudged through the woods. It took a few minutes for her head to clear enough for her body to transform back. When it did, her face was still long in mourning. She grabbed her phone from her pocket and flipped it open. It was dead. She shoved it back into her jeans angrily.

What a cosmic fucking joke.

So, she walked. It wasn't exactly her first time doing so, but today, everything felt a million miles longer to her heavy feet. They dragged through the vegetation, the dirt, the asphalt. A flash of lightning lit up the sky and sparked the start of rain. The water and wind came in with a vengeance but failed to get through to Adelie. She walked slow and steady against the impending elements.

Her head was still fuzzy from everything that had happened, fuzzy enough to not fight when she felt someone come upon her from behind. She vaguely felt a bundle of cloth reach her lips before the world melted away once again.

❖

It was perhaps the second or third time being roused from sleep that day when Adelie realized her hands were bound. She was seated beneath a large tree that shielded her from the brunt of the storm. It didn't seem to make a difference. She was drenched straight through her skin and shivered when the breeze touched her. A figure crouched a few yards away, their back turned against her. Fear chilled her deeper than the rain. She was deciding on whether to scream or stay silent when the person turned around, stood up, and spoke.

"Oh, you're awake, thank goodness!"

It was a man. The voice was gruff, but very familiar. The face, however, was not. It was unkempt, a mess of facial hair and grime. She could hardly even see his eyes from the sheer height of his stature.

"Wh-Who are you? What is going on?"

The man walked a few steps closer and crouched again, this time, a mere foot away, his stench undeniable. Every nerve begged for her to break free of the rope around her wrists.

"It's me, Addie. It's me," he gestured to himself, his large hands patting on his own chest.

"Addie! It's me! C'mere, listen!"

His voice was muffled. She could barely understand him. Part of her didn't even want to. Yet, her body crept closer.

"That's it, that's my girl. Look," his dark eyes focused on her frightened ones.

"I can't stay. You know I can't. I wanted to say I love you, okay? Don't you forget that."

A million memories cascaded down into her brain at the sound of her nickname. So did confusion and elation, but mostly confusion. So much had happened—and was happening—and she couldn't keep up with it all. Nonetheless, it was clear that the person in front of her was undoubtedly her father. No wonder his voice sounded so familiar.

"Dad? What? I was told you were dead, I don't—"

"I know it's all hard to understand right now, but it'll make sense soon."

"I'm happy to see you but I'm so, so confused. Why did you knock me out? Why did you tie me up? Why did someone say you were dead?"

"I didn't mean to make you pass out. I just couldn't let you get away," a flash of despair sparked in his brown eyes.

"What do you mean? Why?"

"I'm getting you out of here, away from your mother. We can start a new life somewhere else," his brow knitted together, but his lips smiled.

Though that sounded amazing, something about this didn't feel right. A father wasn't supposed to make his child pass out so he could tie them up and carry them away. A father wasn't supposed to kidnap his child. Up until a minute ago, her father wasn't even in existence anymore.

"How did you even know where we were? How did you—"

That's when it clicked. Those noises she'd heard, those things she'd seen, was it all him this entire time? Was that his cover being blown, or was that her own mind playing tricks on her?

"Addie, please let me explain, then we can leave here, together," he offered, his hand pulling up a beaten-up backpack, seemingly filled to the brim with things they would need.

"You followed us. You stalked us. You've been here this whole time but never once came home," her voice shook, but she continued.

"You've seen everything that's been going on and never once thought to intervene, to come back? You saw me cry over you and didn't even think to come running? I don't even know what to feel, Dad! *Are* you my dad? You've been a ghost for so long, but I'm just now starting to see through you," hot tears bubbled from her eyes as her voice grew louder with anger.

Shame sagged his features. He dropped the bag to the ground and his eye twitched. Clawed hands dug into the mud.

"Addie, I understand, but please don't be mad. I don't want to hurt you."

She understood that he meant his absorbism, but at this point, she felt she didn't have much more to lose.

"You already have. Untie me and let me go," she ordered sternly.

Owen has, too. He lied to me. I can't trust him anymore.

"I already let you go once. I've let you go countless times. I'm not leaving without you, now. Let me help you," he reached his hand out to cup her cheek, but she turned her face away.

"I don't want this. I was *finally* over you," she spoke through gritted teeth.

"Addie, please, I—ah—"

Adelie looked at him again. His muddy hand now covered his face, but she could see his mouth curled back in a sharp-toothed snarl.

"I didn't know how to come back to you guys. I knew your mother would just keep me from you. Instead, I've watched over you both. I've kept you safe from the world—and me—the best I could."

The sadness in his words was genuine. A river of guilt ran through Adelie, but it wasn't strong enough to wash away the hurt. It only added salt to the wound. A huge, confusing, painful wound.

"Please just let me go. I won't tell anyone," her voice trembled with desperation and fear.

"You're not listening. We need to leave, *now*," his tone shifted to hostility.

Adelie curled her legs up beneath her and subtly wiggled her fingers to get her pocketknife—the one he'd left for her—out from her boot. As he attempted to gather his things before picking up his daughter, his breath came out in growls and groans.

He's going to change form. I might not survive an attack this time around. He's too far gone.

He was looming over her, half-human, half-bear, when a black-and-white shape jumped between them. Adelie gasped when it hooked itself to her father's ankle and made him tumble to the ground.

It was Ace. He bared his teeth and growled to match the beast in front of him, who was still getting to his feet. Adelie took this chance to snag her pocketknife, flip it open, and work at the rope that bound her. Adrenaline bloomed in her system, keeping her from overthinking or fainting. She needed to get away, and fast.

When her father finally stood again, he was the same grizzly bear he'd been all those years ago. He crashed his front half down, narrowly missing Ace, who was more nimble and able to dash to the side in the nick of time. The bear roared in frustration and swung its head to get a bite of the dog. Ace evaded him again, jumping backward and barking to hold the other's attention. Adelie then realized that the brave husky was tryingto lure her father away so that she could make her escape. She worked faster, harder. Almost there.

A mighty bear paw swiped at the canine, one of the claws catching on its cheek. Crimson splashed onto white fur, but still, he barked and ran backwards for the creature to follow him. It gave in to the trap and began to lumber menacingly towards Ace. Rain continued to pelt down, slicking both animals up with mud. Ace turned on his heel and sped off towards the nearby clearing. Though the grass was not very high, it would provide cover for the dog to disappear in. The rope around Adelie's wrists snapped just as the two of them went out of sight.

She immediately jolted up and then fell onto her knees. Her legs and feet had fallen asleep. She fought the pins and needles by getting right back up and running as fast as she could. It seemed that today just wanted to be filled with running, crying, and more running. In all honesty, she didn't even know where she was running to, but she knew she had to get as far as possible from here. Should she go to the police? Should she go home? Should she go to Owen for help?

No. He betrayed me. He lied to my face for months. I'm not sure I even know who he is anymore. He's not my friend.

When her body couldn't take anymore, she buckled under the pressure and landed on the road in agony. The rain mixed in with the tears that refused to stop pouring from her eyes. She sniffled and sobbed and crumpled into a fetal position.

I'm so sorry Maple, Aspen. I don't know if I can do this. It all just hurts so much.

The headlights of an oncoming car flickered through the walls of water. It screeched to a halt, only missing her by a few inches. Two women rushed out of the vehicle and dropped down to Adelie's side. The relief she'd hoped for had been snatched away.

Please just leave me here.

"Oh my god, are you alright? Hello?"

"Honey, help me get her in the car."

Yet again, Adelie's body was being lifted against her will. Again, she felt powerless to stop it. The couple gently lowered her into the backseat and covered her with a towel. In what felt like seconds, she was being guided into a warm, brightly lit home. Once inside, Adelie slid to the floor to sit down.

"Are you lost? Do you need something? Do you know where home is?"

No, I don't.

Adelie shook her head vaguely.

"What can we do to help you?"

"I'd like a shower," was all she could muster to say.

The two women blinked a bit confoundedly but granted her wish. They brought her to their home, guided her to their bathroom and took her dirty clothes. While Adelie stood under the hot water, the kind couple washed and dried her clothes. She must've been in that shower for an hour, just letting the hot water scald her skin so that she would feel something. It didn't work.

What am I doing? Why am I here? Where should I go?

She got no answers. Instead, she stepped out, dried off, and asked for her clothes. The couple obliged and then invited her to sit with them in the living room.

"Are you absolutely sure you're okay? You looked like you'd caught your death. Do you need to go to the hospital?"

The question sparked life back into her emotions, her pain. Adelie's face twisted with sadness.

"Hey, hey, you're okay. Just talk to us," one of the women urged with concern.

It took a heavy breath or two for her to formulate words. Might as well just talk.

"I'm not okay. I'm not. So much just happened and I... don't want to deal with anything anymore," she answered blankly.

"I'm so sorry that something bad happened to you. What's your name? How did you get out there? Are you hurt?"

Adelie looked at her wrists. There was a bit of rope burn but not much else. She'd escaped mostly physically unscathed. Well, except for the scrape on her knee from falling on the street, but it wasn't as bad as the scrape she had sustained after Jeremy's funeral, at least.

"M-My name's Adelie. It's a long story, but if you mean my body, then no, not really."

"Do you need us to call the police?"

"No, no. Please don't."

"What can we do for you?"

"Take... Take me to my house. Please."

It wasn't exactly a true home to Adelie, but it was all she had right now.

"We can do that," one of the women smiled warmly at her.

On the way home in their vehicle, one of the ladies said something to Adelie that she would never forget.

"Sometimes, the easiest thing in life is to give up when you're down, but… You, Adelie, you seem like a girl with fire in your heart. Don't let anything douse it. Keep fighting, okay?"

Adelie had simply nodded in reply. These words couldn't help her in this very moment. She stored them away within herself until there was a different time to use them.

❖

By the time they arrived at Adelie's house, the rain had finally ceased. Though she was still shaken to her core, her mind cleared up along with the clouds.

I hope Ace is okay. I hope my dad is long gone from here.

She thanked the Good Samaritans for everything and waved to them as they drove off. Just down the road, she spotted Owen pedaling towards her on his bike. Where she might've once felt excitement, all she felt was disdain.

"Adelie! Hey! Are you okay? I've been looking everywhere for—"

His bike hit a stray chunk of asphalt, sending him flying over the front of his handlebars. He landed with a shriek. Adelie felt her body twitch in an attempt to run forward and help him, only to settle back into a standing position. She simply watched as he picked himself up enough to walk his bike over to her. He now wore scrapes and cuts on his knees and face.

"I texted and called you a million times. What happened?"

The redhead wrinkled her nose and didn't dare to make eye contact. Owen leaned in worriedly.

"Adelie?"

The sound of her name snapped her head back in his direction, golden eyes aflame. A bomb went off inside her.

214

"My dad is alive. You lied to me. Why did you lie to me?"

Owen turned white as a sheet.

"How did you... Look, I can explain, you have to understand, I—"

"NO! I don't have to understand anything! How could I? I don't understand anything anymore!"

"Please, it was for your own safety, I saw him sneaking around and—"

"You could've just told me, and I would've accepted it! I would've listened! I would've reported him! Or maybe we could've helped him and had him fight your dad!"

"It wasn't that simple," his grip on the handlebars tightened.

"No, because nothing is simple, especially not with you. I found Birch. He's dead—dead because I trusted you and went to that godforsaken lake house! He's dead because of *you*," she pointed at him with an accusatory finger, despite her argument having no true basis.

Owen's face darkened.

"I was trying to find you so I could tell you that we'd found Birch. I didn't think you had found out before that. Adelie, he was sick. Nothing could've changed that."

"I could've spent more time with him. I could've spent more time doing anything other than wasting my time on someone who lied to my FACE for MONTHS."

"When I saw what he was doing, I kept trying to scare him away. I just wanted you to forget your dad. I thought if he was dead, you could move on."

"Yeah, well, now I never will, because he tried to kidnap me. I will *always* be wondering if he's going to do it again, or worse," her voice broke with the last few words.

Owen didn't offer anything else to say. Instead, he stood there, hands fidgeting with his bike and his eyes squinted in pain.

"Where do we go from here, then?"

"We don't. Friends don't lie. Not *once* have I ever lied to you, Owen," his name left a bitter taste on her tongue.

Her mind briefly wandered to when she gave him a fake name way back when. It didn't count. They hadn't been friends yet.

The two young adults stood facing each other for a minute, tension cutting a clear line between them. Adelie heard her front door open, probably her mom coming out to greet them.

"Have fun at college," was all Adelie could muster.

With that, she turned around and stalked off to her house, where, for once, she was almost glad to see her mother. Compared to her father and Owen, she was a saint, even if it was just for today.

"Everything okay? You look like you got soaked in the rain."

"I'm fine, mom," she grumbled, aiming for the stairs to her room.

A hand grabbed hers. Not painfully, but gently.

"Did you and Owen just break up?"

The question took her totally off-guard, but she guessed it was fitting.

"Yeah. We did," she answered, letting go of her mother's hand and heading to her bedroom.

When she looked out the window, she noticed Owen still standing in the same spot, head in his hands. He then hopped on his bike and rode off. That seemed to be what he was good at.

Adelie floated to her bed as the husk of a girl she once was. There was death that day.

Part III

____

FINIS VITAE SED NON AMORIS

*"In three words I can sum up everything I've learned
about life: it goes on."*

- Robert Frost

____

<u>Chapter 1</u>

As the days went on, the weather got colder. So, too, did Adelie's shell. She believed she would be forever encased in ice. No fiery touch would ever succeed in freeing her. It was a protective shield, now. She couldn't allow herself to get hurt again.

Most days were spent in her room, empty and listless. The only thing that brought color to her life were her two kits. Even though they could fend for themselves, now, their importance to her kept her going. Each time they had a visit together, they would stop by the site where Birch had passed on in order to grieve and process their loss.

Sadly, without the aid of Owen and her friends, Mr. Smit's snare empire only grew. Winter was hard enough without the threat of being caught and suffocated. They had to tread extremely carefully. Adelie once got caught by hunters when attempting to bring food for the foxes to eat. They escorted her rebellious, thrashing body out of the forest for her to be picked up by her mother, whose behavior had only worsened.

"I don't understand where this is coming from. You're in your room all day, you hardly touch the food I make you, and now you're giving Mr. Smit a hard time again. Is this because of your break-up with Owen?"

Her mother had staged a sort-of intervention in their living room one night.

"I guess," Adelie shrugged.

Temptation to spill the truth sat at the tip of her tongue. She stifled it.

"Adelie, you need to give me a clear answer. You're acting like a child."

"Then treat me like a child and send me to my room," Adelie snapped back.

"What, to sit there and do nothing with yourself? Oh, no, that's not happening. Starting tomorrow, you're coming to Mr. Smit's shop with me and working," the mother pointed a disciplinary finger at her daughter.

"Uh, no thanks," Adelie huffed.

"You do not have a say in it. It's time you did something useful with yourself."

Frustration prickled at Adelie's insides. Who was she to define what was useful and what was childish?

"*Fuck* you."

Adelie did not even have the power to care about punishment anymore. Her mother surged in front of her and grabbed her by the arms, hard. Hard enough for her nails to leave crescent shaped marks.

"Do you not have a brain? Are you two years old? Do you not even realize that you hurt people with your words?"

Adelie ignored the pain and scrunched her nose in a snarl.

"Do *you* realize? With your words *and* your hands?"

The statement brought a sudden awareness to the mother, who then released Adelie from her iron grip. For a split second, it almost seemed as if she was going to apologize. However, her malicious intent soon returned.

"Deflection. Very mature. Do whatever you want, but tomorrow, you're coming with me, even if I have to drag you out."

When the morning came, she did just that, Adelie leaving claw marks on the front door's frame. When they got to Mr. Smit's shop, it suddenly occurred to her that perhaps she could sabotage him in some way. She'd never had the opportunity to visit his store before. Plus, with her mom there, he probably would hesitate before stuffing her head and mounting it on a wall. Maybe.

The shop was about average size with a register at the far left of the entrance. The carpet was an ugly, rubbery green color. Shelves were filled with skulls and small pelts– rabbits mostly. Some hunting equipment hung on cabin-like walls.

"Ah, so you've brought this one to earn her keep. 'Bout time," Mr. Smit stood with his arms crossed.

He was as tall and menacing as ever, face particularly groomed. He always had a mustache, but sometimes he was scruffier than usual. Perhaps he was trying to look more gentlemanly for her mother's presence. Adelie didn't dare flinch away from his eye contact, even if he *did* share that same shade of blue with his son.

Her mother was put behind the register while Adelie was put to work stocking and arranging shelves. It got relatively busy for a bit, but only for an hour or two. It soon died back down, and Mr. Smit and her mother started to chat it up at the front counter.

"So, how is Owen doing at college?"

The mention of his name caught Adelie's attention, albeit bitterly.

"He seems to be doing alright. Called me last week."

Good riddance.

"That's good to hear. If I had the funds, I would've sent Adelie, too," her mother stated, to the surprise of her daughter.

Adelie continued to stock shelves, her back turned to them but her ears pricked.

"Mm, a shame. I could spot 'ya some money if 'yer desperate," he offered.

"Oh, I couldn't ask that of you, Richard!"

"It'd be no problem. I'm sure my buddies would pitch in, too."

Yeah, you'd like that, wouldn't you? Town hero who got the problem girl kicked out?

The mother didn't answer. She simply stared and smiled at Mr. Smit in disbelief.

"Just gimme a ring if you decide that's what you—and Adelie—want," he made sure to quickly add in her name for good measure.

"Will do. Thank you, Richard," the mother thanked him, a sort of flirty tone covering his name.

The rest of the day was... boring. The store mostly kept quiet, and Mr. Smit mostly hid away in the building's basement. At least Adelie wasn't being hounded by those scary eyes the entire time, but she became curious. What was down there?

It took her a few weeks to build rapport as a worker. She spent most of her free time pondering over ideas. It gave her something to think about, anything but the horrible things that happened last month. She picked up on old hobbies to further distract herself-- drawing, reading, painting. Keeping her hands busy meant keeping her mind busy, too. Nighttime was the hardest part, the quiet allowing the pain to seep back in.

It was yet another workday and stupid conversation between her mother and Mr. Smit. Could she just chop her ears off, please, so she wouldn't have to listen to it?

She decided it was time to try and figure out the basement. Adelie didn't move or talk until she had heard Mr. Smit head to the back of the shop. The door there was marked for employees only. She slowly placed the last mink skull on the shelf and turned around.

"I'm gonna go to the bathroom," she told her mother, not waiting for her to reply before heading to the back of the shop.

"Alright, just get right back to work when you're done."

"Yeah, yeah," Adelie replied under her breath, too low for anyone to hear.

She walked to the door and was thankful that it was directly across from the actual bathroom. Less suspicious that way. Adelie stared determinedly at the basement door for a few seconds. When she reached for the knob, she was shocked to see that it was unlocked. She was expecting to have to put up a fight to get in. Instead, she turned it with ease and stepped inside.

The room was very dimly lit with only a few lamps scattered across the open space. Concrete stairs guided her downwards. Small, blinking red lights indicated the locations of security cameras throughout the large room. None of that scared her more than the contents being stored there.

All the walls were covered in the pelts of animals that no longer existed in this area: black bear, cougar, lynx, bobcat, wolf, and the soon-to-be red fox. Some of the furs had price tags. Some did not. They hung as prizes, proof of the domination of nature. The only thing that gave her solace was not seeing any of the kits' bodies strung up alongside the trophies. Birch's body would've been too dangerous to get a hold of. Their true mother's body had probably been sold a long time ago. Various hunting tools made their home here, too, along with a table and chairs—no doubt where the hunters held their meetings.

I knew you were hiding all this shit somewhere. I guess it was kind of smart to put it in such a conspicuous location. No one would expect it.

When the door clicked closed, Mr. Smits' voice rang out from one of the corners. She knew he was in here, but she still nearly missed a step when his voice bellowed through the darkness with venom.

"You'd better head back up front, little girl. This isn't the bathroom."

Though she internally felt a spark of fear, she didn't let it show. She stood her ground and spoke sternly.

"I'm aware. Tell me, who keeps their stash room unlocked?"

"It's bait for those who want to lure in big catches."

He stepped out from the darkness, only half his face illuminated by the pale lamps.

An intimidation tactic. Adelie had one of those up her sleeve, too.

"Yeah? Well, I won't be caught that easily."

Untucking her phone from her back pocket, she swiftly pulled up the photos of the hunter stomping on the fox from ages ago. She also had pictures of the excessive number of traps in the malnourished woods. She'd waited so long to be able to reveal this black mail material. Now she held out the screen in his direction, images clear as day.

"I've got evidence, eyewitnesses. I'm gonna get you shut down."

"That would be a good plan, but tell me, where's your army? Your friends are all gone and your former 'lover' betrayed you," he crept closer with his hands in his pockets.

"I don't need an army," she argued, though his nearing presence started to make her nervous.

"You're bluffing. I've got men from all over the state—the *country*—that will make you out as a hysterical teenage girl. Think of the media attention. Think of your *mother's* reaction. You wanna end up like your dad?"

Anger bled through fear.

"What do *you* know about my dad? You're nobody. You're an asshole who couldn't even father his own kids," she growled, her hold on her phone unwavering.

Finally, he was looming over her, full of testosterone-filled rage.

"*You* are a spoiled brat that *thinks* she knows everything about everybody—correction, *I* do. You've been testing my patience for over a goddamn *year*. You best hold your tongue."

The darkness hid the tremble in her legs.

"Is that a threat?"

"If you're such a smart girl, why don't you tell me?"

As he spoke, he smacked the phone from her grip, sending it spiraling to the concrete floor. He stomped a heavy boot on top of it, the device cracking pathetically. Air left Adelie's lungs and was replaced with her own form of rage to combat his.

"How *dare* you. I'll scream—"

He clamped his hand around her mouth.

Neither of them noticed the sliver of light that cascaded down the steps. The door had opened. The mother had seen all of it. She was now flying down the stairs. She formed a human shield between Mr. Smit and her daughter, shoving his hand away from her face.

"What the hell is going on here?!"

"Marianne, your daughter is out of control. She—"

"You put your hands on her. You broke her phone. Why, Richard!?!"

"She's got no respect, no respect at all."

"Neither do you. I never want to see you again."

Adelie stood stark still and shell-shocked. Was her mother actually *defending* her?

"Fine. You two ain't shit, anyway. Two-faced bitches—like mother, like daughter."

The mother slapped Mr. Smit's face, a clapping sound echoing through the eerie room. Adelie couldn't believe what she was seeing and hearing. Before she knew it, Mr. Smit had lashed back, a slap of his own hitting her mother's cheek. It nearly knocked her over, the woman falling to her knees.

"*Mom!*"

Though they weren't exactly the closest, it was still surreal to see her only parental figure being beaten by the person they'd trusted for so long. The mother wiped her mouth, lifted her head, and shot Mr. Smit with a look of pure contempt. She looked as if it was taking everything in her to not strike him again.

"Adelie, get our things. We're leaving."

Mr. Smit spat in their direction. Now Adelie was the one who was close to ripping his head off. Instead, the two women remained silent and headed back up the stairway. When the store's lights hit her mother's face, she could already see the start of a bruise. There was something else that startled her more, though.

Her eyes. They looked different. No longer were they condescending. They were sorrowful. No longer cloudy, but clear. They held some kind of knowledge that had been hidden for a long time.

"Let's go home," the mother simply said.

Adelie sat on the recliner in the living room across from where her mom sat on the couch. The ride home had been strange, and things only kept getting stranger. Speaking of strangers, she didn't quite know who the person in front of her was anymore. Mother? Mom? Tyrant? Victim? She guessed she would find out.

"I've been trying to think of how to have this conversation for years, but I guess I'm just going to come out with it. Adelie, your father had a lot of problems. Most came from the absorbism, but not all of them," she sighed.

Adelie suddenly felt everything and nothing at the same time. The simple confession awoke a black hole in her abdomen. Maybe, deep, deep down, she knew about this long ago. Maybe her rose-colored lenses were shattering.

"He was always very good with you. I commend him for that. But he hurt me physically and mentally. He usually didn't mean to, but he did, and always made me into the bad guy in front of you."

Adelie's mind flashed to the growls she would hear at night as a child, to the times she saw her parents talking but couldn't quite hear what they were saying. It made sense that neither of them would've wanted her to know the truth at her age.

"I guess today made me realize it all so clearly. When Mr. Smit hurt me, it brought back so much of the past, and I couldn't keep protecting you from it."

Though Adelie knew this must be a troubling conversation for her mom, she also knew she had to call her out on things, too.

"Protecting? You *became* the bad guy. *You* drove us apart. *You* hurt me mentally and physically. You passed your trouble onto me."

Her mom sat silent for a moment, face seemingly deep in thought. Then, the unexpected happened. A teardrop slid down her cheek.

"I realize that now. I never, ever should've said and done such horrible things to you. You didn't—couldn't—understand. My trying to protect you ended up making things worse. Maybe we could've been closer if I'd just been more honest, but I was afraid of breaking your heart by ruining the image you had of your father. He didn't mean to be the way he was, but it happened," she began to get choked up.

"Why do people keep hiding things from me in order to 'protect' me!?! I'm sick of it! I'm not a child! I can take it!"

"I know. I'm sorry. I'm so, so sorry, Adelie. I wish I could rewind these past few years and do it all over differently, but I can't."

The sentiment barely reached Adelie's heart. Too much hurt, anger, and sadness was encased around it. She sat stewing in her emotions, eyes threatening to spill like her mom's. She didn't know what to say.

"It's okay if you can't forgive me. I just wanted you to know. What happened back at the store gave me an epiphany of sorts. I don't want us to be this way anymore. I want to be better, for both you and me," her mom explained.

"I guess you just like men that hurt you."

Her mom barked out a melancholic laugh at that.

"That might be so. I need to work on myself instead of taking it out on my daughter," she wiped the tear from her face.

Adelie nodded and gripped the chair's fabric tightly.

"I don't know if I can forgive you. I do know that I can't forget everything that has happened," Adelie announced, now making eye contact with her mom.

"That makes sense," Marianne's voice shook in the slightest.

Adelie remembered a time when all she wanted to hear were these words. The want had faded into resignation over the years. Now that she was given this gift, it felt like a white elephant. What should she do with it? How should she feel? Should she come clean, too?

"I've got stuff to say, too. You need to understand why I've been the way I've been."

"I'm all ears."

"You need to promise not to be mad with me, not to yell, not to hit," she demanded.

Surprisingly, her mom reached between them and placed her hand on hers. Adelie flinched at first but then became still.

"I promise."

Adelie took a deep, purifying breath before diving into everything that had happened in the past year. She spoke of the mother fox, the kits she had adopted, how she loved and cared for them. The truth of Mr. Smit's intentions was revealed along with the true nature of her and Owen's friendship. Adelie's chest seemed to lift the more that she spoke. She never thought she could speak to her mother in this way, yet here she was. Time flew as she talked. By the time she'd gotten to everything that had happened with her dad a few months ago, sadness was ebbing from every pore. The dark cloud that had hung above her since the end of summer was back. It rained upon her, spouting tears.

"I never told you any of this because I feared your reaction. I hope this wasn't a mistake. Please don't yell at me or hurt me," she practically begged, now vulnerable and broken for her mom to see.

She felt small beneath her mother's gaze, no more than a little girl waiting to be put in time-out.

Was this the right choice? Will I regret this?

No more words were said, only action. Initially, when her mother closed in, a jolt of fear had coursed through her, causing her to panic. However, it was soon remedied when it was a hug that she was pulled into.

The girl was silent, stoic, blank. Her mind was as empty as her eyes, flames gone. Her mother reached out to her.

"Addie."

Her ears didn't hear her. The mother desperately shook the girl's shoulders.

"Look at me."

Soon, they were both sobbing uncontrollably. Adelie still felt a little panic, perhaps as a reflex, but at this point, what else was she to do? That was when she began to feel the hair on her neck rise.

"Adelie, you've been through so much. I'm so sorry that I never saw any of it. I really, really am. You didn't have to inherit my hurt, but I didn't leave you a choice, did I?"

Adelie's body started to feel heavy with static.

"You don't have to forgive me. I just want you to know that I understand, now."

The world went dark for a moment. When it came back, Adelie was a fox caught in her mother's arms. She couldn't recall any other time that this had happened in the past five years. This was pure, unconditional love, now.

This is real, then. It has to be. My absorbism never lies.

She curled up in her mother's lap to relish in the feeling of being openly loved. It'd been a long time. Though the anxiety of her progressing condition plagued her, she allowed this moment to happen. It was about time. Admittedly, Adelie wasn't so sure about how she felt toward her mother at this very moment. She just knew that someone was on her side again, someone who hopefully wouldn't end up deceiving or leaving her.

<u>Chapter 2</u>

"I can't believe I fell for his tricks," Marianne vented as she ate at the dinner table with her daughter.

"Yeah, it *is* a little unbelievable," Adelie replied.

Marianne snorted between bites of her food. It was Adelie's favorite pasta dish again.

I never thought I'd see the day where we'd talk to each other like this. It's weird, but kind of nice.

A few hours had passed since their cathartic conversation. The two women continued to chat about the things they'd hidden and the things that they now felt with their newfound knowledge. The room felt warm from both the kitchen and the two women's conversations.

"I guess I don't have much room to talk. I was friends with Owen for a long time before I figured out that he was lying to me," Adelie pointed out irritably while swirling up a fork-full of spaghetti.

Her mom took a few moments to reply, seemingly ruminating as she chewed.

"From what you've said, it doesn't sound like he did it to hurt you," she suggested.

"He still did, though," Adelie replied, her mouth full of food but her voice resentful.

"I know. What he did wasn't right, but maybe he deserves to be heard out?"

Even though she didn't want to admit it, her mom had a point, but it seemed to be null now that she didn't have any way to contact him.

"Well, even if I *did* decide to give him a chance, I now have no way of contacting him. Mr. *Dick* broke my phone."

"Shoot, and I can't ask Mr. Dick for his number now, either."

The two of them sighed.

"I need more time to think it over, anyway," Adelie dismissed the rest of the conversation as she put her dishes in the sink.

"As for your father, Adelie, I don't think you should go wandering by yourself any longer. It's not safe."

She was giving her a rule out of concern rather than spite.

"I still need to see the kits, though."

"I could drop you off and keep a lookout for both him and the hunters. The weather's getting very cold now, too."

"Yeah, we could do that."

"I'm going to apply to some other places for a job, too. No way I'm going back to his shop."

Though Adelie was happy about that, a wave of worry washed over her suddenly.

"Mom, is there any way to fight this? Anything? I was looking for dad in the hopes that we could fight this legally, but now I don't know what to do. What they're doing to this town—to the forest—just isn't right, and now I don't even have my evidence," Adelie ranted.

Her mom joined her in the kitchen to start washing the dishes.

"I'm not sure, but I will look into it."

Adelie nodded and helped her dry and put away everything. As she did, her thoughts floated off into the deepest corners of her mind. They came back with a question that she'd forgotten to ask.

"I just remembered something else I've been wanting to ask you about."

Her mom shut off the sink and started to take off her gloves.

"Okay?"

"Why was dad's emotion anger?"

Her mom placed the gloves on the counter and cleared her throat.

"Ah, that makes sense. I don't think we ever told you."

Adelie shook her head and watched her with impatient eyes.

"Well, his mom—the grandma you never got to meet—had him as a teenager. Her family was very disappointed in her but made her keep the baby. When she had him, everyone in the delivery room still felt very angry toward her."

"Oh, is that why—"

"Yes, that's where the anger comes from. Then she killed herself many years later because of the disapproval. They never stopped beating down on her for it."

"That's awful," Adelie reacted quietly.

"It is, and then your dad was put into the foster care system. He hopped between homes a lot due to his condition. Eventually he aged out of the system and did well for himself. We met sometime afterward. He was a good man, but all those years of hardship made his absorbism even harder to ignore," she explained.

Adelie wished that she'd known this a long time ago. That was when she quickly realized that she wouldn't have understood any of it at an elementary age.

"Thank you for telling me."

I'll still always love and miss him, but I see now that he was—is—a very troubled person. I can't place all my cards on him. I've been my own parent before, and I'll continue to be.

❖

Autumn comes along, the tension between Adelie and her mother dropping like the leaves outside. Both mother and daughter got jobs at a local café. Marianne worked in the kitchen, Adelie at the register. She wasn't the cheeriest cashier, but she did her job adequately. Right now, the objective was to make some extra money to possibly get the resources they needed to go after Mr. Smit legally. That, or move out if things got to be exceptionally dangerous. They did, however, get enough money to get Adelie a new phone.

After their shared shifts, they'd drive out to the woods so Adelie could visit the kits and bring them food if needed. Her mother would wait out in the car to keep an eye out for both hunters and her husband. She had to call Adelie and warn her of hunters more than a handful of times. On the contrary, she never made a call about Adelie's father. He'd either left the town or gone into hiding, hopefully.

Adelie tried not to think about it so she could focus on Maple and Aspen. They were thin and had a cough, but she had faith they'd get better. Though she usually brought them something to eat, it was nice to see prey in their den occasionally. It must've been harder to gather their meals without their strongest sibling with them.

For Adelie, it was starting to get harder to keep her grasp on her identity. The absorbism blackouts were getting longer and more frequent. Once, she'd blacked out in the kits' den and woken up in the woods somewhere. It took her a long time to find her way back to the car that day. Once in, she felt woozy and sick.

"Adelie, are you catching a cold? You're not looking so good."

"I'm fine," she'd insisted, forehead pressed against the foggy window.

"Maybe stay at home tonight and tomorrow. I've got some soup from work you can have."

Adelie's nails dug into the seat cushion.

"I said I'm *fine*."

Her mom stopped the car. She turned to Adelie.

"It's getting worse, isn't it?"

Her question shouldn't have caught her off guard, but it did. She kept staring out the window, not knowing how to respond. The beginnings of snow brushed over the windshield.

"I'm right, aren't I? God, you're too young—"

"Yes, mom, you're right. It's getting worse. Happy?"

"Not at all," her voice trembled.

When Adelie looked, her mother's face was full of tears.

"I'm so sorry. We knew from the start that love would be a hard one to live with."

"No kidding," Adelie scoffed quietly.

"I want to say that I'm here if you need me, but I feel like that will only make it worse," her mom responded defeatedly.

"Just keep being like this. I don't want things to be the way they were. Not ever again. Jeremy, the others, Birch—they've all led me to this, too."

Her mom sniffled, breathed in deeply, and nodded before putting the car back into drive.

That night, when Adelie was in the shower, doused in hot water and truly alone, her thoughts ran rampant.

I'm going to leave this world without saying goodbye to my father, without talking to Owen, without explaining things to Jeremy, without taking down Mr. Smit.

She suddenly felt thankful for, and regretful of, so many things in her life. She looked down at her pruned fingers. She recalled the last time her hands had felt like this.

Can't I just go back to that day at the lake house? Can't I just live there forever? Jeremy would be alive and making sandcastles. Colby and Damien would be teasing each other. Owen and Jace would kiss and hold hands without ridicule. The kits would live in the nearby woods. There would be a

By the time she'd drug herself to bed, she'd felt exhausted and sore.

Just live until you can't. That's all you can do.

❖

A snowstorm hit, the first of the season, and a monster of a storm, at that. It blew icy breath across the town, cutting out power with its powder. Animals without a home found themselves amid death itself. Temperatures plummeted into the negatives. Adelie could feel its chill within the house, and she worried for her children. They'd been thin and on the verge of sickness the last time she'd seen them. It seemed that it could only get worse.

The winds went on for hours, days, without letting up. Plows waged war against the snow but still found themselves skirting on the edge of ditches—along with the countless other vehicle victims. Adelie's anxiety snowballed.

"Mom, I need to bring food to the kits. I've got a bad feeling."

"Adelie, I'm sorry, but we can't. The roads are horrible," she answered, eyes glued to the television news.

"I'll walk then."

"And freeze to death?"

"*They're* the ones freezing to death!"

"We need to stay inside. It's not safe. Won't *they* be safe in their den?"

"They didn't look well the last time I saw them," she admitted, nausea weighing down her words.

"I thought you said they were getting better?"

Snow and ice continued to pelt down. It thumped against the roof, filling the stagnant air with sound.

"I don't know. I just don't want to lose them. I can't. I need to make sure they're okay," her voice broke with desperation.

Marianne turned off the tv, shut her eyes, and took a deep breath herself.

"Help me shovel out the driveway."

❖

The two women drove as fast as they could against the storm's whistling howl. Their tires kicked up chunks of ice while serpent-like swirls of snow skated across the asphalt. Windshield wipers fought endlessly against the onslaught of snow. In fact, it was hard to tell exactly where they were going, but they hoped their instincts wouldn't lead them astray. Adelie was especially relying on hers. Her gut told her they were close. Another minute and she was itching to get out of the car. Her teeth chattered and sharpened.

"Mom, here! Stop here," she ordered.

"You're sure this is the spot? I can't see anything familiar."

"Yes! Stop the car!"

As soon as the vehicle was in park, Adelie threw the door open and flew out on four paws. She landed face first into the snow but quickly tunneled her way out of it with vixen expertise. The wind itself seemed to carry her through the trees to her target. Her mom trudged far behind with a shovel in her hand. Adelie ran and ran until her body fell onto its side, lungs heaving and vision blurring. Her consciousness dipped.

No, please, not now!

Hot, anxious breath puffed from the fox's mouth as it tried to fill its lungs with air. It blinked, shook its head, and stood on its feet again. It cowered under the storm and moved to find shelter. Paw prints swiftly disappeared under the snow. The vixen was coming upon a hill when it collapsed.

Adelie returned to her body and urged it forward. Her nose brought her to the den entrance, though it was sealed with snow. She quickly got to digging, something her animal body was especially good at. Amid the unearthing, Adelie's mom showed up just in time to help. Human and fox worked together to clear the way. At last, Adelie poked her paw through and found herself touching open air. A few more swipes and she was in.

Now more of a snake than a fox, she slithered her way through the icy tunnels, the soil now hardened and cold. Aspen and Maple lay curled together in their den. The two of them were shivering and sniffling, relief showing in their eyes at the appearance of their mother. She reached forward and pressed her nose to their foreheads before nudging at their skinny sides.

Get up, we need to go.

The "kits" quickly got the message and untangled themselves from each other to stand up. Their bodies were shaking and scrawny. Looking over her shoulder with each step, the vixen led her children out of their home, knowing she would need to make a new one for them at her human residence. It wasn't safe to stay in the woods any longer.

Bitterly cold air whipped their faces as they emerged from the den's opening. Marianne stopped digging and stared at the three foxes in awe. It was her first time seeing them, after all— though minus Birch. Once they were all freed from their hollow, Adelie kicked in the entrance, snow and evergreen twigs practically erasing the spot from existence. It felt bittersweet. Final, because it was. There was no going back, now.

Adelie turned her head away from the tomb she had just sealed when a wave of absorbism wracked through her once again. A small squeak slipped from her maw when she went down, face-first into the snow once again. Maple and Aspen yipped and poked at the vixen, forgetting their own fragile health. Marianne bent down and gently shook the unmoving fox. That was when it bolted upright with snarling white teeth that even the snow could not conceal.

The human mother and two foxes stood their ground, albeit a bit shaken by the sudden mood shift. The angered vixen curled in on itself, amber eyes flicking to and fro before eventually collapsing once again. The return of Adelie's conscience also brought her animal form back to its feet. She was starting to truly understand her father's struggles. A soft bark fell from her jaws in apology.

Four cold bodies trudged through the mountains of snow on their journey to Marianne's vehicle. The horrid weather showed no sign of letting up, but neither did their determination. Eventually, though, Adelie found herself relying more on her feelings of concern rather than love. This way, she could return to her human form and help Maple and Aspen make their way out of the woods. The two of them stumbled and coughed with each step. Their poor bodies were not faring well and would need to be carried the rest of the way. So, they were.

On the way home, Adelie sat between them in the back seat, arms and coats curled around their tired frames. Once they were back, Adelie decided it would be best to keep the kits in their garage. It was small– just a few feet of extra room beyond the space for their car– but it would have to do. At least they could stay hidden and warm. Adelie could check on them at any time, too, and keep them from damaging anything. This put her at ease.

Some old blankets were thrown on the concrete floor to act as bedding along with some meat and veggies the Hendersons had in stock at home. The sickly foxes did not touch the food. This wasn't too unexpected. It would take them some time to acclimate to such a big change. Adelie lay with them in her fox form to comfort them, her consciousness dipping a few times throughout the night. The risk of this situation began to set in, not only for the kits, but for herself, too. She tried to ignore the worry and just focus on what Aspen and Maple needed right now.

Adelie eventually woke up in her human form the morning after. That was when she saw the two foxes just finishing the meal that had been provided to them. It relieved her.

<u>Chapter 3</u>

The entrance of Spring felt like a breath of fresh air for the very first time in almost a year. There was still the lingering of snow—a reminder of the things still out of place— but there was also new growth, a blue sky, and the hopeful promise for better things to come. The kits were feeling better, and that was a miracle in and of itself.

The cafe was busy today. She was told it got like this during the warmer months, tourists visiting for outdoor fun. Thankfully it didn't seem like a hot spot for Mr. Smit or any of the other hunters. The small shop, home to about six tables, was covered with light hard wood and a large blackboard behind a simple counter. White letters marked their products and the day's specials. A window formed the connection between the kitchen and the front desk, which held pastries behind a glass case.

As the early rays of the Summer to come filtered in, it was clear that Adelie had lost weight and some hair. Still, someone recognized her.

"Adelie? Is that you?"

She perked up from her spot behind the counter and blinked.

"Colby?"

"Yeah! Hey! How are you?"

Her old friend's appearance had startled her, but it wasn't exactly unappreciated. In fact, she even smiled. Colby didn't look all that different. Maybe just a slight maturity to his facial features, but all else was the same.

"I've been doing okay. I'm sorry I never reached out to you guys. My phone got busted a while back and I lost everyone's numbers."

"Oh, that's alright! Do you have a phone now? I could give you mine and all the others' numbers!"

Adelie winced but obliged.

"S-Sure. Wanna input them for me?"

The two of them leaned over the counter together, Colby inputting numbers and Adelie's vision swimming with sudden dread. Now that she had their numbers again, would she contact them?

"Thanks, Colb. Have you been doing well?"

"Oh, have I! College football has been a *blast*. I even have a girlfriend now. Damien is totally jealous," he stated proudly.

The boy's enthusiasm warmed her fragile heart.

"I bet they are. I'm glad you two are still close."

"Me too! We still talk to Jace and Owen, but only sometimes. They've been busy, I guess," he shrugged.

"A-Are they still together?"

"I think so. I hope so! They're just harder to get a hold of nowadays."

Adelie's throat dried up. She swallowed hard.

"Gotcha. D-Do they ever ask about me?"

"They used to, all the time. I'm sure they're still wondering how you've been doing. You should give 'em a call or text sometime. I, for one, am super relieved to see your face after all this time!"

His honest, kind words split her in two. Her teeth chattered. Her balance faltered. He was on her in an instant, strong arms catching her from hitting the floor.

"Adelie, you okay? Was it something I said?"

"Huh? N-No. Well, I mean, yes, actually..."

"Is it--?"

Adelie nodded and fought out of the absorbism outburst as Colby steadied her back to her feet.

"I'm so, so sorry."

"It's fine," she replied, not wanting to make a scene in front of the other customers.

Colby quieted his voice before speaking again.

"The kits, how are they?"

The change in subject actually brought some light to her chestnut eyes. Dim at first, though it slowly brightened.

"Well, Birch died around the time everyone was leaving. I don't really want to talk about that, but I brought Aspen and Maple to my house during a bad snowstorm a couple months ago. They're doing really well," she whispered back.

"Oh... Well, I'm sorry about Birch, but it sounds like you're taking good care of the others. Don't doubt yourself on that– I know how you are with that," he encouraged.

His reassurance was appreciated beyond words.

"Thank you, Colb."

"Don't sweat it. I'm visiting my folks for a week before going back for summer classes. If you wanna hang or anything, let me know. I'll be there."

Adelie nodded, sniffled, and stood behind the register once again. She needed to get back to work.

"Now, what can I get for you?"

❖

Adelie stared at her phone for what seemed like hours that night, contemplating if she should text Owen. Her anger had only slightly faded, but her mom's words rang fresh in her ears. Her head hadn't been clear that day, so she hadn't been open to hearing anything he had to say. Though he still should've been truthful, she remembered the remorse in his eyes like it was yesterday. It was hard to believe that it'd been nearly nine months since they'd last spoken. Before everything, they'd hardly gone more than a few hours without seeing or texting each other. She found herself hesitantly missing that closeness.

I should text him. I should work things out. I should tell him about everything that's happened.

Doubt crept in. Even before the incident with Mr. Smit, Owen hadn't bothered to reach out to her at all. If he felt so bad, wouldn't he have tried?

I didn't either, though. Not sure I would've listened to him if he had, anyway. I scared him *and he hurt* me.

Adelie groaned and turned over in bed, shutting her cellphone and placing it on her nightstand.

Maybe tomorrow.

❖

"I'm going out for a walk. I just need some space," Adelie called to her mom with her hand on the front door handle.

Said mom came rushing up.

"You got your phone?"

"Yep."

"Put on sunscreen? Here, take some water—"

"Mom, it's just a walk. I'll be fine."

Being fretted over in such a healthy, protective way was a weird feeling for Adelie. Weird, but pleasant.

"I know. Okay. Just be safe, though, please. If anything starts to happen, call me."

"I'll be fine. See ya in a bit."

The redhead walked down her driveway and followed the sidewalk. She wore jean shorts complete with a tank top, light flannel, and, of course, her trusty lace-up boots that concealed her pocketknife. Sighing, she walked on, hoping the movement and fresh air would help her come to a decision about Owen.

The sun felt nice, and the wind smelled of soil. As the street clung to the woods, nostalgia colored her view. She saw herself and the kits weaving through the trees. She heard the jingling of Owen's bike pedaling along, herself in tow and laughing at Owen's antics. She spotted Jace, Colby, and Damien disabling fox traps in the distance. Sadly, she also saw the ghostly shadow of her father, neither human nor animal. The nostalgia turned to panic. She froze and gripped her knees to stop herself from falling. The sun suddenly felt scorching hot, the comfort gone. Her ears heard Birch's snarly, dying breaths.

Stop. This is supposed to be my home. Stop it!

Chasing grasshoppers. Rolling in mud. Catching fish in the river.

Think of the good stuff. Think of what makes you happy.

Meeting Jeremy. Helping Owen. Being helped by Jace, Colby, and Damien. Carving pumpkins. Understanding her mother. Fighting against Mr. Smit. The lake house. Getting drunk with friends.

Adelie started to walk again with a little more pep in her step. She stepped off the road and into the forest, following an invisible path. Her feet led her to the duck pond. This was where she and Owen had first talked, and where he told her about her dad. It felt unreal but she could practically hear the rain as she sat on the surrounding rocks.

Though it can hurt sometimes, I need people in my life. Especially now that I don't have much time left to be with them.

Adelie took out her phone and flipped it open. She scrolled to Owen's number, finger lingering across the keys.

I want to talk to him. I want to hear what he has to say.

She stared at his name for a long time, trying to find the exact words to send to him. Eventually, she got it.

<u>11:32 AM</u>

<u>Adelie</u>: hey. its adelie. can we talk?

As soon as it was sent, she stuffed the phone away in her pocket and covered her eyes with her palms. All she could do was wait, now. She laid herself across the rocks and crossed her hands over her stomach. She relaxed for a few minutes before a sound in the bushes spooked her. That unresolved fear of her father resurfaced, pushing her to get back home. The brisk walk to her house helped to clear the uncertainty from her mind. She'd made a decision and stuck with it— that was what counted. Even if he ignored her, at least she knew that she'd tried.

Aspen and Maple comfortingly curled around Adelie in her bed that night.

❖

A week passed and Adelie could not bring herself to meet up with Colby. A month flew by and no word was had from Owen. Adelie felt herself sink ever lower. The closer she got to her mom, the farther she fell from her human reality. Day by day, her absorbism worsened, but she pushed herself to work at the café. They were rounding on enough money to pursue Mr. Smit's actions legally and she didn't want to let go of that last shred of hope. She even had enough fight in her to dismantle a few traps. Prey animals were starting to really pick the land clean of its vegetation. It was a sight for sore eyes, but it begged for Adelie's help, and who was she to say no?

Even if I lose myself before we can go against Mr. Smit, I'll keep coming back here for as long as I can. I can't give up on my real home. The kits wouldn't want me to. Their true mother wouldn't want me to, either.

Soon enough, it'd been two months since Adelie had texted Owen. Summer was at its peak while Adelie was at her lowest. Different kinds of traps were being brought back into the forest, and fast. It seemed they were going for any scrap of fur they could get their hands on, now. It was devastating to know that this wasn't the first time they'd resorted to such selfish tactics. To hunt irresponsibly was to disobey the very will of the Earth. Even the trees looked disappointed. The uneven scale of nature weighed heavily upon their branches, causing them to sag and snap. Their etched, bark faces soon became chewed to ribbons by those not kept in control by Nature's sweep. The canopy widened and brought the sun crashing down to the floor below. It cut the ground like light caught in a magnifying glass.

Today, Adelie let out her frustrations by throwing stones into the duck pond. She tried to make them skip at first. Now she just wanted to throw as many as she could, as hard as she could. Geysers of water erupted from her efforts. The feathered inhabitants flew away in fear. She didn't mean to scare them.

I was a fool to think Owen might come back.

A splash and an angry scream.

The forest is dying. So is my body. I can't control any of it.

She dropped down to her knees. She saw her reflection in the muddy water.

Who even am I anymore? I don't—

"Adelie?"

Her name in someone else's mouth sent her spinning. The voice was familiar. Painfully. She nearly fell into the water as she turned around.

Owen was standing a few yards away.

Chapter 4

Were her eyes deceiving her? It wouldn't be the first time. Owen's back was hunched with hesitance and his arms were stretched in front of him as he spoke.

"Okay, I know how this looks, and how we left off—"

"You're here. How are you here? Are you real?"

Owen paused and stared at his former friend. Adelie was frazzled from head to toe.

Please, mind, don't play any more tricks on me. I can't take it.

He walked a little closer. Adelie stayed where she was and watched his movements closely. His eyes seemed genuine.

"It's me. It's really me. I promise," his hand made its way to his chest, where he clutched at his heart.

Adelie nodded slowly and sank back down to the riverbank.

"You're back. You didn't answer my text," was all she could mutter.

"Oh, uh, I've honestly been without a phone for a while," he scratched the back of his neck in embarrassment just like he used to.

Upon closer inspection, Adelie noticed how his clothes hung on him, how his face seemed almost sunken in.

Adelie felt some of her old self returning the more that she spoke to him. She could almost forget what had last transpired between them. Almost.

"I guess we've both been worse for wear, huh?"

"You could say that again," he huffed.

"Come, sit," she patted the ground beside her.

Owen, though shocked at her acceptance of him, obliged. The two of them sat quietly for a few minutes, the wind their only ambience. He fiddled with his fingers nervously.

"Adelie, I want to—"

"Owen, I'm sorry—"

The pair stopped themselves after they'd spoken in unison. Their eyes met, brown to blue.

"Please, let me go first. I owe it to you," Adelie said, not really asking.

Owen couldn't have stopped her if he'd tried.

"It was wrong of me to be so angry with you. I should've heard you out. I'm sorry. I'm ready to listen, now, if you'll tell me."

"Nah, you were right to be pissed with me. I never should've done those things. I never should've lied."

"I've learned recently that sometimes lies are made with the best of intentions. It doesn't take away the hurt, but they can be forgiven," Adelie breathed out.

"I'm not sure I even deserve to be forgiven. I'll still tell you, though. I'll tell you everything," he replied, his face dark.

"DON'T LISTEN TO HIM!"

Yet another voice rang out from the woods, birds flying away in its wake. It was louder, deeper, more terrifying than Owen's. Both of them stopped talking, eyes searching for the source. Adelie's stomach churned. Her heart knew who it was.

A tall figure crept out from the bushes several meters away. It didn't look human. It didn't look like an animal. Owen moved in front of Adelie, arms shielding her protectively.

It was her father. He was back and seemed even worse than before. She didn't know how he'd even stuck around this long.

"He's just gonna sell you more lies; don't you know that? You're smarter than that," he growled, creeping ever closer.

Fear flooded Adelie's system. Owen stood his ground, chest puffed out and brow furrowed.

"I guess he just wants another rematch after all," her father scoffed.

Adelie's fear soon changed to confusion.

"A rematch? Owen, what is he talking about?"

Owen kept quiet, his body and mouth rigid.

What else has he hidden from me?

"Ah, so he hasn't told you yet. What a deceitful boy!"

"You don't know anything about me. All *I* know is you've been nothing but a bad memory for Adelie. You should leave. For good this time," Owen snarled in return.

Adelie felt the hair on her neck start to rise. Her father barked out a scornful laugh.

"How *dare* you. She's my daughter. She'd leave you in a heartbeat."

"That would be her decision. Let her make it on her own. Leave her *alone*," Owen demanded.

Owen's protective love transformed her. Her fox-body cowered behind his human one. Her father grew angrier. The situation was becoming dangerous.

"Watch yourself. I'm a man with nothing left to lose," her father warned, his body growing larger and furrier by the second.

"I'm telling you to *leave*," Owen's voice deepened with newfound aggression.

"I'm not leaving here without her. Not again. Not to you," the beast declared, mouth now full of glittering, sharp fangs.

Adelie's consciousness wavered. Was this really happening?

"I WON'T LET YOU TOUCH HER," Owen yelled, his voice cracking with emotion.

A roar from Adelie's deepest nightmares resounded around her. When she blinked, she swore she'd been in that ancient courthouse this whole time. Instead, she was still in the forest, her fox body on all fours and Owen standing in front of her. Her father crashed to the ground on mighty bear paws that rumbled the duck pond.

"Adelie, go–!"

Owen's shout was cut short by one of those paws slashing across his chest. His guttural scream pierced her nervous system. She dashed from beneath him just as he fell, his blood coloring the pond's brackish surface. The bear slipped on the bank's mud, giving Owen a moment to move. Though in obvious pain, he scrambled to his feet and ducked behind a boulder. The bear groaned in annoyance and leapt on top of the rock, bounding off it and rounding on Owen in one swift movement. Owen clutched his chest—just like he'd done with Adelie mere moments ago—and spit blood from his bleeding lip in the bear's direction. He used the boulder as leverage to stand up and run. Adelie watched the scene unfold from close by.

Both of these men had hurt her. Both of them had lied, disappeared, and returned as different versions of themselves. One she shared blood with. One she shared her deepest, darkest thoughts and secrets with.

The bear tripped Owen and grabbed him by the ankle with its teeth. It dragged the screaming boy through the dirt.

She wanted to move, but her body wouldn't let her. She didn't know what she should do. That is, until she caught a flash of the bear's eye looking at hers. It was dark, black, even. It was different than it'd been back at the courthouse. Then, though black, a shred of humanity had still been buried in its irises. It had still been her dad. He'd come through and stopped himself. Now, when she looked at the creature, she saw nothing but rage. Nothing was left. This was it. There was no coming back from this. There was no love. There was no father. However, there was still a friend being mangled under this bear's monstrous form. There was still Owen.

There was only one thing she *could* do.

The bear mauled Owen, its jaws breaking the arm he used to protect his face. He yowled in agony as more of his blood spilled to the forest floor. Heavy paws pressed down on his abdomen. A stranger's words emerged in Adelie's mind.

"Sometimes, the easiest thing in life is to give up when you're down, but... You, Adelie, you seem like a girl with fire in your heart. Don't let anything douse it. Keep fighting, okay?"

Adelie's body turned human again. Her fingers slipped into her pocket and pulled out her knife.

A box appeared in the father's hands. He opened it, revealing a pocketknife.

"I always had this to keep me safe from those who might harm me. When you get a little older, it'll keep you safe too."

Adelie held the knife to her chest and closed her eyes. Her face twitched. She didn't have time to think— only act.

Dad, I hope you'll forgive me. I hope you'll find peace. If I die, then know I died trying to free you.

Everything seemed to slow as Adelie hurled herself atop the boulders. Owen's screams continued to echo with the beast's growls. The smell of blood was thick. She gave a final look at the scene before throwing herself atop the bear and gripping his fur for dear life. Time snapped back to normal as she did so. The animal roared in confusion and swung its head around, teeth snapping at the air.

Adelie screeched as she curled her arm around its head and drove the knife into the animal's throat, stabbing it over and over again. She squeezed her legs around its form to keep herself from falling as it bucked defiantly. Again and again she punctured its neck until she was able to slice a clean line through it. Blood bubbled up as the bear cried in pain and rage. Owen lay beneath it all, face stunned and covered in red.

Eventually, the bear was able to throw her from its back, Adelie thudding against a tree trunk. The wind was knocked from her and she lay motionless for a few seconds. When she opened her eyes, the bear was upon her, crimson pouring from its windpipe. It was attempting to lift a paw when a final, sad whimper left its throat. Its body buckled and collapsed onto its side.

Adelie took this chance to get back up, one hand cradling her bruised side while the other searched the ground for her knife. She quickly found it and held it above her head with both hands. She was preparing to land a final blow when a deep breath escaped the wounded animal. Looking down, she saw its eyes were fluttering shut and its muscles were loosening.

The young mother held her distressed baby, worry and fear plain on her face. She looked to her family members for help, but they only frowned and called for a nurse. All too soon, those family members had vacated the room completely, leaving an air of disgust behind them. As the teenager held her son, she felt his skin changing in her arms. He was soon covered in fur and sporting a long muzzle. She'd vaguely heard about absorbism before but had never heard of it running in her family. Yet another thing to ridicule her for.

The bear cub lashed out and scratched her chest. Red marks formed across her collarbone. She teared up with pain but held him close to her.

"Shh, it's not your fault," she whispered.

Peace washed over the animal, a peace that Adelie had never seen in anyone—or anything—before. When its soul left its body, both relief and guilt took over her. She let the knife fall from her fingers as she dropped down next to her father. She buried her face in his fur momentarily and remained surprisingly composed. When she wiped her face, it became smeared with his blood. Owen's weak voice stopped her from continuing.

"A-Adelie—?"

Adelie moved her attention to her injured friend. Though she was shaking, she lifted Owen's torso and held his head up. He was utterly soaked in crimson, some his, some her father's. He undoubtedly had at least a broken arm and several fractured ribs. His ankle was probably broken, too. He was still conscious but wouldn't be for much longer. His eyes were fluttering like her dad's had just been. Surprisingly, he still had the strength to speak.

"Did you—is he–?"

"Yeah. It's over," Adelie responded gruffly.

"I'm sorry," he sighed and sagged in her arms.

"Owen, I'm gonna get help, okay? Please, stay with me," she pleaded.

With one hand she held up her friend and with the other she took out her phone. She called 911. When the call was done, she tucked it back in her pocket and hoisted Owen up. He tried to stand, but his ankle made it too painful. Instead, she supported his weight and carried them both to the road to wait.

She left the knife with its rightful owner. There was death that day.

❖

An ambulance ride later, both Adelie and Owen were being treated at the hospital. Adelie's injuries were relatively minor. She had some major bruising but no broken bones. Doctors cleaned her up quickly. Owen, on the other hand, was in bad shape. Her suspicions were correct: deep scratches across his chest, a broken arm, ankle, and a couple broken ribs. His arms and torso were covered in extensive bruising and he'd lost a lot of blood.

Adelie waited outside of his room, leg bouncing anxiously with her face in her hands. Marianne was there, too. She'd been called shortly after they'd arrived at the facility. Adelie was done being examined and the two of them finally got to talk. Marianne had only heard the short version of the entire story. The white hospital halls flickered with yellow light. Everything was squeaky clean. Adelie could practically see her face in the shiny floors.

Marianne touched Adelie's shoulder. The redhead jumped and revealed her face.

"Adelie, what exactly happened? How is Owen here? I feel like there's more than what the doctor and nurses said," she asked with deep concern.

Adelie nodded slowly, eyes flicking around as she tried to sum up the ordeal. Her brain was already trying to repress this day.

"I-I had gone out to the woods for a bit while you were working. I know I shouldn't have. I'm sorry. I'm so stupid," her face grew angry with self-hatred.

Despite the growth in the last few months, the daughter still expected her mom to be angry, to scold her. Punish her more than she had already been punished by her actions. Instead, her shoulder was being rubbed comfortingly.

"It's okay. I'm just glad you're alright."

Adelie sniffled and continued.

"Owen showed up while I was at the duck pond. We were talking and then... dad showed up. He was angry. He wanted to take me away again. Owen stood up for me and they fought. I..."

The next part was hard to get out. It clogged up her throat. After taking a deep breath, the words were able to flow out of her mouth in a whisper.

"I had to kill him. Kill dad. He wasn't himself anymore. I used... the knife he gave me a long time ago. I'm sorry," Adelie's lip trembled.

The hand on Adelie's shoulder squeezed harder but it didn't hurt.

"It's not your fault. I'm sure you did what you had to do. Owen could've died," Marianne said through newfound tears, her free hand clutching her own face.

"I know... but then why does it still feel so wrong?"

"Because he was your father, regardless of everything."

"Yeah. I guess so. It just really sucks," Adelie stared at the tile floor.

After a few hours, a nurse approached them. Both women wiped at their faces and focused their attention on them.

"I know you two are not immediate family, but his biological father refuses to come. You can go inside if you wish. We had to perform surgery on his arm and ankle."

A myriad of feelings whirled in Adelie's head but she pushed them aside so she could see her friend. She could be angry about Mr. Smit later. Inside, Owen was in a hospital bed and hooked up to fluids. He had a couple white braces on, and his eyes were closed. The sheets on his lifted bed were light blue. A ring hung in a half-circle around him, the curtains pushed to the side to allow entry. A window on the far right let sunlight into the room just above two visit chairs.

"He's resting, as you can imagine," the nurse explained.

Marianne spoke to the nurse as Adelie stood by Owen's bedside.

"He's gonna be alright, isn't he?"

"Yes. He's sustained quite a lot, but he's young and strong. He just needs to stay under our watch for a little while so he can recover enough to go home."

Adelie held Owen's good hand. It had scratches on it.

"You've been through a lot too, young lady. Perhaps you should go home and rest? He's safe here with us," the nurse suggested to Adelie gently.

"Good luck persuading her," Adelie's mom laughed lightly.

"I see. Well, I'll be back to check on you guys in a bit," they said as they left the room.

Now that they had privacy, Adelie's mom hugged her daughter from behind.

Adelie didn't feel the hug. She just stared at Owen. She internally urged him to wake up. To talk to him again. To make sure he was okay. To thank him. To get the story he was going to tell her before they were attacked.

She decided it was a selfish thought and stayed in the room with him instead. Noise only came from nurses, the beep of Owen's monitor, and her mother's sobs while she grieved her deceased husband. Adelie didn't have any more tears left.

The two women slept on cots in Owen's hospital room that night.

❖

When morning came, so, too, did Owen's consciousness. Adelie immediately stirred from her fitful sleep. In a second, she was at his bedside, her hair in knots.

"Hey," his voice cracked out.

"Hey. How are you feeling?"

"Like shit," he laughed a little.

"Me too. Do you want your nurse?"

Owen shook his head. He groaned as he tried to make himself more comfortable.

"So, my old man didn't show up, huh?"

"No. I'm sorry."

"Figures. Whatever," he replied casually, though his tone said otherwise.

"I wanna talk. I wanna say the things I didn't get to say yesterday," he declared with a wheezing chest.

"Maybe we could talk later. Your ribs must be killing you."

Words were tumbling from Owen's mouth anyway. She pulled the privacy curtain around them as a shield.

"I didn't mean to lie. I don't know why I did, other than to try to keep you safe. That didn't work out so well. I guess I've just been lying my whole life so it's what comes easiest to me," he admitted shamefully.

"Are... there other things you've lied about? With me?"

It took Owen a few seconds to answer.

"Yes, there's something else," Owen replied in an exhale.

"I never, ever meant to hurt you, Adelie. Please know that. You mean so much to me. You're my best friend! I found out about your dad and I saw him. I saw his true colors and I didn't want him to get to you because he was just so far gone—" he rambled on, sweat beading on his forehead and his heart rate monitor beeping faster.

"Then I went to college, and everything got worse. I fell apart with Jace. I couldn't do it. My dad was in my head—still is—and I was scared I was gonna become him and hurt everyone around me. I started drinking. A lot. I failed my classes and got kicked out. I was on the streets for a while until I found my brother, Andres. He helped me. He got me a bus ticket to come back here and talk to you. I haven't stopped thinking about you since last summer," the heart monitor continued to speed up.

Marianne had woken up and peaked inside the privacy curtain. Owen paused, chest heaving with the heaviness of his words and the severity of his injuries.

"What's going on?"

"Mom, can you keep the nurses out? Please?"

Her mom sensed the urgency of the conversation and nodded. She stood watch at the door. Adelie turned her attention back to Owen.

"I'm listening," she put her hand on his leg gently.

The sight made Owen grit his teeth and close his eyes.

"I'm just so, so sorry, Adelie. I can't say it enough. I've been hurting and I'm sure you have, too. This is so hard for me to even talk about. It's always been my job to hold onto things, I guess. Ever since I was a kid," his free hand rubbed at his forehead.

"Tell me. You can be honest with me."

"It's so hard. It hurts," his voice was strained with the effort of honesty.

"I know. I won't hurt you, though," Adelie reassured.

"I never had a dead friend with absorbism. That was a lie, too."

His heart rate quickened even more. His face twitched. The whites of his eyes turned black and spilled hot tears all over his cheeks and bedsheets. A floodgate had been torn open.

I've never seen him cry before. He looks different. What's happening?

"I just, I—I—"

He covered his face, but one hand wasn't enough to conceal everything. His teeth chattered and sharpened, much like how Adelie's would. She stared incredulously. When he moved his hand again to speak, fur was sprouting around his now canine-like eyes. His voice came out in short, sharp, congested spurts.

"I'm sorry! I'm so sorry! I'm sorry!"

Black and white fur spread across his arms and poked through his hospital gown. The casts were the only things to not get engulfed in it. Owen continued to shake and gasp as his body shrank, face narrowing, fingers conjoining together into paws. The new form lay upon the bed with a whine. The heart rate monitor and fluids came undone and hung limply.

A dog was sitting in front of her. A black and white husky. It was Ace. Owen was Ace. He whimpered and stared at her with remorseful sky-blue eyes. Adelie vaguely heard her mom telling a nurse to give them a moment.

"Adelie, I can't keep them away much longer. What is going on?"

Adelie couldn't answer. She kept staring at Ace—well, Owen. He'd been an Absorber this entire time. A million things started to make connections in her mind.

His mother died in childbirth. His emotion must be sadness. That's why I've never seen him sad or crying. He's hid it. He's been hiding it his whole life, so he hid other things, too. He saw me on the news at the courthouse when I was little. It probably scared him even more into hiding.

She thought back to those encounters in the forest, his absence at Jeremy's death and funeral, the impeccable timing of Ace defending her from her father's attempted kidnapping. It all made sense.

This is what my dad meant by a "rematch." He must've tracked him and fended him off numerous times, even before last summer. It's not like he didn't have plenty of things to be sad about with Mr. Smit around. He kept his morale low.

The longer Adelie stared and pondered, the more and more nervous Owen looked. He curled in on himself and whined, not daring to look her in the eyes.

He saved my life. He's been sad for so, so long, yet he stuck with me and protected me. I get it now. I'm not mad.

"Owen, I forgive you."

His ears perked at that. He sat up.

"I forgive you. I forgive everything. God, it all makes sense now," she leaned in and hugged around his neck.

A cry escaped his throat at the affection. He clung to her and dug his nose into her shoulder.

"It's okay. I forgive you, Owen," she squeezed him tighter.

She'd never felt closer to him. Her absorbism soon took over and she wrapped around him, fox tail curling over him in comfort. She didn't have to say anything else.

I love you. I forgive you.

The two canids enveloped each other in warmth, acceptance, and love. Marianne checked on them and was shocked to see the scene in front of her. Yet, she found herself smiling. Things started to make sense to her, too. She quickly walked out the room to make sure no one else disturbed them.

Owen was the one to turn back first. He sniffled and wiped at his face. Adelie curled up in his lap and let him pet her.

"I was so scared to tell you. I couldn't. I've always been told not to," he hiccupped.

"B-But, I'm glad you know, now. Thank you for forgiving me," he held her close and rested his cheek on her soft fur.

When she eventually changed back, she carefully gave him a hug. However, not carefully enough. He winced and yelped with pain.

"Okay, let's get the nurse back in here now, mom," Adelie called out.

Marianne heard her and opened the door. A flock of nurses came flooding in. Adelie moved away just in time for them to overcome Owen and get him hooked back up to everything. They also gave him a scolding or two. He smiled sheepishly and scratched his neck. Adelie shrugged and sent him a teasing grin. He grinned back.

<u>Chapter 5</u>

Being in the hospital meant that Owen had a lot of idle time to kill. So did Adelie. Naturally, she visited him every day after her work shifts, sometimes staying overnight. She filled him in on the status of her and her mom's relationship. Marianne would bring them food and movies to watch in his room. Their friendship had returned to its former glory. Maybe it was even stronger than before. They talked incessantly, continuing to catch up with each other's lives.

"How long were you out on the streets after being kicked out of school?"

"I lost track of time. Probably two or three weeks before Andres found me. Honestly, I think my absorbism was the only thing that saved me. I was in a dark place. I still kind of am, but it was way worse. I was sad all the time. That dog nose helped me find food," he laughed wryly.

"Hm. We'll have to fatten you up once you're done with this hospital food," Adelie half-joked.

"I think your mom's already trying to. You've seen all the stuff she's been bringing in. I'm not exactly complaining, though," he clarified as he bit into some chips.

"Me neither," she agreed as she chomped on some gummy worms.

The notion of being brought food reminded her of the two kits she was caring for back home. Owen didn't know about that yet. She stopped eating.

"So, a few weeks ago, I had to bring Aspen and Maple to my house during a snowstorm. They were sick and definitely wouldn't have lasted the night in that weather. It was almost impossible to even drive through the backroads," she explained.

Owen hung on her every word, eyes wide.

"Wow... are they still at your place?"

"Mhm, they're in our garage. They're doing good. I only wish I could take them back to the woods. Of course, it's not really safe there anymore. Your dad has continued his antics," she sighed.

"Of course he has," he rolled his eyes, "but I'm excited to see the kits again.I'm glad to be back," his annoyed expression turned into a smile.

The smile faded after just a few seconds.

"Still, I miss our friends. I miss Jace. I really fucked things up," he vented.

"How so?"

"I dunno. Just had my dad in my head all the time. I got into drinking more than I should have," he sighed.

"Oh," Adelie breathed.

"I hurt him. All I was doing was hurting him. It's for the best that I left."

"You don't know that. Have you talked to him since then?"

"No. He's better off without me," he looked away.

"You don't know that! I bet he'd hear you out. *I* heard you out, after all," Adelie encouraged.

It took him a moment to respond. His body had become rigid but was soon relaxing again.

"That was kind of you," he admitted, a smile returning to his face.

"Maybe. I dunno. After this, I think I'll return to my brother. He said I could live with him. Maybe then I'll reach out to Jace again," he said, thoughts running behind his eyes.

"I think that's a good plan. I wish I could come with you."

"Me too," Owen replied wistfully.

"It's okay. My mom and I have to stay and kick your dad's ass."

Owen laughed at that. Adelie kept talking.

"So, did you lose your phone while you were...?"

"My dad shut it off when I was kicked out of college. Then it got stolen. Not fun."

"Damn, I'm sorry."

"It's alright."

Speaking of phones...

"Y'know your dad smashed my phone while you were gone? I had to get a new one," she informed him with a nonchalant tone.

Owen stiffened and looked like he was about to spring out of bed.

"He did *what!?!*"

Adelie was, but also wasn't, surprised to see him react so strongly. Gentle hands pushed him back down. He breathed heavily and grit his teeth.

"It's fine, it was a while ago. Besides, you can't be doing that while you're still recovering," she urged.

Owen followed her order and laid down but his face remained angry.

"He's such a piece of shit. That kind of stuff was normal for me, but for *you?* No. That's low, even for him," he spat out.

Seeing Owen this angry was definitely something new for Adelie. Well, he was angry during the fight with her dad and she had seen small snippets of it in the past, but this felt different. More personal.

"Yeah, it was... pretty shitty of him. It was because I showed him those pictures I took of them stomping on that fox. Dumb move on my part, but–"

"Don't take the blame. It's not your fault. It's his. He can go fuck himself," he growled, unbroken arm's hand clenching the bed sheets.

While they were on this subject, Adelie decided she might as well tell him what *else* happened that day.

"He also... slapped my mom too. He was trying to silence me with his hand when my mom got him off of me."

Owen's heart monitor beeped faster.

"H-How *dare* he. He can go to Hell for that. For everything he's ever done to me, to you, my brother, and to this town. He deserves to be dead," the words were tossed out in rapid succession from snarling lips.

It was nice to see Owen being able to freely say these things but he needed to calm down for his health's sake. Maybe she shouldn't have mentioned these things. She should've realized how upset he would be.

"Hey, I agree with you, but I'm okay, right? My mom's okay too. He hasn't bothered us again since then, either."

Her words slowly pulled the outrage from his features. His face deflated and he threw his head back against his pillow.

"I should've stayed. I should've been here. I know we got in that fight, and you wouldn't have wanted to see me, but... Maybe I could've stopped all that from happening," he sighed somberly and stared at the ceiling.

Adelie reached forward and squeezed his hand.

"You don't know what would've happened. Plus, if that hadn't happened, my mom and I might've not had our talk. Not saying it was okay, but please don't worry about it. I just thought you should know," she urged him.

The injured boy lay quietly for a few moments before nodding. He turned to her, those angry eyes now empty.

"I'm sorry. Anger has been an issue for me since getting more into drinking," he apologized with genuine guilt.

Adelie shook her head and held his hand tighter.

"I'm sure that's hard. You have the right to be that angry. Your father is an awful, awful person. I'll never forgive him for the things he's done, especially to you."

He sucked in a deep breath and then exhaled. He smiled and replied with humor rather than sorrow.

"Yeah. Like you said, his nickname's 'Dick' for a reason, right?"

There he is. There's the Owen I know.

"No doubt," she grinned, recounting the texts they had sent to each other long ago.

He grinned back. She let go of his hand and leaned back in her chair. A thought occurred to her.

"It's almost funny how both of our lives have had to be... *carved* around our absorbism. Dealing with it hasn't been funny, but just the fact that both of us have so much in common, more than I ever thought we did."

They both looked up at the ceiling while they talked. Owen laughed a little, his sour mood now gone.

"Yeah, you're right. I love Jace and the others but I've never bonded with them over these things, y'know? I didn't have anyone to talk to about this until now. I never thought I'd get to meet the girl from the news, much less be her friend."

He was talking about the courthouse fiasco. A twinge of pain filled her chest but quickly dissipated. In fact, she smiled wider than before. That was simply his way of giving a compliment.

"I never thought I'd get to be friends with the former high school bully... Speaking of the others, why didn't you tell us about you being Ace at the lake house?"

Owen fiddled with the bed cover.

"I've always been told to keep my true self hidden. To lie, even to my friends. I was so close to saying it but Jace beat me to the punch. After he kissed me, I shut myself down. 'Another time', I thought. Stupid me."

Adelie looked away from the ceiling to gawk at Owen in disbelief.

"Wait, so even Jace doesn't know?"

He shook his head.

"No. My father doesn't know, either. Only you, your mom, and my brother know."

Adelie blinked and settled back in her seat to focus on the ceiling once again.

"Wow. You really have been good at concealing yourself. I imagine you've had to… really stifle your emotions to do that?"

Owen visibly shook and nodded fast.

"Yeah," his voice cracked with vulnerability.

The sound broke her heart.

"You don't have to anymore. Not with me or my mom, at least."

His lip had begun to tremble, transformation trying to take hold, but it stopped. His smile returned.

"Yeah. Thank you."

"Don't mention it."

Another quiet moment passed between them. Owen nestled more into his bed to try to get some sleep. He said one more thing before doing so.

"When we get to your place, we should try to find our friends' phone numbers. Bringing us all together again would be good," he suggested, though a hint of hesitance lined his words.

Adelie guessed it was due to his relations with Jace. She was proud to hear this nonetheless.

"Yeah, that would be good. I actually already have their numbers. Colby came through town recently and put everyone's numbers on my new phone."

Owen looked surprised, relieved, but also still nervous.

"Oh, even better. Yeah, we'll do that," he replied, seemingly pushing past his uncertainty.

❖

Once Owen was literally—and figuratively—back on his feet, he was discharged. Back on his feet was an overstatement, actually. Between the cast on his leg and the one on his arm, his movement would be restricted for a while. The Hendersons brought him to their home to stay for as long as he wanted. The living room couch became his bed, blankets and a large pillow set out for him.

The three of them ate dinner together as a family for the first time that night. It'd been a long time since there'd been a third member in the Henderson home. It was full of laughter and... *warmth*, something Adelie had been starved of for so long. No longer did she need to pretend and hope that her father would be sitting at this table with them again. He was at peace, somewhere he should've been a long time ago. Now *Owen* could be at peace where he belonged– within safe walls and at Adelie's side.

This being said, she was surprised by Owen's words that evening.

"You guys can send me out as soon as I'm better. I don't want to be a bother," he urged as Adelie helped him lay down.

"You're the farthest from it. I promise," Adelie said as she handed him a blanket.

Owen made himself comfortable and sighed.

"Alright, if you're sure."

"Of course I am, now hush and go to sleep," she teased and stood up.

Owen waved his hand playfully.

"Yeah, yeah, alright," he laughed and closed his eyes.

Adelie clicked off the nearby lamp when a lightbulb of her own lit up. She stood still in the darkness for a minute and took a deep breath. Owen had opened one eye when he realized she was still standing by him.

"I do have a question for you, though," Adelie piped up.

"I'm all ears."

"How have you not started to lose yourself to absorbism yet?"

Owen was quiet for a few moments.

"I guess I've just stifled myself so much that it's prolonged my life. Funny how that works."

"I see… I've been having a lot of trouble hanging on, lately," she sighed.

Owen sat up and looked her way. He couldn't see her very well, but he could feel the desperation in her words.

"Really, are you sure you want me here? I don't want to cut your time even shorter," he worriedly replied, blue eyes trying to find golden ones in the dark.

"No. I don't want you to go. I'd rather only live a day more with those I love than live forever and be alone. I should've learned that lesson from the start. I made that mistake with Jeremy. Never again."

❖

Owen saw Adelie's first bout of uncontrolled absorbism the very next morning. She was heading down from her room when she abruptly stopped and fell onto the steps. Adelie gasped and pushed at her forehead but to no avail, teeth chattering and fur beginning to emerge all over her body. Her friend tried to get up from the couch but couldn't on his own. Panicky blue eyes watched from afar.

"A-Adelie? Are you okay?"

He didn't get a reply. She was soon replaced with a wild fox. He was helpless, unable to move under the restraint of his casts as it flew down the stairs and bashed right into the back sliding glass door. It rolled onto the floor, limbs flailing with abandon. It jumped to its feet and looked around fearfully, teeth visible as it screamed. The sound shook Owen to his core. He'd seen her dad taken over by his animal form before, but to see Adelie going through it was absolutely haunting. Owen was about to call out for Marianne when she popped out of her bedroom. The mother became just as paralyzed as Owen, eyes staring at the animal like it could've been a ghost.

"Oh my gosh, Adelie?"

There was nothing in the fox's amber eyes, just animalistic fear and agitation. Marianne looked around frantically and settled on grabbing one of the blankets on the couch. She swept it up and held it in front of herself, creeping closer to her transformed daughter.

"It's okay, it's okay," she repeated while slowly walking over in its direction.

The closer she got to it, the more distressed it became, screeching and wrapping its tail around itself defensively. A few seconds later, it was bolting past her. To Marianne's luck, she was able to jump on and cover the fox with her blanket. It kicked around erratically, claws almost poking through the fabric, but not quite. The mother struggled to keep hold of the animal but she wouldn't give up. She remained crouched over it, hugging it tightly, body bouncing when an especially good kick was placed. Tears were streaming down her face. Owen tried to get up again. Marianne spotted him.

"No, Owen, don't. You'll only hurt yourself more," she ordered.

He looked as if he wondered how he could feel any more emotionally and physically hurt. His scleras started to darken. It wouldn't be long until he transformed, too.

Marianne choked on sobs as the fox slowly calmed down, muffled screeching and fighting gone. She held its swaddled form in her arms like a newborn child. Wheezing breaths could be heard from underneath the cloth. It tugged on Owen's heart. His teeth chattered. He remained silent, waiting to see what would happen next. Marianne continued to cry. Eventually, the blanket unwrapped itself, Adelie's body gradually returning and slipping out from underneath it. She simply stared at the ceiling, face emotionless. Marianne clung to her. Owen held his breath. Adelie spoke plainly.

"It was bad, wasn't it?"

The weeping mother nodded her head against Adelie's chest. Owen began to shift as he settled back down onto the couch. Fur grew through his clothes.

"Yeah, it was," he answered just as plainly.

Adelie's face twisted in defeat.

"I figured."

❖

Owen continued to stay. He was able to remove his casts after two more weeks. Adelie switched form constantly. She stopped working at the café. Her mom did the same. She'd faulted her daughter too many times to not spend as much time with her during her last days. They would make do.

Adelie, despite her ever-growing condition, wanted them both there with her. If she could sacrifice herself for the kits, surely, she could sacrifice herself for them, too. Besides, when she *was* able to stay present, she felt very happy and content. Almost felt like a kid again.

However, when she did shift without human conscience, Owen and Marianne now had to resort to locking her in her room to wait out the storm. Even Aspen and Maple had to stay away from her. The wild fox paced around and screamed. It scratched the walls and tried to dig under doors. It shredded her bed sheets. Often, they'd come back to the room to find her asleep amongst the feathers, sometimes human, sometimes not. The whole process was exhausting for both parties. Still, they wanted to support one another, so they allowed it to become a routine for yet another week.

Unbeknownst to Adelie, during that week, Owen had been reaching out to Damien and Colby, courtesy of Adelie's phone. He didn't have the strength to talk to Jace directly, but his friends were gracious enough to do that for him. Arrangements were set in motion for the gang to meet up again, and the scheduled day was soon upon them.

Owen was so thankful that Adelie was feeling well enough to go outside. The two friends wandered out to the Hendersons' front yard. Adelie tucked a thin red hair behind her ear and smiled. It had been raining lately, so it was nice to have a sky void of clouds. Even so, she had grown to feel physically cold most days, so her other hand clutched at the jacket she wore over her casual wear.

"It feels good out here," she commented.

"Yeah," Owen agreed, though his eyes were transfixed on the end of the neighborhood's road rather than on the weather itself.

Adelie wasn't subdued enough to not notice this. She poked his shoulder.

"Hey, what're you staring at?"

Owen twitched at the question. When he didn't answer after a few moments, Adelie only grew more determined to get to the bottom of the boy's behavior. She completely turned her body in the direction of his stare. Despite everything, her stubbornness was far from gone.

"You're acting weird. Is something going on?"

The raven-haired boy glanced at her and opened his mouth. He appeared to be struggling to put his words together. Adelie watched his peculiar stuttering, but soon enough, she was now the one to become very interested in scoping out what was happening at the end of the road. A vehicle had turned the corner and was heading toward them– a familiar one. Adelie gawked at the sight of it.

"Wait, is that...?"

Owen turned around to see Jace's vehicle tumbling down the crumbly asphalt road. He cracked a smile at Adelie's reaction, but his eyes showed apprehension. Colby and Damien stuck their heads out opposing windows on the car and waved their arms in greeting. Adelie's pale, flushed face brightened like the sun that hung above them, bringing color to her cheeks. She almost couldn't believe what she was seeing. It'd been such a long time, and it was such a pleasant surprise to see them again— now more than ever. The redhead shook Owen's shoulders excitedly. His head swung back and forth.

"You— how did you put this together?"

She stopped shaking him to allow him the chance to speak. He blinked quickly to override the dizziness and pushed stray hairs from his eyes.

"I stole your phone. I figured you wouldn't mind," he admitted with a snaggle toothed grin.

Adelie didn't get the chance to reply. Their friends rolled into the driveway, Damien and Colby practically leaping out of the vehicle toward Owen and Adelie. Colby was about to swoop Adelie up into a hug when Owen jumped in between them. Colby skidded to a stop.

"You can't be doing that, remember?"

Owen was obviously referring to Adelie's condition. Colby nodded slowly with a sheepish smile.

"Oh, right, sorry," he apologized, the embarrassment expression quickly turning into a mischievous one.

"You're not off the hook, though."

Owen's blue eyes blew wide as the taller boy scooped Owen up with extreme ease. Colby squeezed him tight enough for the smaller boy to nearly choke. Meanwhile, Damien had stepped toward Adelie much more calmly. She gladly accepted his hug just as Colby was setting Owen back on the ground.

The driver, of course, was the last to emerge from the vehicle, his pale hands finally losing their grip on the steering wheel. Jace stepped out and into the sunshine, shade from the tree near Adelie's window spreading darker dapples along his skin. He looked at Owen, whose legs refused to stop shaking. This eye contact was long overdue, *closure* long overdue. A few yards stood between the two boys. The group backed away to give them some space. Adelie held her breath, her friends appearing to do the same. How would this reunion go?

There was silence, only silence. Well, except for the fluttering of birds and the creaking of branches that swayed with the steady breeze. The light gel in Jace's hairdo failed to stand up to the wind, threads of brown hair sweeping across his forehead. Owen's dark mop of hair grew messier than usual. He succeeded in stepping a few feet forward with his hands stuffed in his pockets. Blue eyes momentarily veered away from green ones. His voice crawled from his lips as if tied to an invisible string, tugging back over and over to stutter the words that came out.

"Jace, I-I know I r-really messed up. Y-You don't have to stay, but–"

Owen hadn't noticed Jace stepping closer as he spoke. The trembling boy hardly had time to look up before Jace was upon him, pulling him into a tight hug. Owen's eyes widened and blinked in shock as his head rested just past Jace's left shoulder. Jace held him close, his own head resting on Owen's opposing shoulder. The others watched on.

"I'm so glad you're okay," Jace replied before Owen could even catch his breath.

When he did, the beginnings of tears were pricking at the corners of his eyes. His mouth twisted in confusion.

"But... But I treated you so badly. Why?"

"I knew you were in pain, that you didn't mean it," he paused to lean back, one hand petting Owen's back soothingly.

"When you disappeared, I tried my best to find you but couldn't. Now you're here and I–" he pressed his forehead to Owen's, "I'm so relieved."

"Jace," was all Owen could say, practically no louder than an exhale.

He withdrew his hands from his pockets and gripped the back of Jace's shirt like he might fly away at any second. Their noses bumped together.

"I'm sorry. I'm so, *so* sorry. I'm sorry," Owen repeated through a hitched throat.

Hot, salty tears were now rolling down Owen's cheeks. Jace pulled back to wipe them away but halted when black and white fur began to sprout across Owen's face, the sclera of his blue eyes turning dark. The brown-haired boy blinked in shock and took a step back. The group nearby shuffled over to see what had happened. Everyone's jaws dropped except for Adelie's.

Owen peered down at his trembling hands, which were now melding their fingers together into paws. A few teardrops landed on them. Chattering canine teeth bore through his gums. The ashamed Absorber lifted his head and flicked his eyes between Jace and his friends, who were staying a reasonable distance away from the transforming boy.

Apologies continued to fly out of his chapped lips while his body shrank and hunched over. The bridge of his nose grew longer into a proper muzzle. Thick fur grew over his clothes, concealing the last bits of his human essence. He struggled to continue to talk as his mouth stretched, but he pushed himself to speak.

"I-I'm sorry. I'm sorry. This is something else I kept from you all– please, please don't leave, I–"

His last words were cut off by the completion of his husky form. Ace stood before them, tail between his legs and pricked ears flattened. He looked at the humans with a pleading stare. Damien massaged his forehead and was the first to speak.

"Wait, so you were Ace this whole time?"

Owen tucked his head into his chest fur.

"Holy shit," Jace whispered and combed his brunette hair back.

Fear shown in the husky's eyes at Jace's reaction.

"Oh my god... that makes sense now. Plus, you're so *cute* like this," Colby added, stepping closer and crouching down to Ace's level.

The positive praise made Ace's tail wag slightly, but it wasn't enough to show that he was completely accepted yet. Damien and Jace appeared to be lost for words, Damien still rubbing his forehead and spouting out questions.

"You're an Absorber? How– How did you keep this secret so well?"

Since Owen could not speak for himself yet, Adelie stepped in.

"I only found out about this after he came back to see me. He's got some good reasons... but he can tell you those himself once he's transformed back. For now, though," the redhead walked up to Ace and scratched a spot behind his now pricked ears.

"How about we show him some love, huh? This hasn't been easy for him."

Colby gladly followed her suggestion and joined in by scratching under the husky's chin. Damien walked over and trailed his hand along Ace's back fur. Regardless of the confusion in his eyes, he still smiled. Adelie felt the hair at the back of her neck rise. The dog's tail began to wag a bit more, though it held back as it waited for the last person to interact with it– Jace. He stiffly stood beside the scene and simply stared for a few seconds. Adelie glanced up with worried eyes whilst the other two boys kept their attention on Ace. Would Jace reject him?

Before she knew it, Jace had made a fell swoop down to the husky and was giving him a side hug on one knee. It was clear that he was still as puzzled as Damien was about the situation, but there was still love in his eyes– acceptance. While Jace squeezed him tight, Owen's tail wagged impossibly fast. Adelie's body shook and fell backwards, tugging her hand away from petting the now-happy dog. Everyone stopped to turn their attention to her. She transformed much more quickly than Owen into her fox form, most likely from how severe her symptoms had become. Thankfully, she was able to keep her consciousness clear. Lifting herself up, she strolled over to the larger canine and leaned against his side happily. The dog yipped and whined excitedly, paws tamping the ground beneath him.

It wasn't too long before Owen was rising onto his hindlegs to stand above his friends as his human self. Fur drew back to uncover his regular skin and clothes. Front, furry toes peeled away to become hands once again. That long dog muzzle retreated backwards into a human nose. When his normal eyes were revealed, they were crying tears of joy rather than sadness. A beaming grin plastered itself across his face. Much like he and his friends had done to Adelie back at the lake house, the boys circled him and pulled him into a group hug. The vixen weaved around one of his legs. She fought to hang onto her consciousness for her friend's sake.

Owen held his face in his hands as he sniffled and caught his breath. When he faced them all again, he accepted the hug wholeheartedly, stretching out his arms to tangle them in his friends' embrace.

Chapter 6

Jace, Damien, and Colby stayed at their respective homes but came to the Henderson home often. Owen texted his brother about his promise to stay until his friend's final day. A few more weeks passed, summer fading into fall. A few times they caught glances of Mr. Smit from Adelie's upstairs window, but no confrontations.

Adelie dreamt often. She saw visions of those she'd loved and lost. She saw them beckoning to her, hands and paws soft and welcoming. When she woke from such dreams, pain and dread immediately seized her. Nothing could soothe the crying outbursts of pain that resulted from it. Even Owen's canine form did little to comfort her.

Sometimes Adelie shifted in her mother's arms, claws scratching, teeth biting. This only made her hold her daughter tighter. Eventually the vixen would tire and fall asleep in her lap. Her human form was becoming harder and harder to come by. At this point, most of her day was spent pacing her room or sleeping.

It was just after 8 AM on a Sunday. Adelie was asleep in her room upstairs. Jace, Damien, and Colby had arrived and were sitting at the dining room table with Marianne and Owen.

"I think… we should start talking to her about what *she* would like to do. I don't think she's really said," Owen sighed and ran a hand through his thick, dark hair.

"Yes. She deserves to make that choice," Marianne agreed.

"As if she'd ever let any of us decide that for her," Damien added with a light laugh.

The sentiment made everyone smile, even for just a moment. What felt like an eternity of silence followed that, only to be disrupted by Owen's voice once again.

"Well, let's go see her, then."

Everyone stood up from their chairs in mutual agreement. The climb up to Adelie's room felt ten years long. Old family portraits smiled at them all along the way, but Owen didn't feel happy. He didn't really know how to feel. He just knew that he had to help his friend however he could, even though he knew he'd be torn to shreds at the end of it all– just like the bed set in Adelie's room.

When they walked in, they were surprised but relieved to see that she was laying blissfully asleep while still in her human form. None of them had ever seen her this peaceful before. Even her mother hadn't since Adelie was just a young child. Adelie contrasted with the state of her room. The curtains at her window were pathetic and falling apart. White walls were covered in deep scratches, splinters of wood collecting on the floor.

These things made it even more apparent that arrangements needed to be formally planned.

It was sunny outside. The windows had to be kept shut due to the risk of her fox-form escaping, but he could tell that the wind was blowing gently. Orange and red leaves dusted the front yard from the giant tree that sat against the house. A few soft, white clouds hung in the blue sky. It was perfect weather. A lump formed in Owen's throat.

"Adelie, hey," he soothed her awake, hand rubbing gently at her shoulder.

"Hm?"

"It's us. You should wake up. It's so nice outside," he fought to sound cheery.

She shifted a little and rubbed at her eyes. He was relieved when she opened them without crying. Sunlight hit her pupils and shriveled them.

"The sun's out," she noted as she looked toward her window.

"It is."

Adelie rose from her bed and leaned against the window frame. Everyone could see how much her body was dwindling. It was ghostly. Though her personality remained the same, the fight in her had disappeared. Owen let her bask in the warmth of the sun for a few moments before breaking the ice, and his heart.

"Adelie, I think it's time you tell us what you'd like to do. Where you'd like to go, I mean."

"Yeah," she answered quietly.

The group looked to Adelie expectedly, hanging on every breath she took. She almost laughed at the looks on their faces.

"Well, don't look so desperate, now," she joked.

She inhaled deeply while the others struggled to smile. Cracking her fingers while filled with thought, she followed up with her answer.

"I think going farther north would be nice. Somewhere over the bridge. I feel like I never got to see enough of it. Then I wouldn't have to worry about that anymore, y'know? It would be my home."

Those words made everyone teary-eyed. Owen clutched the fabric of his jeans and clenched his teeth. Fur was trying to poke through his skin.

"We could just drive up there and pick a spot. Find a trail, maybe. Follow it until it feels right. Away from people would be best. Somewhere secluded," Adelie continued to speak through a stream of consciousness, brown eyes fixed on the sight of Fall outside.

They turned amber in the sunlight.

Not even two days later, it was time. Adelie was finding it hard to eat. To see such a capable person in such a state tore everyone's hearts from their chests. The profound presence of grief in the home was enough to make Owen constantly change form.

Adelie used some of her last ounces of strength to open her bedside drawer. She pulled out five envelopes. She'd been writing letters while being left alone in her room. When she was human, that is. She gave a last glance at the space that had held so many memories despite its short time in her life– her room. It was falling apart, too.

When Adelie's bedroom door opened, she was adorned in a yellow sundress. Small white flowers were scattered across it. It was as if she were dressed for a casket. In a way, she was. In another, it was far from it.

Owen greeted her, slightly taken aback at the stark difference of the dress when compared to her usual clothing. She held out the envelopes to him. They each had a name inscribed on the outside.

"I wrote these for everyone, but you guys can't open them until after, okay?"

"Oh, alright," he agreed and took the letters from her hand gently, as if the statement hadn't made his heart even heavier with hurt.

Before heading downstairs, she pulled the fox figurine that Owen had made her from her dresser. It felt like a lifetime had passed since she received it. She pressed it to his chest.

"Keep this to remember me by," she somehow managed to make her voice both happy and somber.

Owen cracked a small smile.

"You act as if I could ever forget."

They went downstairs together and placed the letters on the kitchen counter. Owen placed the wooden fox on the living room coffee table. He'd come back for it later. Adelie walked around the house to take everything in for the last time. She felt absorbism wash over her every few seconds. She used every bit of energy she had to fight it off for now, especially when thinking about her lost loved ones. Everyone watched Adelie make her rounds of the house without interruption.

The family portraits that journeyed toward her bedroom.

Dad, I hope I get to see you. We'll both be at peace this time.

The Halloween group photo in a frame on the coffee table.

I've missed you, Jeremy. Maybe when we meet again, you'll forgive me.

She closed her eyes and let her mind drift to memories of Birch.

I love you. I hope to see you again soon. Maybe I'll have more kits in my new life.

Caramel eyes opened again. She laced up her trusty boots. The group backed her up. Marianne and Jace grabbed their car keys. Owen could hardly breathe, but he tried to for Adelie's sake.

"Ready?"

"Yeah," she answered without hesitation, "are you?"

"Not really," Owen admitted.

"It's okay," she squeezed his palm.

Crossing the bridge really did always feel like entering a different world. It'd been several years since Adelie had done so. Her last time was a camping trip with her parents when she was much younger, yet it still felt like it was just yesterday. Beyond the dueling Great Lakes' waters was a land of nearly pure wilderness and wildlife. It was just the place for a vixen's fresh start. After St. Ignace, they were all greeted with rocky hills that clung to the sides of the main road. Wildflowers stretched desperately toward the dying warmth of Fall.

Adelie rode with her mother, the kits in cages in the backseat. The boys traveled in Jace's vehicle just behind the Hendersons. Mother and daughter were silent for quite a while. Their relationship would've never been perfect, even if it weren't for the absorbism, but at the very least, it was an improvement. It wasn't something that had to drag down Adelie's rest any longer.

As if on cue, Marianne spoke once they reached the swerving roads of the sand dunes. It was obvious that she'd been holding back tears this entire drive, even if she didn't want to admit it. Pale knuckles held tight to the steering wheel. The sun spread its light across the lake just to the driver's left side, glittering the waves with white.

"I'm sorry, Adelie."

This was something the redhead had heard many times at this point, but it never stopped giving her relief. She had waited so long to hear those words. At first she wasn't sure how to handle it, but now she welcomed it gladly. This time, though, it made her sad. There was so much more to this "sorry," maybe even more so than the first time it was said after leaving Mr. Smit's shop. It was Marianne's last chance to say it, her last chance to show just how much she regretted the time lost to her own selfish behavior.

Adelie, too, wished her mother had come to this conclusion long ago, but what was done is done. She had let go of her resentment long ago– especially for her own sake.

"All is forgiven now, you know that," Adelie reminded.

"I know," Marianne exhaled, "but I didn't want to leave you without saying it just one last time."

❖

It wasn't until the group was about two hours into their drive that Adelie began to feel the extreme *pull* of something, surely nature beckoning her to her new home. As soon as Adelie asked her mother to pull onto an unpaved side street, they all knew that this was it. The vehicles tumbled down the dirt road slowly to allow Adelie to find her bearings. Clouds of dust flew up from their tires as autumn leaves fluttered to and fro in the air. Trees of all colors surrounded them, creating a tight tunnel of beauty. The foxes' auburn coats would surely match their surroundings perfectly.

"Here," Adelie urged after they'd traveled a decent distance from the main road.

Marianna guided the car to the side of the road and brought it to a stop. Jace followed suit. Adelie, of course, was the first one to step outside. She closed her eyes. The air was crisp, cool, and comforting. It smelled almost like that first day back at Orchard Hill, but better—more *alive* somehow, the tanginess of evergreen and maple ever present. Fresh wind blew on her face and caressed her cheeks lovingly. The forest here was thriving, so different from the one she had once come to know. She was thankful. Everyone clambered out from their seats and looked to Adelie for guidance.

"We'll go this way, but I need to let the kits out, first," she answered their silent question while opening the backdoor of her mother's car.

Aspen and Maple hopped out as their cages were clicked open. There was no doubt that they would follow their mother with the utmost loyalty. A couple of the boys stared at the pair in awe, having never seen them before. Adelie took a moment to ensure that everyone was behind her before venturing into the forest.

The hum of neighboring wildlife filled their ears. A nearby river also made its presence known through an echo of running water. Small litterings of leaves covered the forest floor with sporadic clumps of color. They crunched under the force of the group's hike. Red coats and cream tail tips became part of the scenery. Now the humans were the only ones who stood out.

After some time, they all made it to a small clearing. Ferns swathed the area, withering, though they would surely return as green as ever in the spring. There was an undeniable sense of peace here, of safety, of joy. Geese flew in a "V" overhead, while some songbirds would stay to tough it out during the upcoming winter months. Aspen and Maple sniffed about, obviously finding much to hunt and scavenge for. It seemed they wouldn't have to worry too much about famine or disease here, at least not more than what was to be expected from nature's cycles. Man's influence here was minimal.

Adelie took a deep breath and straightened out her back. She was so glad to have been able to make it all the way in here without changing form yet.

"This. This is what I want," she made her decision clear, "I guess I should start the rounds, huh?"

She began with her mother. The two women embraced each other, and Adelie swore she was just a kid again, hugging her mom as if she were the wisest person in the world, the one that would always be the brightest light that carried her through her life, her biggest support. That light had dimmed for a long time. In fact, it was almost extinguished. A small spark was all it took to allow it to illuminate Adelie's life once more, even if it glowed with a different hue. Even so, it was time for her to let it go completely. She no longer needed it. She had created one of her own.

Moving on to Colby, Damien, and Jace, she was trying to decide who to hug first when Colby stepped in and tugged the four of them into a group-hug. She laughed and stretched her arms as wide as she could to accommodate them all. Never had she thought she would be surrounded by friends this true. She hoped that friendships really did last more than one lifetime. This lot meant more to her than words could ever say.

After hugging her mother and other friends, Adelie turned her attention to Owen with a serene smile and opened her arms to him. The teary-eyed boy fell into her embrace immediately, clutching her as if he could stop her from transforming– from *leaving*– but, no. That would be selfish, not to mention impossible. It still didn't stop him from holding onto her for dear life. He hunched his back and dug his face into the crook of her neck and shoulder, sobs racking his body just as much as his absorbism was. Maybe she should've been crying too, but no tears would come. Adelie wrapped her arms around him and gently tapped his back.

Though she would absolutely miss all these important people from her human life, she felt at peace. Utter peace. Maybe this was how her dad had felt when he died.

"Y-You're so brave, Adelie. The bravest person I–I know," Owen's slightly muffled words spewed out between gasps of breath.

"Don't sell yourself short. You're brave too, much braver than the Owen I met two years ago," Adelie reassured him with a light laugh.

A small chuckle broke through his clogged throat. He pulled away and looked at her, bits of fur sprouting across his face and his sharpened teeth chattering. His brow was furrowed, and he tried to hide his grimace with a genuine smile. Blue eyes bore a million emotions. He held one of her hands.

"I'll make sure to remember that," he promised.

"Good. You better," Adelie demanded with a poke to his ribs.

Owen's body sometimes shied away from the familiar manhandling by his friends, but not this time. It was Adelie's last chance to do it. He'd let her have that one for free. He sucked in a deep breath and wiped at the tears on his face.

"I'm sure everyone else here will remind me, too."

Damien nodded toward Owen at the statement. Colby shook Owen's shoulder in agreement. Jace stood closer and held Owen's hand. The dark-haired boy smiled thankfully at his companions and boyfriend. He then simply stared at Adelie for a few moments, taking in those last few seconds of their friendship. When Adelie's body buckled like falling building blocks, he knew it was time to truly say goodbye.

"I'll miss you," he added as he helped her stand up straight.

"I'll miss you too. I'll miss all of you," she replied as she graciously accepted his help and glanced around at the others.

She just had two more souls to say goodbye to now.

Adelie crouched down to be at Aspen and Maple's level and relished the look in their eyes, the beauty of their being. She had succeeded in keeping these two safe. Hopefully she could continue to do so in her new life. Another wave of absorbism shook her failing body. She was on her knees now. The two foxes wove around her, rubbing her lovingly.

"I'd say goodbye, but it's not really goodbye for you two, is it?"

The red-haired girl bowed her head down to allow them to kiss her face.

"Thank you. I love you both," she gave them one last look before standing up again and facing the rest of the group.

"I love *all* of you."

The Earth felt like it was shaking beneath her when a powerful burst of her disease spread throughout her body. Her knees shook and she stumbled backwards. Everyone rushed in to stop her from falling. The five-person circle all looked to her with concern and sadness in their eyes. Owen fought hard to keep himself from transforming, his free palm pressed to his own forehead. Safe in the arms of the others, Adelie reached up and gently removed Owen's hands from his face. Blue eyes widened with shock at her next words.

"It's okay. Don't fight your feelings. Let them happen, then let them go. That's what I've learned the most, I think."

Owen nodded fast and he started to allow those hot tears to tumble down his face. More fur grew atop his skin and clothes. Everyone grouped into a tighter circle around the trembling girl.

She shut her eyes. The sun bathed them all in warmth and Adelie swore it spread right through her from the touch of her loved ones. She could feel herself beginning to fade. Chestnut eyes opened and flickered between the others' faces.

"I love you, mom. It's nice to be able to say it and mean it again. Thank you."

Marianne delicately moved a few auburn hairs from her Adelie's face. She was on the verge of an absolute wreck, but she did her best to contain it for now. To lose both one's husband and daughter would be excruciating to get through, but this was not about her right now. It was about her daughter.

"I love you too, Addie."

Funny how Adelie was fine with her calling her that, now. She continued her goodbyes.

"I love you Jace, Damien, Colby. Thank you for being there for me."

"We love you too, Adelie," Colby sniffled, the other two boys smiling through tears in agreement.

When Adelie looked at Owen, he could see the light leaving her eyes.

"I love you, Owen. Thank you for changing. Thank you for caring. Keep it up, okay?"

Owen clenched his teeth as his breath hitched in his throat.

"I love you too, Adelie– and I will, I promise."

It was all such a relief for Adelie to be able to give and receive these words. She allowed herself to melt into their group embrace, eyes closing for the last time. The autumn breeze soothed her once again.

I only wish I could've loved for much longer in my life, but at least I got to do it, no matter how fleeting. Some can't say the same.

Red fur began to spread throughout her body, though this time it didn't grow through her dress. White teeth sharpened. Dark ears and a bushy tail showed themselves. Her entire figure was shrinking into its canine attributes. A smile danced across her lips as she spoke her final words.

"I'm sure we'll all meet again. Just not too soon, or I'll be mad," she sprinkled her statement with humor, enough so that it made everyone laugh through their grief.

In seconds she had disappeared within her sundress and fallen out of the group's hold. The yellow fabric fell to the ground, momentarily concealing the animalistic movements beneath it. Soon enough, a long muzzle poked out, amber eyes shooting across the small group in confusion. It scurried out from under the dress and walked around the humans cautiously.

The kits swarmed the vixen, the three of them sniffing each other and snickering quietly. As the tearful group watched this interaction, Owen collapsed into a puddle of tears. His breath heaved and cracked under the weight of his bittersweet grief. On his knees, he held Adelie's flowery sundress in his hands, holding it close and transforming into Ace without a fight. The dog curled himself around the dress and whimpered into the fabric. Marianne and Jace knelt down beside him and petted his fur. The saddened mother bit her lip in anguish, her body shaking with the toll of losing the last of her family. Colby and Damien kept track of the foxes through bleary, tearful eyes.

Aspen and Maple followed the older vixen around the circle of humans to give each of them a good sniff. Her body tensed apprehensively with each encounter, tail tucked behind her and slowly wagging with uncertainty. Damien, instinctually, reached to pet her, but soon drew his hand back when she barked and skittered backwards. The vixen then backed into Owen and spun around in surprise. Owen lifted his face from the sundress and stared at his permanently transformed "friend" with melancholy eyes.

The two canines looked at each other, one wild, one completely tame. After the initial shock, the fox slowly inched closer again, curiosity now taking over her movements. The dog stayed still as stone. Everyone watched as the two of them made proper contact this time around. Amber eyes glittered with interest, and when both canines looked at each other, the husky swore a glimmer of caramel had swirled around those thin pupils.

As the vixen stooped towards Owen, a narrow muzzle met a broad one, dark noses bumping in the slightest. All of the husky's whimpering had now left him, finding this last interaction to be a comforting sign. It was only a matter of seconds, but it would definitely become ingrained within Owen's memories forever. She was going to be just fine.

The vixen gave Owen one last sniff and flick of the ear, followed by thin legs trotting away from the cluster of humans. Maple and Birch flanked her sides as the three foxes began their journey into the wilderness.

Sobs and sniffles halted at the sight of the fox family starting their new lives. Owen slowly returned to his original form alongside his companions. He wiped his drying eyes. Jace wrapped his arm around his boyfriend's waist. Marianne fought her tears with a smile. Colby gave a wave of goodbye, along with that goofy grin of his. Damien simply took in the moment with a deep inhale. The foxes didn't spare even a passing glance, evidence of their new, truly free nature. There was no death that day.

They would never be seen again, but would surely carry on.

ABOUT THE AUTHOR

Kassandra Keator

Kassandra knew from a very young age that writing would be her passion. In Kindergarten, she wrote small photo-story books and presented them at Show-and-Tell. This grew into full-fledged short stories in elementary and high school. The idea for *Orchard of the Fox* came to her during her freshman year of high school.

Now, after several years of change and progress, she has succeeded in writing a story that is very near and dear to her heart. Though she is from South Florida, she now resides in Northern Michigan. The wilderness continues to inspire her.

THE ABSORBISM SERIES

Stay tuned for *Den of the Mongrel,* Owen Smit's story!